"I wanted to talk to you."

In response, Matt held up the latest edition of the *Babbitt* and Layne winced. So much for not antagonizing him.

She stepped off the low retaining wall to the patio below. "I didn't have anything to do with that article. Not directly, at least. Noah Wilkie, the *Babbitt's* social reporter, overheard part of what my aunt was saying at the gala, so he may have mentioned it to one of the other reporters."

"I see."

"But I'd still like to apologize, and also about my aunt getting so upset. It wasn't like her, but she's been through a lot. And she..." Layne trailed off. She was in danger of starting to babble, and she reminded herself of her plan to treat Matt Hollister as a fact to be researched, instead of a sexy guy who turned her brain into a mass of overreacting neurons.

Dear Reader,

Welcome to my second book in the Those Hollister Boys series, about the commitment-wary sons of Sullivan Spencer "Spence" Hollister, known in the tabloids as "S.S. Hollister, the man with an ex-wife in every port." Spence has children and ex-wives all over the world and is a hedonist who lives on charm and an enormous fortune.

Matt followed his father's fun-loving footsteps, and for years he partied hard and pursued extreme sports. But now that he wants to run his grandfather's charitable foundation, his reputation is getting in the way. He's thrown another curve when Layne McGraw shows up, wanting answers about a suicide and theft connected to Matt's own stepfather.

Classic movie alert: I love old movies, and in my last letter I recommended *Hobson's Choice,* released in 1954. Because *Challenging Matt* includes a mystery, I'd like to suggest watching the 1953 film *The Blue Gardenia,* with Anne Baxter and Richard Conte. There's a hint of romance, and a whole lot of suspense in that movie.

I hope you enjoy reading *Challenging Matt.* I look forward to hearing from readers and can be contacted c/o Harlequin Books, 225 Duncan Mill Road, Don Mills, ON M3B 3K9, Canada.

Wishing you all the best,

Julianna Morris

JULIANNA MORRIS

—

Challenging Matt

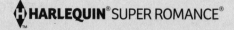
HARLEQUIN® SUPER ROMANCE®

Recycling programs
for this product may
not exist in your area.

ISBN-13: 978-0-373-60857-7

CHALLENGING MATT

Printed in U.S.A.

ABOUT THE AUTHOR

Julianna Morris grew up wanting to be a writer and started her first novel in sixth grade. It was about an injured ballerina, and needless to say, it's an incredibly maudlin tale that will never see the light of day. When Julianna isn't frantically busy with family, cats, dogs and her computer, she's baking bread, traveling or pursuing one of her other hobbies. She could probably get everything done if she only had forty hours every day and didn't have to sleep....

Books by Julianna Morris

HARLEQUIN SUPERROMANCE

*Those Hollister Boys

Other titles by this author available in ebook format.

To the memory of Aunt Polly and Uncle Del.

CHAPTER ONE

"HERE YOU GO, LAYNE," said Kit Carson, tossing a copy of the *Puget Sound Babbitt* on the desk.

"Thanks." Layne McGraw smiled at the lead mail-room clerk.

"Look at the intrepid explorer, pushing his trusty steed. Or is that just a mail cart?" taunted Regina Sorkin, who thought it was a hoot that Kit was named after a famous explorer.

"And if it isn't The Kitchen Corner's smart-ass columnist. I see you have more bandages on your fingers—did you screw up another recipe?" Kit returned, appearing annoyed as he pushed his cart forward.

Layne looked at her friend. "Why do you do that?" she asked. "You know how much it annoys him."

"*Because* I know how much it annoys him," Regina replied, unrepentant. "You'd think he'd be more ambitious with a name like Kit Carson."

"He's happy running the mail room. People don't always *want* to earn a bigger income or get a more impressive job title."

Regina shrugged and headed back to her own desk, most likely annoyed with Kit for not being ambitious enough to notice her as a woman. Layne felt bad for her—unrequited love was hell. Still, she didn't think it was right to torment someone over their career choice…the way her family tormented her.

She leafed through her copy of the *Babbitt* and spotted signs of her work throughout the weekly regional news magazine. Whenever someone had trouble finding information, she got it for them. She took pride in knowing her facts were triple-checked and documented.

Pulling out her lunch, she munched on a sandwich as she read. It was always fun to see how the information she'd researched translated into print.

"I need some things checked for my next op-ed," said Carl Abernathy as he walked up and dropped a file onto her desk. His eyebrows rose as he spotted her half-eaten sandwich. "Peanut butter again?"

"Peanut-butter sandwiches are great. They're easy and don't have to be refrigerated. And they're healthier than the greasy-spoon burger and fries *you* eat every day." Layne grinned, knowing she was one of the few *Babbitt* employees who could sass Carl and get away with it.

"I'm an editor—I have to eat like one. Don't you go to the movies?"

"From what I've seen, those editors just chomp on cigars and yell a lot. You have the yelling part down all right. Of course, that isn't healthy, either. Though I'm sure a cardiologist would disapprove of the burger and fries even more than the yelling."

Carl's eyes narrowed. "I don't yell, I suggest. And don't pay attention to what your famous mother says—it takes the fun out of life to worry about everything you eat. My God, it must have been dreary growing up with a heart doctor for a parent."

"I survived," Layne said wryly.

It wasn't a surprise that Carl knew her mother was a renowned cardiologist; practically everyone at the *Babbitt* knew about Barbara McGraw...the same way they knew her father was a top orthopedic surgeon, and that she had three megasuccessful siblings. At one time or other, the magazine had done articles about each of them.

"What's this?" Layne asked, pulling the file toward her.

"Just an editorial I'm writing on endangered species here in Washington State. Look at it after lunch."

He hurried away and Layne glanced through the folder. She liked Carl; he was a good editor and uncompromising on journalistic integrity. A year after she'd started working at the *Babbitt,* one of the columnists was caught using her research notes verbatim without giving her credit. It was a firing offense and while Layne had wanted to feel bad about the incident, she couldn't because Doug was a snake. He'd not only been copying her work for several months, he had patted her butt in the elevator. But he'd only done it once—her father had taught his daughters excellent self-defense skills.

She scrunched her nose at the memory. Both

Regina and Annette Wade, who wrote the nuptials column, had wanted her to report Doug the first time he'd plagiarized, but Layne had figured he'd get caught sooner or later, and she wouldn't have made points by being a complainer.

"Layne, I have two recipes for your aunt to test." Regina held out a couple of sheets of paper. "They were awful when I tried to cook them myself. I brought them over earlier, but I didn't want to talk about it with Kit around. The usual pay rate—two hundred and fifty a recipe."

"Great. What are they?" Layne asked. Her aunt was struggling financially and when the freelance chef who'd done some of the *Babbitt*'s recipe testing had retired eight weeks before, she'd suggested Aunt Dee as a replacement.

"A tropical chiffon cake and pecan sticky rolls." Regina glanced down at the first-aid strips on both her forefingers. "Jeez, I can't wait until Carl lets me do hard news and takes me off this fluff stuff. *A cooking column.* Almost nothing I try comes out. Hell, I can't cook any better than you."

"Sad but true." A shared lack of culinary skills was one of the things that had cemented their friendship. "I'll set it up with my aunt."

"Fabulous. She could make them on Saturday or Sunday, and the staff can taste test both on Monday." She checked her watch and made a face. "I'm going to lunch—maybe I'll meet tall, dark and handsome while eating sushi."

"Check his ring finger before losing your heart. Now that we're thirty, tall, dark, and handsome is often married."

"*Also* sad but true. See you later."

Picking up the phone, Layne dialed her aunt's number.

"Hey, Aunt Dee, just a heads-up. Regina has two recipes for you to test this weekend." She glanced at the tropical cake and made a face. "One is for sticky rolls that should be easy enough with all the bread you make. But the dessert is complicated. It's a cake with a mousse filling and whipped frosting and a gazillion ingredients."

"That doesn't sound too difficult."

So said the woman who'd once baked all the pies for the church's harvest dinner fund-raiser, at the same time creating a pumpkin costume for Layne to wear in her school play. As a kid, Layne had spent far more time at Aunt Dee and Uncle William's house than she did at her own.

Uncle Will.

Would she ever stop missing him so terribly? Maybe it was because of the *way* he'd died. She still found it hard to grasp that he'd committed suicide.

Layne chatted with her aunt another few minutes and then went back to work, trying to push the sad feeling away. It didn't seem possible that Uncle Will had been gone for almost seven months; the wounds were still too raw and she missed him too much.

ON SUNDAY AFTERNOON Layne arrived at her aunt's house and rang the bell.

"Darling!" Her aunt hugged her as if they hadn't seen each other in a week, instead of attending church together that morning. Dee then peeked into the two bags of groceries she'd brought. "You don't have to bring the supplies."

"It comes out of Regina's expense account."

It was true, but Layne would have paid for everything herself, rather than have her aunt lose any of the money she got for testing. Things hadn't been easy for Aunt Dee since Uncle Will's death. She rarely talked about money, but what she earned as a successful graphic artist obviously wasn't enough. In a worried moment, Dee had confided that she'd taken out a second mortgage to pay off other debts, but Layne could tell she was still struggling financially. Her aunt had even mentioned that she might need to sell the house.

Layne sat back and watched her aunt work, making notes for Regina and marveling at how easy cooking looked when someone else was doing it. She didn't think it was the equipment, though her aunt had every gadget imaginable. Uncle William had designed the kitchen for his wife years ago and it still looked great, with lighted quartz countertops, hardwood floors and commercial-grade stainless-steel appliances.

Three hours later the cake was assembled and the sticky rolls were on the counter, rising.

"Regina will be eternally grateful," Layne said. "I'll take them to work tomorrow and save you a trip into the city. And I'm sure they'll cut a check for you right away."

"Thanks."

Layne stretched and glanced around the warm, inviting home. Her stomach clenched whenever she thought that Aunt Dee might be forced to sell the house. Some of her happiest childhood memories were here, spent with her aunt and uncle and feeling completely accepted. It wasn't that her parents and older siblings didn't love her, but they were always pushing her to be something she wasn't.

"I got another email from Mom about that medical research assistant position at the university," Layne said idly. "She has it all mapped out—I can work with Dr. Clark and he can be my faculty advisor while I get my doctorate."

"You don't want a doctorate."

"According to Mother, I do. She doesn't care what I study…as long as it's somehow connected to the medical field and I become Dr. McGraw."

Dee sighed. "I love my sister, but she has tunnel vision when it comes to this stuff. Don't let her push you, Lani. Just keep doing what makes you happy."

Lani.

Layne smiled at the nickname that only her aunt and uncle had ever used.

Dee absentmindedly wiped the stone counter she'd

already cleaned twice and Layne frowned. "Is something wrong? You've been distracted for weeks."

"I…oh, nothing."

"Come on, I know you too well. Fess up."

Her aunt smiled weakly. "It's just that lately I keep feeling as if William is in the house. In his office, walking up and down the hall or up the stairs. Or lying next to me in bed. Sometimes I can even smell his aftershave."

The unexpected mention of her uncle made Layne's stomach drop. "That's what Grandmother Adele said after Granddad was gone. I'm sure it's normal."

"Maybe, but I can *feel* him, Lani, the way I always used to know he was home. It's as if he's looking for something or trying to tell me something. Some people believe a soul can't rest if they have unfinished business."

"Is that what you think it is?"

"I don't know." Dorothy gathered the dish towels she'd used that evening and threw them into a laundry hamper. "But it started when I received that letter from Peter Davidson, so what better time for Will to come back and haunt the place?"

"*What* letter?"

"I'll get it." Dee dried her hands and went out, returning a couple of minutes later.

Layne read the note from her uncle's former partner, a scowl growing on her face. "How dare he? This is emotional blackmail." She stared at the letter in disbelief. "Agree to sell Uncle Will's company under the terms he offers, or he'll drag the embezzlement case up again?"

Aunt Dee's face was pale. "Yes. But wouldn't making accusations against William be libel?"

"I'm not sure. It's possible you can't libel someone who's…uh…"

"Dead?" Dee finished flatly. "Maybe. But Peter is basically saying I'm not due *anything* because of what happened, and he'll make a stink about it if I don't go along. That was William's company, too. He'd be so upset if he knew about this."

"Uncle Will was never actually indicted for embezzling."

"I know. But I haven't gotten anywhere with the police or the Carrollton District Attorney's office on clearing his name. After they decided he killed himself, it seems as if they just stopped investigating. I even heard one of them say 'he must have been guilty' the night Will died. I've called and called and nobody will even talk to me any longer."

Layne let out a pent-up breath. "Maybe they think you're just trying to throw doubt on the suicide verdict to get Uncle Will's life insurance."

"God knows I need the insurance money—it's probably the only way I'll hang on to the house—but that isn't the only reason. I *hate* people thinking Will would steal from his own clients. And now this letter from Peter.… I've been dragging my feet, but I have to make a decision soon. He's working for the Eisley Foundation as their chief financial officer and doesn't want to deal with Hudson & Davidson any longer. His stepson resigned three months ago to take over as director of the foundation from his grandfather."

Layne nodded, recalling Matthew Hollister's connection to her uncle's company. The notorious playboy, Gordon Eisley's grandson, had started working for Hudson & Davidson almost a year and a half before, a case of pure nepotism on Peter Davidson's part. Though Uncle Will had been annoyed about it, he hadn't objected. And not long before his death, he'd admitted that Matt Hollister had worked hard and seemed to have a decent business head on his shoulders.

Layne had only seen Matt Hollister in person once, when he'd come to Uncle Will's funeral. A ripple of whispers had run around the church when he'd arrived, sitting in the back. He had slipped out early without speaking to the family, but at least he'd come; Peter Davidson hadn't even sent flowers.

"Aunt Dee, what did *you* think of Matt Hollister?" she asked.

"We've only met once at a company Christmas party. It was just a hello and goodbye encounter— the other women were crowding around too much for anything else."

"But what about when Mr. Davidson married Matt's mother?"

"We didn't go to the wedding. It was a small, hush-hush affair on Catalina Island to avoid publicity—you know Katrina Eisley's reputation for being a recluse. Marrying into the Eisley family was a big deal for Peter. Between his new father-in-law and famous stepson, he joined a small, very exclusive social circle."

Layne returned Peter Davidson's letter to her aunt. "I've done research on Matt Hollister for some of the reporters at the *Babbitt.* I can't imagine he's really reformed. His father, S. S. Hollister, is one of most outrageous hedonists in the world and they seem cut from the same cloth."

"Except the son never married, and the father can't stay out of divorce court. Anyway, I sort of understand why Peter claims I'm not due anything from the sale of the firm…."

"*I* don't," Layne said stoutly.

"Unfortunately the math appears to add up. The embezzlement crashed the value of the company and Peter repaid every penny of the stolen money from his own pocket. At the end of the letter you can see he's offering to give me twenty-five thousand dollars as a goodwill gesture, but that's all."

"It's hard to believe you wouldn't be due several million at the very least. The property alone is worth a fortune."

While Dee didn't say anything, Layne thought she agreed. Her aunt had never dealt much with money, focusing on art while her husband went into business after getting out of the navy. They'd seemed to have the perfect marriage, but Layne wasn't naive enough to think there hadn't been occasional problems.

Dee sat next to her and traced a pattern in the quartz countertop. "The thing is, I know how good you are at research and putting pieces of information together. And I've been thinking…if anyone can prove Will was innocent, it's you. And then I could challenge Peter about the sale and be able to pay off the mortgage before I have to sell the house. Will and I built this house together—I don't want to lose it."

Layne froze.

Okay, so she was good at her job. That didn't make her a criminal investigator. And what if she proved Uncle Will *had* embezzled from his company? How could she tell Aunt Dee? It might hurt even more to know for sure.

"Uh, about the mortgage," she said. "The house means a lot to me, too, and I have some money saved—"

"I can't accept it. This is my problem," her aunt said predictably. "But if you *could* find out the truth, it would help in more ways than one."

"What if you don't like what I find? I'm not saying Uncle Will was guilty, but you never know."

"I need the truth, wherever it leads." Dee put a hand in her pocket, her mouth tense. She was a lovely woman, with golden blond hair and warm blue eyes that had twinkled brightly before her husband's death. She resembled Layne's mother in physical appearance only; eleven years separated them and Dorothy's nature was far more artistic than her older, brisk cardiologist sister's.

"All right," Layne agreed reluctantly.

She loved Aunt Dee dearly and had loved Uncle Will. She *couldn't* say no. Her aunt and uncle were the ones who'd made her feel special when she was growing up with a star athlete brother and beautiful twin sisters who could charm the paint off walls. Her parents were so brilliant and accomplished themselves, they hadn't known what to do with a daughter who was merely average and didn't fit in. It was Uncle Will and Aunt Dee who'd understood her.

"Good." Dee slowly opened her fingers. "This is the key to William's home office. Maybe you can start with the stack of boxes that Peter sent over from the company. I haven't had time to open them because there's been too much to deal with. I know the police went through everything before it was packed, but they were looking for things that made William look guilty, not anything to show he was innocent."

Heart in her throat, Layne took the key. The metal seemed to be burning a hole in her palm and she quickly hooked it on her keychain. The answers might be in her uncle's office…but it was also the place where he'd died.

Was that why Aunt Dee was imagining that she'd heard him around the house?

Layne lifted her chin.

Ghosts weren't real, but if they *did* exist, she could never be afraid of Uncle Will. He might even help her discover what had happened to him.

CHAPTER TWO

MATT HOLLISTER HANDED a stack of files to his assistant, who gave another stack back to him in return.

"They're the latest reports and the daily correspondence, boss," Gillian said. "I couldn't help the delay—the mail came late this morning."

"I understand. Did you learn more about who my appointment might be? You mentioned the name seemed familiar."

"I can't think of anything. I just wish the temp covering me on Wednesday had put down L. McGraw's first name and a contact number."

"It's not your fault." Matt flipped open the top file filled with correspondence. Beneath the file were reports on various projects the Eisley Foundation was spearheading. "Anyhow, it's probably someone with Heifer Project International. I spoke to one of their supporters recently about becoming a sponsor."

"I guess we'll find out." She smiled and left him to work.

Matt read through the letters and memos, making notes in the margins for Gillian, setting some aside to handle personally. Half were pleas for money from outside organizations—with descriptions of their programs and how additional support from the foundation would benefit them. The other half were about existing Eisley Foundation projects…and pleas for more money.

He sighed.

It wasn't easy seeing how much was wrong in the world, and trying to do something about it was like trying to drain a bottomless pit. Kids, the environment, the homeless, animals… The list was endless, along with the heartbreak.

As for the reports Gillian had given him, he would read the material in depth, before making any decisions. When he'd taken over the director's seat, he'd starting looking at the long-term projects list—some no longer seemed viable, so he had auditors examining their expenditures, and experts evaluating their merits. Project leaders were screaming, upset about the scrutiny. Nevertheless, the reports were starting to arrive.

"Come in," he called at a knock on the door.

Gillian poked her head inside. "Hey, Matt. Reception called—your three o'clock is here. They told me L. McGraw's first name and you aren't going to like it."

"Then it isn't one of the Heifer Project folks?"

"Nope. L. McGraw is *Layne* McGraw, that's why it sounded familiar. She's works for the *Puget Sound Babbitt.* I see her name at the end of articles—you know, 'research provided by staff member Layne McGraw.'"

"Maybe she's branching out into reporting."

"I'm so sorry," Gillian said. "There's a procedural list on my desk for handling calls, saying you aren't doing any interviews. The temp must have forgotten to follow it."

"This isn't your fault," Matt assured her, determined not to be one of those hard-assed managers who blamed other people for everything. But he *was* frustrated; the *Babbitt* was one of several publications that seemed to go out of its way to be annoying. Once upon a time he'd provided steady fodder for the gossip page; now their columnists were gunning for him. They kept publishing editorials, voicing concerns about someone with his reputation running the Eisley Foundation. They weren't the worst of his critics, but they were bad enough.

Hell, it wasn't as if he didn't have any qualifications for the job. He had a degree in business administration, and his grandfather had always planned to have a family member assume control of the foundation one day—Matt had even worked there before leaving for college. Besides, a lot of wealthy people were philanthropists, their only credentials being the ability to spend money.

Nevertheless, Matt had to admit things would be easier if everyone took him seriously. His grandfather had deliberately kept the foundation private so he wouldn't have to be accountable to anyone except the Internal Revenue Service, but it wasn't as simple as that for Matt. The Eisley Foundation didn't operate in a vacuum, it needed serious people involved, and those serious people didn't want their names linked to a notorious playboy—especially one with his reckless reputation.

"I can send her away," Gillian offered.

"That's all right, I'll handle it."

She left, giving him a few minutes to stew. When she returned, there was a young woman at her heels.

"Ms. McGraw, this is Matt Hollister." Gillian introduced them. She sent him another apologetic look before heading back to her desk.

Matt stood and assessed his unwanted guest. The *Babbitt* reporter had masses of silky brown hair and green eyes in a pixieish face. She wore khaki slacks and a green shirt, and couldn't be more than five foot three in her stocking feet.

"You've wasted your time, Ms. McGraw," he said. "The assistant who set the appointment forgot that I'm not giving interviews right now."

Layne McGraw blinked. "I don't want an interview…that is, I'm *not* a reporter. I'm here for personal reasons."

"You don't work for the *Babbitt?*"

"I'm a researcher there, but this has nothing to do with the magazine. I have some questions, just not work related. Questions, that is." She seemed nervous and dropped into a chair without being invited. "Uh, that's some view," she said, pointing to the window.

Matt automatically turned his head, though he was well acquainted with the view. The Eisley Foundation building overlooked North Seattle's Lake Union, and the vista was spectacular, especially on a sunny June day. At the moment a sea plane was coming in for a landing and three crewing teams were skimming across the water, rowing in rhythmic precision.

"The foundation has been located here for twenty-five years," he explained, anticipating her first inquiry would be about a charitable organization operating out of a multimillion dollar property. "We were part of the restoration efforts for the immediate area. This was a historic structure that was empty for twenty years until we purchased and renovated it for our use."

"That's great, I love old buildings. What I wanted to ask about…" She hesitated, looking even more uncomfortable. "It's about your new chief financial officer. And the company he owns, and uh, where you worked for over a year."

Matt kept his expression neutral. Peter Davidson was a straight-up guy who'd married his mom four years ago—Pete had made Katrina Eisley genuinely happy, possibly for the first time in her adult life since her very messy, very public divorce from Matt's father. And Peter had given Matt the job he'd needed to prove to his grandfather that he was serious about changing his life and taking over the foundation.

"What about Mr. Davidson?"

"I know he's related to you and that he's now on staff here."

"While our staff isn't of public concern since we are a family-endowed foundation," Matt said carefully, "Mr. Davidson's salary is one dollar annually. Basically, he's donating his valuable time."

"Uh…sure. But as I said, my questions are about his financial management firm. As I'm sure you recall, his partner was accused of embezzling from the business seven months ago."

Matt's eyes narrowed. He and his stepfather had worked with the Carrollton District Attorney and outside auditors to clean up the mess at Hudson & Davidson. Not only that, Peter had personally assured every single client they wouldn't suffer any loss because of the thefts. His stepfather had come out of the whole thing squeaky clean, though the betrayal of his friend and business partner had deeply wounded him. Matt had even remained at the firm longer than he'd planned to help sort everything out.

"Again, I have nothing to say. It's time for you to leave, Ms. McGraw."

Frustration and another less-defined emotion were visible on Layne McGraw's face. "Please, you worked there when the thefts occurred and you're related to Peter Davidson, so I hoped you would be able to get me in to see him or tell me more about the case against his partner. The police and D.A.'s office have refused to release any information and Mr. Davidson is harder to see than the governor."

"I'm sorry, that isn't my problem. This is a private office and you've been asked to leave."

"Please, I didn't start this right. Let me tell you why I'm asking. Mr. Hudson was my—"

"I'm not interested," he interrupted.

"Don't you want to know if there's more to what happened than what it looks like?"

Something in her quiet question troubled Matt, but he pushed it away. "We *know* what happened." He lifted the receiver on his phone and gestured with it. "Now, shall I call security and have you escorted out, or will you go on your own?"

"No, I'll go."

When she was gone, Matt dialed the number of his security chief. "Connor, a young woman just left my office. Her name is Layne McGraw. Slim, dark hair, not too tall, wearing a green shirt. Will you make sure she exits the building and doesn't bother anyone else?"

"Right."

The phone clicked off without a goodbye, which was Connor's style. He was a blunt, transplanted Irishman who'd been the Eisley family and corporate security chief for fifteen years. Matt had gotten to know him quite well during his wild college days—Connor had expressed his opinion of spoiled rich kids on a regular basis, particularly when bailing him out of trouble. If Matt's father had been more like Connor, Matt probably wouldn't have wasted so many years playing.

Swiveling in his chair, he looked at the view the McGraw woman had admired. Unlike most of his half brothers and sisters, he'd thrown himself into their father's playboy lifestyle. But at least he didn't have a bevy of former wives and children and girl-friends strewn around the world like good old S. S. Hollister. He'd taken his share of lovers, but he'd always been careful to keep things casual, only dating sophisticated women who had as little interest in domesticity as he did himself.

Matt pinched the bridge of his nose. He might not have been as notorious as his father, but he'd done his best to have fun and duck responsibility for a long time. And now that he wanted to do something important, his former stupidity was getting in the way.

He leaned back for a moment, thinking about everything that had happened over the past few years.

First his oldest brother had gotten married. Admittedly, it had only caused a small blip on Matt's radar, mostly because he'd believed Aaron was just as cynical about marriage as he was himself. But then Matt's closest childhood friend had called with the news that he had Lou Gehrig's disease, and ALS was virtually a death sentence.

Matt remembered how he'd hung up after the call and stared at the cast on his leg, broken in a stupid, reckless accident. There was nothing stupid or reckless about Terry—he'd simply gotten sick and there was nothing anyone could do about it. So Matt had hobbled to the wall and punched it so hard he'd cracked two bones in his hand.

He flexed his fingers.

Maybe it was a good thing he'd had a broken hand in addition to his tibia. Being injured had made him slow down, forcing him to deal with the reality of his best friend's illness, instead of throwing himself into parties or another extreme sport to forget that Terry could die soon. And gradually, Matt had begun thinking about his grandfather's philanthropic foundation. The Eisley Foundation funded medical research, and if he became the director, he could push a project to help find a cure for ALS. Even if it didn't help Terry, it could help other people with the disease.

His grandfather had been hard to convince. Gordon Eisley had finally agreed that if Matt could hold an outside position for a year, he would retire and hand over the reins. During that time they'd worked together every Saturday, with Gordon showing him the ropes. It turned out that for the past decade his grandfather had done little more than review requests for money and sign checks, rather than actively overseeing the foundation's projects.

Matt intended to be far more involved.

LAYNE DROVE TO her aunt's home in Carrollton, Washington, and parked in the driveway. For almost a week she'd spent every free moment in her uncle's office and wasn't any closer to discovering answers than before she'd started.

She'd found nothing to either support her uncle's innocence or to suggest his guilt, and it had quickly become evident that she needed more information on the supposed crime to even know *where* to look. With the police and District Attorney's office refusing to cooperate, speaking with Peter Davidson had seemed necessary; when he'd proved elusive, she'd given Matt Hollister a shot.

Sighing, she got out and went inside. Normally Aunt Dee worked at home doing commercial art for a greeting card company and other freelance contracts, but today she was on duty at the gallery where some of her paintings were for sale.

Going into her uncle's home office, Layne sat in his leather executive chair and felt the familiar rush of grief. Tears had streamed down her face the first evening she'd spent there. The room still smelled like Uncle Will, with a hint of the pipe tobacco he'd smoked once in a while, and the dark roast coffee he'd drunk by the gallon. Or maybe it was just her imagination, wanting to feel closer to him.

She tried pushing the sliding keyboard tray farther under the desk, but it caught on the cord and wouldn't go all the way. With a sigh, she left it alone, turning again to the boxes Uncle Will's partner had sent over from the company. Aunt Dee hadn't exaggerated… there was a large pile against one wall, filled with everything imaginable. Layne had only catalogued the contents of a few, but the careless way they'd been packed infuriated her—things thrown in, papers crumpled and items broken, as if drawers had been upended and surfaces hastily swept off.

It was thoughtless and cruel, because no matter what the firm had believed about William Hudson, his wife shouldn't have been subjected to something so unpleasant after his death. Thank goodness Aunt Dee hadn't had time to look in the boxes or it would have upset her terribly.

Layne pressed her lips together; she'd completely blown the meeting with Matthew Hollister. However briefly, he'd worked for Hudson & Davidson and could have given her information about how they operated and facts about how the embezzling occurred, but instead she'd gotten nervous. And it certainly hadn't helped when he'd learned she worked for the *Babbitt*.

Her cell phone rang and she dug it out of her purse. "Yes?"

"It's me, darling."

"Hi, Mom."

"I just talked with Sheldon at the university. He says you haven't spoken to him about that position on his genetics project team."

Layne gritted her teeth. Maybe she could pretend she was losing the signal, except her mother would just call back. "Mom, I'm not interested. I love my job at the *Babbitt* and I'm good at it. Why isn't that enough?"

"This is a once-in-a-lifetime opportunity. Here, speak to your father."

"Layne," said Walter McGraw's deep voice. "If you aren't interested in genetics, I'm sure we can find another medical research study you could join."

She wanted to scream. "Look, I'm at Aunt Dee's right now. Could we talk about it on Sunday when I come to dinner? I promise you can nag for at least twenty minutes before I say no again."

"We just want the best for you."

"I know. Gotta go, Dad," she said hastily, hating his hurt, offended tone. "Love to you both. Bye."

She turned off the cell and dropped it back in her purse. For Pete's sake, she was offended, too. Nothing she did would ever be good enough for her parents.

Layne leaned her elbows on the desk and studied the records she was keeping of everything found in the boxes so far; she didn't want anything to go unnoticed. The rest of the office would receive an equally careful inventory and review. Most of it was deadly dull, but research wasn't always exciting. It was more of a one-foot-in-front-of-the-other sort of activity.

An hour later she heard her aunt arrive home and went out to the kitchen to greet her—Aunt Dee cooked as a stress reliever, so she was in the kitchen a lot these days. Layne was just glad she earned money from the *Babbitt* part of the time for testing recipes. It wouldn't fix her financial woes, but maybe it would help stave off disaster for a while.

"Hi. How was the gallery?"

"Fine. How was meeting the gorgeous philanthropist?"

"So-so." Layne wrinkled her nose. "Matthew Hollister is good-looking, but he isn't *that* gorgeous."

Liar, screamed her conscience. Matt Hollister was tall, dark and stunning. With his expensive suit, black hair and gray eyes, he could have walked off the cover of a men's fashion magazine. Of course, he'd graced the cover of more than one magazine and scandal rag when he was still carousing...usually with a woman and a juicy caption. In person he was magnetic, one of those guys who made you want to tear off your clothes and throw yourself into his arms. Her sisters could get away with it, but her? Not a chance. She wasn't Quasimodo, but she was hardly in Matt Hollister's league.

"Anyway," she continued. "Mr. Hollister wasn't in the mood to talk. He practically had me thrown out of the building. His security guy showed up as I got off the elevator in the lobby and I thought he was going to pull a gun on me. Followed me clear out to the parking lot and watched me leave."

"Are you all right?" Aunt Dee exclaimed.

"I'm fine. I'm probably overreacting, since he didn't actually do anything. He was just menacing, in this quiet, intense sort of way. I bet he just *looks* at someone and they skedaddle."

"Lani, I know I asked you to investigate, but it isn't worth you taking risks. I don't want you getting hurt, and William wouldn't have, either."

"I'm not taking any risks. It was just a conversation. Though I did hope Mr. Hollister would talk about the company and anything he might have seen or heard about the case. I mean, he worked at Hudson & Davidson through the main part of the investigation, so he must know *something*. I thought he could at least get his stepfather to meet with me, only he didn't give me much chance to talk. But I can tell you one thing, Matt Hollister sure got uptight when I mentioned Peter Davidson. What can you tell me about Mr. Davidson? I don't remember him very well."

Aunt Dee pulled several items from the refrigerator, frowning slightly. "He was focused and dedicated. We became friends with Peter and his first wife at William's last posting in Guam. It was Peter who suggested that Will go back to school and get a degree in accounting when he left the navy. That way they could go into business together when they were both out of the service."

Layne scribbled a note on her pad. "I see. Is that why Mr. Davidson moved to the Seattle area, because you guys were here?"

"Yes, though by that time Shelley, his first wife, had died in an accident. I think that's why he didn't come to the house that much—it reminded him of those years when we were all so close."

Not close enough, Layne added silently. Peter Davidson had hung his old friend out to dry the minute a whiff of scandal appeared.

"Anyway," Aunt Dee said, "Will started an accounting firm when he got his degree instead of going to work for someone else, and when Peter took twenty-year retirement from the navy, he moved here. William sold him half the company so they'd be equal partners. By that time Peter had already made a fortune on the stock market."

Layne stared at her aunt who was working at the

sink. "You mean the company originally belonged to Uncle Will? I thought they'd started it together."

"In a way they did—they expanded beyond accounting and the company grew exponentially after that, with huge corporate accounts and an A-list of wealthy clients."

"I see." Layne gazed out at the wooded backyard. The house faced on a shallow creek gorge and the yard took advantage of a divine natural setting. Whenever possible over the past seven months she'd helped with the upkeep of the property, though Aunt Dee was awfully touchy about it. "But if Mr. Davidson came out of the mess so clean, why won't his stepson talk about what happened?"

"Who knows? It could mean anything from a bad relationship with his stepfather to concern about negative press coverage—it isn't necessarily sinister."

"I suppose."

Matt Hollister had annoyed Layne, mostly because he was rich and spoiled and no doubt playing at philanthropy the way he'd played at everything else. There *were* men like him who'd changed their ways, but they weren't usually thirty-two and in the prime of their life.

"I wonder how long he's going to last running the Eisley Foundation?" she mused aloud.

"Is it important?" Her aunt put a plate of Cobb salad in front of Layne.

"Not really, though it isn't as if he *earned* the job."

Dee sat down with her own salad. "The Eisley

Foundation does important work. Mr. Eisley earned a fortune in the shipping industry and lumber business, then funneled half of it into humanitarian causes."

"I know, he's the Andrew Carnegie of the Pacific Northwest," Layne said, waving her fork. "But that's the grandfather, not the grandson. After getting out of college Matthew Hollister mostly partied hard, drove fast and dated supermodels."

Her research on him wasn't flattering. Honestly, why did some women think a man who partied every night and risked his life in race cars and doing other dumb things was sexy? Except…Matt Hollister *was* sexy, his exploits notwithstanding. So sexy he'd tied her tongue into knots. She had to view him as a fact to be researched, instead of letting her feminine instincts jump in and turn her into a stuttering idiot.

"It's a private foundation, Lani. Mr. Eisley can name anyone to the job. Including his grandson."

"I suppose." Layne took a bite of salad. *Mmm.* It was loaded with blue cheese, hard-boiled eggs and bacon, along with thick chunks of avocado. Not to mention her aunt's homemade croutons, with fresh-baked yeast rolls on the side. "This is so good," she murmured.

"It isn't hard to make."

"You don't think anything is hard to make."

DOROTHY HUDSON SMILED, trying to hide her concern. Her niece looked tired, no doubt from the late nights she'd spent in Will's home office. Perhaps she shouldn't have asked Layne to investigate, but it was hard not knowing why her life had fallen apart. And while she didn't want to be mercenary, she'd lose everything they'd built together if she didn't get more than twenty-five thousand dollars from the sale of the company.

She'd talked herself hoarse to the police, calling every day and asking if they'd made any progress. Finally they'd referred her to the Carrollton D.A.'s office, who'd told her in no uncertain terms that while the case was technically open, the only continuing investigation would be to find the stolen money. But it kept bothering her. How could she accept what other people said about William, rather than what she felt in her heart? And lately she could barely sleep for thinking about it.

She believed he was innocent, didn't she?

Sure, a few years ago, Will and Peter had built an expensive new complex for the company. The cost was astronomical, but they'd felt it presented the right image to clients. But then Will's father had gotten sick. The elder Hudsons hadn't had health insurance, so she and Will had helped out to make sure the best treatment was available. Their savings and investments were depleted, putting them in debt for the first time in years.

But millions of people had debts and didn't resort to theft, and Will had always been so optimistic and scrupulously honest; it was one of the things Dorothy had loved about him. Suicide and embezzling were the last things she would have expected.

"I have to say that Eisley Foundation building has the most scrumptious view of Lake Union," Layne said, distracting Dorothy from darker thoughts. "If I was Matthew Hollister, I'd just move in and make his office my living room. I nearly died of envy on the spot."

Dorothy cocked her head. "Don't you like your house?"

"Yes, and I wouldn't have my garden in North Seattle, so it evens out. He was defensive about their upscale location, but I already knew the stuff he spouted about the Eisley Foundation restoring the neighborhood."

"They've been criticized over the years for being there," Dorothy admitted. "People forget how bad that area used to be. They just see that it's pricey real estate and question a charitable trust operating in the middle of so much affluence."

Layne gasped in mock horror. "You mean the press criticized old Mr. Eisley, too? I thought he'd been granted sainthood."

"Almost. What did you hope Mr. Hollister could tell you?"

"More details about the embezzlement, for one thing. The police won't release the evidence against Uncle Will or anything else about the thefts, and it's difficult to investigate when you don't have a clue what you're trying to find out. But I'll get another chance to talk to him."

Dorothy pushed her salad around on her plate; she

was rarely hungry these days, but she'd wanted Layne to have a good meal and her niece would have refused to eat alone.

"If Mr. Hollister threw you out, what makes you think you'll have another chance?"

"I was hoping you'd ask."

A smile brightened Layne's face and she hopped down from the bar stool. A moment later she slid a copy of the *Babbitt* across the counter—it was open to the "Local Doings" section of the weekly publication. New Director of the Eisley Foundation to Attend Mayor's Charity Gala read the headline of the top article.

"The gala is tomorrow," Layne explained.

"How is that going to help?"

"Easy, I'm going, too. We always get two tickets to these events at the *Babbitt.* Naturally the social reporter gets one, but nobody wanted the other, so I grabbed it. Want to go with me? It admits two people."

Dee didn't hold with formal mourning periods where women wore widow's weeds and did nothing but charity work for years, but that didn't mean she felt like going to a party, especially something like the mayor's gala.

"Can't you go with someone else from the magazine?"

"I guess. Noah Wilkie is assigned to cover the event, only his wife is pregnant and the smell of food is making her gag. He suggested I go with him when he found out I was interested. Christine thinks it's a great idea—she doesn't want Noah attending with just anyone." Layne put a finger on the magazine and drew it back toward her. "I'd never hit on a married man, but what does it mean if other women think their husbands are absolutely safe around you? Christine would never be okay with Noah going to a gala with one of my sisters and *they* wouldn't run after a married guy, either."

Dorothy regarded her niece with affectionate sympathy. Layne was lovely, but she'd grown up in the shadow of two strikingly beautiful sisters with classic figures and innate feminine allure. The rest of the family was tall, Layne was small and petite. At best she wore a B-cup bra, and she was direct, rather than flirtatious.

"It means you're special," Dorothy assured. "And you have real friends. I remember you getting a present for someone named Christine before you'd even met her."

"That was for their new kitten. The Wilkies have never had pets and didn't have any toys or other supplies."

"You mentioned Christine was pregnant. What have you gotten for the new baby?"

"Oh, I found a terrific set of…" Layne stopped and looked puzzled. "How did you know I'd gotten her something?"

"Because I know you. Now, tell me why Noah wants someone to attend the charity gala with him."

"He feels it appears less threatening to bigwigs if a social reporter comes with a date."

"'Social' reporter?" Dorothy restrained a laugh. "Is that another name for gossip columnist?"

Layne chuckled. "More or less. Noah is the worst gossip I know. Anyhow, I'd much rather go to the gala with you, especially since I don't want anyone at the *Babbitt* knowing about this. Come on, Aunt Dee, we wouldn't have to stay for long. And even if Matt Hollister won't talk to me, he might talk to you."

"All right, I'm convinced. What's your plan?"

"We'll quietly approach Mr. Hollister and try to get him to agree to another meeting in a less public place."

Dorothy ate a bite of salad. "What if he won't?"

"Then I'll think of something else. Don't worry—besides the stuff in the office, there are public records and other places to search. You gave me the names of the employees you could remember and I'll interview them if needed. And maybe there's a way to get the rest of the names, even if Mr. Davidson won't cooperate."

"They may not talk to you, either."

"I'll figure it out. I just wish I knew more about how the embezzling happened."

Dorothy nibbled a bite of dinner roll.

The sensation of Will being in the house was even stronger than before, sometimes she even smelled the shampoo he'd used and his pipe tobacco, or heard the low murmur of his voice. Or maybe it was just her imagination and a guilty conscience because she hadn't cleared his name and it was the only thing left she could do for him.

She just hoped Layne could find the answer soon.

CHAPTER THREE

On Saturday evening Layne smoothed the front of her dress as she regarded herself in the mirror. Her aunt had just finished doing her hair for her, twisting both sides and fastening it with enameled combs that matched the green silk of Layne's evening dress.

Still peering at her reflection, Layne turned sideways and sighed. Thin ribbon straps crisscrossed over her shoulders, holding her dress up, and the thing sort of swirled to her waist, and then to her feet. But nothing, not even a clever bra, could give her a respectable silhouette.

"I didn't want to buy something new that I'd never use again, but I don't want to be a laughingstock. Do you really think no one will guess this started life as a bridesmaid's dress?" she asked her aunt.

"Honestly, it's fine without the cape over the shoulders," Aunt Dee replied. "And naturally that bow had to go."

"Yeah, that looked stupid on me. I'll never forgive Carla for making me wear it. You'd think she'd be nicer to her own cousin."

She twisted, trying to see the back of the dress.

Aunt Dee had removed the girlish bow and created a slim belt to cover any evidence of its removal, saying it would make the "lines" of the gown more classic. Since her aunt was an artist with exquisite taste, Layne would have to take her word for it. She didn't object to wearing pretty clothes every now and then, but too much froufrou made her resemble an over-decorated birthday cake.

Leaning forward, she checked the light makeup her aunt had applied—just a few touches to her lashes and eyelids, along with lipstick. "And you're sure I don't need any other makeup?"

"Not with your complexion."

Layne collected the matching purse that came with the dress. "Then we'd better get going. I'll never look as good as you, anyway."

"Nonsense. You're lovely." Her aunt smoothed a hand over her midnight velvet gown. It was high at the neck, with crisscross straps down the back that made it look classily provocative. "I haven't worn an evening gown in ages."

"It's for a good cause."

They walked out to the car and Layne patted the roof of her classic 1966 Mustang. Much to her parents' displeasure, her aunt and uncle had given it to her as a high school graduation present. The light turquoise color wasn't original, but it suited Layne. The Mustang had been Uncle Will's first car and they'd carefully restored it for her, including the installation of the latest modern seat belts with shoulder straps—they'd been indulgent, not reckless.

She drove downtown to the fancy hotel where the gala was being held. Inside she produced her invitation and they were motioned into the ballroom. Layne wrinkled her nose at the assembly; big, glitzy parties with "the beautiful people" were way out of her comfort zone. Nevertheless, she circulated with Aunt Dee around the room, keeping watch for Matthew Hollister.

It was an hour before they saw him. She nudged Aunt Dee. "There he is."

"Surrounded by women."

"Maybe that's why he never got married. I mean, who'd want to deal with that every day?"

Dee didn't reply as they maneuvered closer. They'd almost succeeded in getting within speaking distance when Matt noticed Layne and his expression froze. He drifted farther away, and they spent the next twenty minutes trying to get near, while he kept finding ways to shift himself away from them.

She looked at her aunt, expecting to see frustration, but something very different was smoldering in Dee's eyes. She rarely got angry, but now she was furious. "He really thinks he's important, doesn't he?" she muttered.

Layne eyed Matt, tall and elegant in his suit, surrounded by his harem of adoring women. He actually appeared dignified, a major feat for a man who was famous for a bare-chested photo in a hot tub, tipping a champagne flute to the camera.

"I suppose it's a question of perspective. He's rich, his mother is from one of the oldest families in Seattle and he's famous in more ways than one. In his world, he *is* important."

"Well, I've had enough," Dee said abruptly, but instead of turning for the exit, she thrust her glass into Layne's hand and determinedly marched toward Matt Hollister.

Uh-oh. Layne quickly calculated how much wine her aunt had actually consumed, and realized it was quite a lot. Dorothy Hudson did *not* hold her liquor well.

"Layne, you made it."

Harried, she realized it was Noah Wilkie. "Yeah. Hi, Noah." She put the two glasses she held onto a waiter's passing tray. "Hate to run, but I need to..." She gestured vaguely as she hurried toward her aunt.

"And what are you going to do about it?" Dee was demanding as Layne reached her.

Matt smiled charmingly, though when he saw Layne, his eyes began to glitter. "I'm sorry, Mrs. Hudson, I don't know what you're talking about. And this is hardly the setting for a business discussion."

"It's as good a place as any."

"Aunt Dee, please. Not here, and not this way," Layne said a low, urgent tone. While the admiring crowd had faded away at the prospect of an emotional scene, Noah had followed and he was watching the confrontation with a curious expression.

"*Aunt* Dee?" Matt repeated, raising an eyebrow.

"I'm sorry, I should have told you. I was going to, but then you weren't…uh…."

"I remember," he said grimly.

"Peter Davidson is your stepfather and you worked at the company," Dee announced. "You must be able to tell me more."

"Aunt Dee, Noah Wilkie is here," Layne told her urgently. "Remember what I told you about Noah? He works at the—"

"I'm entitled to information, Layne. I'm tired of being put off, with one excuse after another."

Noah had obviously perked up his ears and Layne grimaced. Terrific. Aunt Dee was running her mouth off in front of the biggest gossip in Seattle. Even if he didn't write about the incident, he was bound to mention it to someone at the magazine. It was part of the reason she'd wanted to attend the gala with her aunt, instead of Noah.

"Layne, Aunt Dorothy, I didn't know you were coming tonight," exclaimed a familiar voice.

It was Layne's sister, Jeannette, looking flawless from the top of her blond head to the tip of her Prada shoes. *Her* gown wasn't a recycled bridesmaid's dress; it was probably a designer outfit that had cost a fortune. She could afford it as a fast-rising pharmaceutical executive. As for the shoes, Layne only knew they were Prada because Jeannette never wore anything else.

"Hi, Jeannette. I didn't know you were coming, either." She *should* have guessed, though. It was the sort of high-toned party Jeannie attended all the time.

"Oh, yes, the mayor invited me. My company is a major contributor to his favorite charity." Jeannette turned and gave Matt a dazzling smile. "Matthew Hollister, right? I'm Jeannette McGraw, senior vice president of the Wilcox Pharmaceutical research division. It's so nice to meet you."

Layne glanced at Matt Hollister, seeing without surprise that he no longer appeared annoyed. Men were usually overwhelmed when they met one of her older sisters—Jeannette and Stephanie were extraordinarily beautiful and successful. So maybe it was a good thing Jeannie had shown up and provided a distraction. Aunt Dee was looking puzzled, but calmer, while Noah appeared starstruck at the sight of so much womanly perfection.

"Would you like to have a drink with me, Mr. Hollister?" Jeannie asked.

"Delighted, but call me Matt."

"And I'm Jeannette. I'm very interested in the business model you want to apply to the research on finding a cure for ALS. I've never heard of a nonprofit using that approach." All at once she looked at Layne and Dee apologetically. "But how rude of me. You were speaking with my sister and aunt. We can have that drink later."

Matt gave them a cool glance. "No need to wait—we're done."

Their voices faded as they walked away and Layne nudged a dazed Noah with her elbow. "You're married, remember?"

He dragged his attention away from Jeannie's shapely backside. "What...that's ridiculous. I'm crazy about my wife."

"Good. Jeannie has broken more hearts than I can count. All she needs to do is smile and they shatter."

"Is she really your sister? You don't look at all alike."

"Yeah, she really is." Layne was resigned to the question. She took after her father's maternal grandmother. If she hadn't looked so much like Great-Grandmother Harriet, she might have suspected she was adopted, or that she'd been sent home from the hospital with the wrong family. There was no justice to being the little sister in more ways than one—both Jeannette and Stephanie topped her by at least five inches. Her mom, too.

Oh, well.

She mentally shrugged; it could have been worse—she could have looked like Great Grandmother Petra.

"Come on, Aunt Dee," she said. "Let's go home and have hot chocolate and some of the biscotti you baked yesterday."

Dee spared a single glance in the direction Matt had disappeared with her other niece. She looked deflated and embarrassed. "All right."

Layne hurried her out, hoping Noah would be

so consumed with the memory of Jeannie's flaw-less femininity, he wouldn't remember the interesting bit of dialogue that had come his way. After all, even though Matt Hollister didn't seem bothered by press coverage, she knew the rest of the Eisley family abhorred being in the news for anything except ribbon cuttings and Eisley Foundation success stories.

CHAPTER FOUR

MATT CHATTED WITH Jeannette McGraw at the bar as they waited for their drinks. She was tall, articulate, intelligent and had a stunning smile. Basically, the type of woman who had always attracted him, yet he kept picturing *Layne* McGraw in his mind.

Jeannette's pint-sized sister was irritating, but she had a quiet freshness that was appealing at the same time. Not that it mattered. Things had just gone from a headache to a major problem. What were Layne and her aunt after, and did Jeannette have anything to do with it?

He looked at the beautiful blonde and saw nothing but a prowling female looking back at him. It seemed improbable that she knew anything about her sister's activities, or she wouldn't have interrupted.

"What was that again?" he said, realizing Jeannette had posed a question.

"I, uh, asked if you knew of any other nonprofit organizations applying a business model to medical research?"

"There's at least one, and they've had encouraging results. I read about it a couple of years ago and thought the concept was intriguing." Matt didn't add that it was when he'd been laid up with his broken tibia. He'd gone out with a high fever and racking cough to a slope nicknamed the Devil's Widow Maker; he was lucky he hadn't broken his fool neck instead of his leg.

He glanced across the large ballroom. Had Layne and her aunt gone home, or were they lingering, hopeful he would relent and give them what they wanted? It had only taken him a second to recognize Dorothy Hudson—she wasn't the kind of woman you forgot. With her classic beauty she could have stepped from a delicate hand-carved cameo.

"So, how do you know my sister?" Jeannette asked. She laughed lightly. "I was surprised to see her here—this sort of party isn't her scene. She's a backyard barbecue sort of gal. Probably complete with tofu burgers. Not that she cooks, but she has vegan friends who do."

"I'm barely acquainted with Layne."

"That's good to know. I wouldn't want to step on her toes…if you understand what I mean?" She was obviously trying to be delicate, but there was a distinct invitation in her eyes.

Matt was tempted, despite her connection to the Hudson scandal, yet the subtle slap at her sister had put his teeth on edge. He was tired of predatory games. Honestly, he'd heard women stick a verbal knife in one another—some would do anything to get ahead—but between sisters it was particularly distasteful.

"I understand. Do you plan to stay in pharmaceuticals or go elsewhere?" he queried, deliberately moving the subject away from flirtatious topics. Few women could match Jeannette McGraw, but at the moment, he simply wasn't interested.

Though disappointment flickered in her expression, she began describing her work. Ironically, that was when she seemed most genuine. Her polish and sophistication weren't unique, but her apparent commitment to developing new antibiotics was admirable.

"So both of your parents are doctors," he mused after a several minutes. "I imagine that influenced your career choice."

"Yes." The playful invitation had vanished entirely from her eyes, which told him she was smart enough to get the message without him needing to be blunt. Whether she knew *why* he'd lost interest was another question.

Matt swirled the golden liquid in his brandy snifter, then set it on a tray. "It was very nice meeting you, Jeannette, but I have a check to write for the mayor's favorite charity."

"I hope we'll run into each other another time."

"Certainly."

Matt quickly made his charitable contribution and headed out to the parking garage, hoping to see Peter before he went to bed. He also wanted to speak with Connor, though the Eisley security chief rarely seemed to sleep in Matt's experience, so getting there early enough wasn't an issue.

The city streets were still teeming with people as he drove to his grandfather's estate. His stepfather and mother lived in a wing of the mansion, while his grandparents lived in another. It wasn't an ideal arrangement, at least for Peter, but he'd agreed because it was what Katrina had wanted. At the security gate Matt stopped and nodded as the guard stepped forward.

"Good evening, Mr. Hollister. We didn't expect you tonight."

"It wasn't planned, but I have some business to discuss with my stepfather."

"I believe Mr. Davidson is taking his evening stroll. He passed by a few minutes ago, headed toward the water." The guard gestured to the southwest.

"Thanks, I'll see if I can catch up."

Matt parked and hurried down the moonlit path. Growing up he'd roamed every inch of the grounds and could find his way blindfolded. There were acres on the estate, with fine gardens surrounding the house, and the rest in natural woodland crossed by a meandering creek, yet it had seemed like a prison when he was a boy. Nobody would admit it, but his mother had been virtually agoraphobic back then. And she'd tried to keep him confined to the estate as well. It was his grandparents who'd insisted he go to boarding school.

Terrence "Terry" Jackson had been Matt's only

friend. As the son of the head groundskeeper, Terry had come to work with his father during the summer. They'd spent every minute together, discovering ways to beat the security system, goofing off and having fun.

Matt's mouth tightened.

Damn it, Terry had children and was a dedicated teacher. A new ALS research project to discover a cure, however well funded, was just a shot in the dark. They both knew it was unlikely to yield results in time to help him.

"Peter, it's me," Matt called, seeing his stepfather's silhouette near the high, tree-lined bluff overlooking the Puget Sound. The moon hung above the horizon, painting everything in silver light and shadow.

"Matt, you're the last person I expected to see tonight. Didn't you go to the mayor's gala?"

"Actually, that's why I'm here. Dorothy Hudson was there as well, asking questions about the embezzlement case. And her niece Layne came to my office yesterday about it."

He heard Peter's sharp intake of breath. "What did you tell them?"

It seemed an odd inquiry, but it was an odd situation. How many people had a business partner who'd embezzled several million dollars?

"Very little. They want details about how the thefts occurred, and probably some other information. Apparently the police and the Carrollton D.A.'s office won't speak to them, so they're going elsewhere for the answers."

"I've tried to protect Dorothy from as much of the ugliness as possible," Peter said irritably. "You'd think she'd appreciate what I've done instead of re-opening the wounds. William stuck a damned knife in my back and took the coward's way out when he got caught. It's as simple as that."

"His suicide must make his death harder for her to deal with," Matt murmured.

"That isn't my problem."

The harsh response made Matt uncomfortable, but he tried to put himself in Peter's shoes. His stepfather felt betrayed and angry and wanted to put it behind him. And he was struggling to make his marriage work, which was no picnic considering Katrina's problems. Matt adored his mother and would do anything for her, but he wasn't blind. She hated to have her name in the press, and she didn't leave the Eisley estate except for a few exclusive social gatherings.

"I appreciate your telling me about this, son," said his stepfather. "I recently told Dorothy I want to sell the company, so perhaps it's just a momentary aberration on her part. She's a nice woman, but she operates largely on emotion, rather than logic. Her artistic temperament, I suppose."

"Yes, of course. I'll see you sometime next week."

They shook hands, yet Matt was more unsettled than ever as he headed for the small house where Connor O'Brian resided on the estate.

Connor's choice of residence was another puzzle. Matt understood why his grandfather would want his security chief living close by; he just wasn't sure why Connor had accepted the arrangement. Yet as he stepped to the rise and looked down at the place, nestled against the dark outline of forest behind it, he wondered if the small stone house reminded Connor of Ireland. It *had* been built by Gaelic craftsmen, along with the mansion and high limestone walls surrounding the estate.

He didn't have a chance to knock on the door since Connor opened it as he approached. "Do you have an early warning system when people arrive?" he asked the older man.

"Dog. Beats electronics any day."

"Oh. Do you ever sleep?"

"Only on alternate days. Come in, Matt."

Like the carriage house exterior, the interior probably looked little different from when it was built. There were white plaster walls, natural wood beams exposed in the ceiling, and the broad planked wood floors were polished smooth by over a hundred years of use. The furniture was basic and solid with no decoration. Matt's own penthouse apartment was stark, but Connor's living room gave the word new meaning.

"Hey, Finnster," he called to the rottweiler lying on the floor. The dog raised his head, let out a faint woof of greeting and settled back again. "This place is pretty bare, Connor. You've lived here, what, fourteen years?"

"I like being able to leave at a moment's notice. Helps if you don't have a lot of nonsense weighing you down."

Matt had few physical possessions himself, having moved around on the party circuit for so many years, but he had a sneaking suspicion it wouldn't take Connor more than a minute to do a fast fade out the back door.

"Do you expect to pick up and leave any time soon?"

"You never know. What brings you here? I figured you'd go home with someone from the party."

Matt's jaw hardened. Every time he attended a public function or dated a woman, it started a frenzy of speculation about his social life, which made it that much harder to be taken seriously at the foundation. Did the gossip columnists and everyone else expect him to become a monk, simply because he was handing out money for charity? And why would his sex life affect his ability to take his grandfather's place?

"Not tonight," he said shortly. "I'm here to talk with you about the woman who came to my office yesterday. She was at the gala, along with her aunt, Dorothy Hudson. It turns out Layne McGraw is William Hudson's niece. Dorothy is his widow. I want a security check on them both."

"You should have a preliminary file in a couple of days."

"Thanks." Matt glanced around the small cottage. "I don't get it. Why haven't you bought your own house?"

Connor patted Finnster on the head. "My needs

are simple and this place meets all of them. There's plenty of room for my dog. I do my job, your grandfather doesn't bother me and I've saved practically every penny he's ever paid me. Since my services don't come cheap, that's a healthy chunk of money. And that's on top of the Eisley company shares I've received as bonuses for services rendered."

"But you're stuck…*here.*"

"It's only a prison if you can't leave," Connor said. "People make their own jails. It's too bad your mother trapped you in hers."

Denial rose in Matt's throat, but he choked it down. Connor knew everything about the family; if they couldn't trust him by now, something was very wrong. He got up and headed for the door, then turned around. "Connor, what do you think of my stepfather?"

"Think of him?"

Matt frowned. He'd never heard that careful tone in Connor's voice before. "You investigated Peter when he began dating my mother—you must have an opinion."

"I found nothing in the background sweep that indicated a problem."

"But you don't like him."

Connor's face was expressionless. "I don't like very many people—it's a hazard of the job. I'll let you know when I have a report on the two women."

"Thanks." Matt headed toward his car again, still frowning.

Just because Layne McGraw and her aunt were

asking questions about the embezzlement case, it didn't mean anything was wrong. The D.A.'s office hadn't doubted William Hudson's guilt, so surely they were satisfied with the evidence. The idea that Matt might have missed something himself was disturbing—should he have seen things the police hadn't?

Don't you want to know if there's more to what happened than what it looks like? Layne McGraw's question had been echoing in Matt's head, and he tried to push it away. It was natural William's family wanted to believe in his innocence; it didn't mean he *was* innocent.

IN THE BEDROOM Layne always used at her aunt's house, she kicked off her shoes and wiggled her toes in relief, grateful she'd decided to stay the night. She hated pumps. And nylons. She hadn't worn nylons since her job interview with the *Babbitt.*

No doubt the women Matt Hollister dated were fashion mavens who wouldn't be caught dead without stockings, and probably silk to boot.

Layne glanced at her reflection in the mirror, chagrined as she recalled Matt's expression at seeing her sister. Her green silk dress hadn't looked that bad, but she couldn't compete with Jeannie. And why she cared when the man in question was Matt Hollister, she had no idea.

Layne lay down on the bed, unable to stop thinking about the gala. At least Hollister had kept his cool better than her aunt; having Aunt Dee confront him was astonishing, but it was an indication of how desperate she felt.

The house was silent and Layne rolled over to stare at the dark ceiling, thinking back to the nightmare almost seven months before. Uncle Will's suicide note hadn't sounded like him, just a brief typed message, with no personal word to his wife of twenty-nine years. He'd always handwritten his letters; even his business correspondence was drafted first by hand. Back in December she'd told the police she questioned whether her uncle had actually written the so-called suicide note, but they'd dismissed her, claiming a suicidal person didn't necessarily follow their normal pattern. Maybe, but she still wondered.

A picture filled her head of Uncle Will laughing on the Friday after the Thanksgiving holiday, not long before his death. They'd been making sandwiches from leftover turkey and he was talking about the future as if he didn't have a care in the world. A few days later discrepancies were found in his client records, a handful of newspaper articles were published, accusations were made against him….and then he was found dead, before he was even arrested.

Yet if it wasn't suicide, it had to be murder.

She hadn't discussed the possibility with Aunt Dee, though it must have occurred to her, as well. And it would mean someone had gotten in and killed Uncle Will in his home office. *If* that had happened, it was mostly likely someone he'd known well…someone he'd trusted. Someone like Peter Davidson, the partner with whom he'd shared the business. The friend who'd turned his back on his old buddy as soon as the suspicion of embezzlement was raised and was now trying to get away with all the proceeds from selling the company.

It appeared Peter Davidson had emerged from the scandal with a spotless reputation. But what if he *was* involved? It could mean he was a thief and potential murderer.

Damn.

Layne got up and pulled on a robe, deciding she might as well get some work done since she was too restless to lie still.

Sleep these days was elusive. Her uncle had kept meticulous records and documentation on everything, but his company records were in terrible shape thanks to the way they'd been packed, and most of the home records were boxed and stored in the upstairs storage room next to the master bedroom suite. No doubt Uncle Will could have put his hands on whatever he wanted, but she didn't know what she was looking for and she couldn't ignore a single scrap of paper in case it was important.

Sitting at her uncle's desk, Layne read through her notes and the logs she had made of what she'd found. It all seemed innocuous. The personal items that weren't damaged she had set aside for her aunt—others needed fixing and some were damaged beyond repair.

At the moment it was nearly impossible to make

any progress without knowing *what* she was investigating. The police department claimed they couldn't release anything because it was an open case and had to be kept confidential. The excuses might be valid if they were treating it as an ongoing investigation. But they weren't, and she suspected somebody with influence was blocking her access.

And who could that influential person be?

Peter Davidson?

If so, it was no wonder Aunt Dee hadn't gotten anywhere. The authorities probably didn't realize the way they were acting was enough by itself to make her question if they had something to hide. The few newspaper articles about the scandal were no help; they were vague and talked about missing money at Hudson & Davidson, but it had all happened so quickly and with Uncle Will dead, they'd shifted to fresh stories.

Layne pressed a finger to her temple as she read an unfinished memo Uncle Will had scribbled a few days before everything fell apart. There was no address or salutation, so the intended recipient was a mystery.

Come on, she urged her tired brain, trying to determine if there was any significant meaning in the bold, strong lines of her uncle's handwriting. But there was nothing she could see, and she put it on the stack to read another time when her head was clearer.

Tucking her legs under her, she leaned back in the comfortable executive-style chair and closed her eyes.

Talk to me, Uncle Will, she pleaded silently. *If you're here in the house the way Aunt Dee seems to think, you must have a reason.*

IT WAS JUST after 5:00 a.m. Sunday when Connor O'Brian parked across the street from the Hudson home in Carrollton, Washington, his gaze sweeping up and down the neighborhood.

He could barely remember a time when he wasn't on alert, watching for the next threat to come his way, whether it was a gang of Dublin street brats when he was ten, or a group of mercenaries when he was working in covert ops. Working with half of the alphabet soup intelligence agencies in the world had educated him in more ways than one.

After his father's death his family had moved to Dublin, and with his mother working several jobs, he'd gotten into more trouble than he cared to think about. It had taken several close calls with the law and a new stepfather with iron nerves to keep him out of more serious trouble. And he'd never even thanked Grady for any of it.

Connor massaged a jagged scar above his knee that had almost ended his career when he was twenty-two. Maybe it would have been better if it had; now his memories were a maze of scars…deaths that ought to have been prevented, friends lost and innocence destroyed. Espionage was a hard road once you'd started down it. Working for the Eisleys had come as a welcome break. Instead of international intrigue, he now dealt with ordinary intrigue. The motivations were often the same, but the scale was smaller. But then, one person's life was just as important to them as another, so maybe scale was moot.

The rising sun showed details of the house—large and comfortable, in an affluent neighborhood—and he snapped several pictures. His staff was already doing a full background sweep on Layne McGraw and Dorothy Hudson, except there were things you couldn't learn about people from a security report. He had his own methods, somewhat unorthodox, for getting a read on a situation.

A faint whine came from the passenger seat of the Jeep.

"Not yet, boy," he said to the large rottweiler.

Finnster whined again, his gaze fixed on the house opposite the Jeep. He was smart; he knew his master was watching that house. There were few men that Connor trusted as much as the highly trained dog.

Finn was the closest thing he had to family in the United States. Everyone else was in Ireland. His stepfather had died of heart failure earlier that spring and his mother had moved back to Dún Laoghaire to be close to her daughter. As a rule, Connor spared little energy on sentimentality, but he regretted Grady's passing more than he cared to think about. He'd always thought they'd have more time to know each other better.

Catching a flash of his reflection in the rearview

mirror made Connor's mouth twist in a humorless smile. Time? He was fifty-four now, and Grady had been nearly eighty. When were they *supposed* to become closer—on his rare, brief visits back home?

Still, his lost opportunities with Grady were the reason he didn't want Matt to trash his relationship with Peter Davidson unnecessarily. He didn't personally like Davidson—wealthy men sometimes took detours around moral issues and Peter was too polished for his taste—but he was a prize compared to S. S. Hollister. Connor snorted. Now, *there* was a man he had absolutely no use for...and for a long time it had looked as if Matthew would become just like his father.

Connor focused his camera on the classic Mustang parked in the driveway. It was the same car he'd seen Layne McGraw driving when she left the Eisley Foundation building. Something about her name had bothered him from the beginning, so he'd pulled his file on Peter Davidson after Matt's visit to his house and found a reference to her in Hudson's obituary, which was included with Davidson's file.

William Hudson is survived by his beloved wife, Dorothy; nieces Layne, Stephanie and Jeannette McGraw; and nephew Jeremy McGraw...

The obit didn't discuss William Hudson's suicide, or that he'd been facing arrest and indictment for embezzling.

The rottweiler whined again.

"Patience, my friend," Connor murmured, watching for signs of waking in the household, perhaps a curtain moving or a light coming on.

Ah...or miniblinds being opened.

Finnster nudged Connor's elbow.

"All right. Let's see how they react to you."

He checked the microphone on Finn's collar to be sure it was secure, tested the receiver in his ear, then let the dog out of the Jeep and tossed him a folded newspaper. He made a gesture with fingers, giving the command. The rottweiler drifted across the street and dropped the paper on the driveway before running to the front door, scratching and barking. When it opened, he pivoted and dashed back to the newspaper.

Layne McGraw followed, yawning. She put her hands on her hips and grinned at Finn. "What are you doing, making all that fuss out here? It's Sunday morning—don't you know people are catching up on their sleep?"

Finn nosed the newspaper forward a few inches. The newspaper routine was a maneuver they'd used more than once—how someone acted with a dog was revealing. Besides, Finnster was a good judge of character; his approval could be measured in how close he let someone get to him.

Finnster barked eagerly. He crouched down and cocked his head to one side, looking at Layne.

The ham.

Rottweilers had a reputation for ferocity in some circles, but Finn could make himself into a clown, scrunching up his face and using his eyes with the skill of a silent-screen actress. It was why Connor had picked him as a puppy.

"It's very thoughtful of you, boy, but that belongs to someone else. Aunt Dee doesn't take the paper. Did you go for a walk with someone and get away?" The girl's voice was amused, coming clearly through the radio receiver in Connor's ear.

Finn yipped again. "It's all right, I'm harmless." She held out her hand. "Give me a sniff. I probably smell like my aunt's cat, but JoJo is okay with dogs as long as they let him be the boss."

Finnster allowed himself to be coaxed and was soon on his back, legs waving in the air as he got his tummy rubbed, along with the place behind his ears that turned him into mush. He was in canine heaven.

Rolling his eyes, Connor belatedly lifted his camera and began shooting pictures.

"What have you got there, Lani?" he heard another voice ask a minute later.

Startled, Connor realized he'd missed Dorothy Hudson's arrival. Damn it all, he couldn't afford to get soft. He eased down in the driver's seat to be less visible and continue taking photos. Since Layne McGraw had seen him the day she'd come to talk to Matt, she might recognize his face if she got a good look in his direction.

"He's a marshmallow, Aunt Dee," Layne declared. "His owner probably took him out for a run and he got away. See? He's dragging a leash and brought us somebody else's newspaper. Maybe the house looks like his home."

"What a good boy." The newcomer added to the caresses Finn was receiving.

If possible, the rottweiler melted further, wriggling along the flagstone driveway to position himself equally between them. His hind legs were even paddling, a sure sign of his pure and complete surrender.

Connor flipped through the Davidson file and found a picture of Dorothy Hudson. The woman petting his dog was just as beautiful as the woman in the photo, though her smile didn't have the same merry quality. In fact, something about that sad smile reminded him of his sister back in Ireland, who'd never really gotten over her husband's death.

"What should we do about him?" Layne asked, drawing Connor's attention. His instincts told him that Layne McGraw and her aunt were decent people, an opinion Finnster would certainly endorse. Yet even decent people did strange things, and they could make serious trouble with the best of intentions.

"Let's see if he has a license tag."

Time for their exit strategy. Connor lifted a dog whistle to his mouth—it was outside the audible range for humans—and blew three short blasts, followed by another two.

What the…?

Connor stared. The bloody animal barely twitched an ear, instead he reached out a leg and pawed Layne McGraw's knee. He was utterly ignoring the command to leave…the toughest guard dog in the state, with highly specialized and unique training, had been corrupted by a pretty girl and her aunt.

Connor sent the command again and Finn finally scrambled to his feet, cocking his head as if he'd heard something.

He barked twice, looking intently down the street and dashed away before the two women could grab his leash.

Scowling, Connor drove after him. Two blocks away he stopped, leaned over and opened the passenger door. Finn climbed in, panting from running, tongue happily hanging from one side of his mouth.

"You should be ashamed of yourself," Connor scolded. "Do you have nothing but fur between those ears?"

Finn didn't appear abashed. He settled down with a pleased sigh and wagged his tail the way any other dog remembering a treat would wag—certainly not like an animal that had been schooled to follow whistled commands without question. *The first time those commands were given.*

Connor wasn't superstitious, but he couldn't help wondering if the whole thing was an omen.

Perhaps the McGraw woman and her aunt were going to be an even bigger problem than he'd anticipated.

CHAPTER FIVE

"I WONDER IF Jeannie spent the night with Matthew Hollister?" Layne said as she pulled into her parents' driveway.

"You think she'd go home with a man an hour after meeting him?" Aunt Dee asked. She didn't exactly have a hangover from drinking too much at the gala, but she looked a little worse for wear and had been quieter than normal.

"I have no idea, but you saw her expression when she met him, and he's been linked with several women since returning to Seattle." Layne parked next to her brother's Acura and behind Steffie's Lexus. Only Jeannie's sporty BMW was absent. She looked at the house and sighed; usually she tried to get there when dinner was already on the table, but Aunt Dee liked to arrive early.

"Come on, Lani. It's just Sunday dinner with your parents," Dee chided as they got out, each collecting their contributions for the meal. In Aunt Dee's case, fresh home-baked rolls and dessert, with Layne's contribution being sparkling cider, a pint of cream and two pounds of Seattle's Best Coffee beans.

"I know. That's the problem." Inside the house Layne dutifully kissed her mother and father and greeted Steffie and Jeremy. "Isn't Jeannie coming?" she asked, giving her mom the coffee and putting the cream and cider in the fridge.

"I'm here," Jeannie called as she sailed through the front door. "I got held up at the office."

"It's Sunday," Layne said, nibbling on a piece of celery from the vegetable tray. "Doctors may be on call 24/7, but don't executives get the weekend off?"

"Hey, I work in the real business world, not a two-bit joint like the *Babbitt*." An uncomfortable silence followed and Jeannette flushed. "Oh, Layne, I didn't mean anything by that."

Layne shrugged and popped a piece of cauliflower in her mouth. It was hardly a surprise how Jeannie and the rest of the family felt—working at the *Babbitt* wasn't prestigious or high paying and would never make her famous. But what was wrong with just being good at your job?

One of these days she'd meet a terrific guy and they'd have two or three kids. She couldn't be the kind of mom who baked cookies—she was too lousy of a cook—but she'd get them from a great bakery and go to all their school programs and accept whoever they wanted to be. You could do that when you were an everyday person rather than a famous heart doctor or supremely confident orthopedic surgeon and expected all your kids to be supercharged versions of yourself.

It wasn't even that she resented her parents' careers—they'd helped thousands of people over the years—but she wanted something like what her aunt and uncle had shared. Though Uncle Will's company had become hugely successful, it was his marriage that had meant everything to him. Besides, she was tired of feeling as if she'd failed her family because she hadn't been born as gorgeous and ambitious as the rest of them.

"Uh, well, can I get anyone a drink?" Layne's father asked. He was a big believer in smoothing over discord.

A hasty chorus of requests followed as Layne stepped down into the open great room to where most of the trophies and awards her brother and sisters had gotten were displayed, among them Jeannie's Phi Beta Kappa key, a letter of appreciation to Dr. Stephanie McGraw for saving the governor's wife, and Jeremy's track-and-field Olympic gold medals. His silver and bronze medals weren't on display— anything that wasn't the best wasn't good enough in the McGraw family.

"Layne, I'm *sorry*," Jeannie said from behind her. "I just don't understand why you can't work at a national magazine or major newspaper, at the very least."

"You're just making things worse, sis," Jeremy told her, giving Layne a hug. "I personally want you all to quit your jobs and come work on my campaign next year. How about it, Layne? We can be the fighting

McGraws, righting wrongs and bringing justice to a weary world."

Layne loved her family, but sometimes she wished she lived in Timbuktu and only saw them on major holidays. "Save the campaign speeches, Jeremy. I'm staying at the *Babbitt*."

"Here's to our next U.S. congressman," declared Barbara, handing Layne a glass of her favorite sparkling water.

Everyone dutifully raised their beverages and echoed the toast. Layne was certain Jeremy would be elected; he got everything he went after—like going to the Olympics.

"So when are you getting married, Jeremy?" Aunt Dee asked as they sat down to dinner.

"After Lissette is back from Antarctica and has finished her study on the emperor penguin."

"It must be hard, knowing she's down there in an observation station for the winter. It gets to almost a hundred below freezing, doesn't it?"

"Yes, but Lissette has been looking forward to being on an Antarctic research team for years. I couldn't ask her to give up something so important because we're getting married."

Layne cast a grateful glance at her aunt as Dee continued asking questions.

The meal was one of Barbara McGraw's healthy offerings—chicken breasts with mushrooms and asparagus in a light garlic wine sauce. Delicious, naturally. Barbara wasn't an inspired cook like her sister, but when she did something, she did it very well.

The expected pitch about going to work at the university came when Layne was helping her mother wash up after dinner.

"Dear, Jeannie shouldn't have said that earlier about the *Babbitt*," Barbara murmured quietly, casting a displeased look into the great room where her husband and three eldest children were playing bridge.

"I'm not sure she can help herself. At least with me."

"Perhaps. Relationships between sisters are complicated. But we're all concerned that your talents aren't being fully utilized at the *Babbitt*. I realize you love research, that's why I spoke to Sheldon about your joining the study team he's forming."

"It's not the same kind of research, Mom," Layne returned drily. For a brilliant woman, Barbara could be quite dense when she chose to be.

"But it's still uncovering information and learning new things. And if you went after your PhD, just think of everything you could find out. All sorts of new facts about diseases and how to cure them. Give Sheldon a call and talk to him."

"I can learn new facts at the *Babbitt* without writing a dissertation and God knows what else is involved in getting a doctorate."

Barbara's eyes opened wide. "Layne—"

"I'm kidding, I know what's involved in getting a

PhD," Layne said hastily. Her mother would have a stroke if she believed one of her children didn't know every step, in detail, of getting an advanced degree. "But I'm not going to change my mind, I'm happy at the *Babbitt* and that's where I'm staying."

"Stubborn," Barbara muttered. "You've always been just like your grandmother that way."

Layne gave her a bright smile. "Gee, Mom, that may be the nicest thing you've ever said to me."

ON TUESDAY EVENING Layne was settled at Uncle Will's desk, logging more items from his old office at work. She had a feeling she was missing something, she just didn't know what.

Mostly she needed more information.

Maybe if Aunt Dee got the autopsy report she could approach the investigation from a different angle. Of course, that was a long shot, too. Right now she was operating on her aunt's belief in her husband, and her own vague sense that something wasn't right about what had happened. After all, where was the missing money? Aunt Dee sure didn't have it, and in his letter Peter Davidson had made a point of telling her he'd personally repaid the stolen funds from his own pocket.

Moodily, Layne flipped on Uncle Will's computer. It went through the regular start-up routine and she figured it hadn't been turned on since before his death.

Then Layne frowned.

Who *had* turned the power off? Aunt Dee avoided computers like the plague and certainly wouldn't have known how to turn it off properly. The police? Maybe if they'd confiscated the CPU and returned it, but it was unlikely they'd hook it back up again. And why would Uncle Will write and print a suicide note, then turn the computer off when he'd always left it on?

Maybe somebody else had been in the office… like a murderer.

You're reaching, Layne thought impatiently.

After a few minutes Uncle Will's favorite screen saver appeared—mostly pictures of Aunt Dee shifting one to the next—and Layne wiggled the mouse to show the desktop again. She opened Microsoft Word and looked at the recent document list. It was really old stuff and she was relieved not to find a saved file of the suicide note.

Next she opened Windows Explorer to look for files. There wasn't much there, except a number of image files. She clicked on the first one, which turned out to be Aunt Dee in her wedding gown, nineteen and luminously hopeful. The next picture was of Layne as a toddler at the reception, held high in Uncle Will's arms, dashing and handsome in his navy uniform. She pressed the print icon, wanting to take a copy home, but nothing happened. After ten minutes of investigation, she stared at the computer, puzzled.

"What do you think about that, JoJo?" she said to

Aunt Dee's cat. He was lying across a corner of the desk, methodically cleaning his paw.

"Think about what?" Aunt Dee asked. She stood at the door, looking like a Victorian lady in her long flowing gown. Her hair was loosely braided, and the thick gold plait hung over one shoulder, tied with a blue satin ribbon. She could have passed for twenty-five, instead of a woman close to fifty.

"Oh…the computer doesn't have a print driver for this printer."

"Speak English, not computerese."

Layne pointed. "This computer hasn't been told how to talk to that printer. Did you buy this device in the past few months?"

"Me?" Dee let out a short, humorless laugh. "You have to be kidding. I haven't been in here since that night. Besides, you know how I feel about computers."

"The same way I feel about oysters."

They shuddered together.

Yet Layne glanced at the printer again and frowned. It seemed strange that Uncle Will would type and print a brief suicide note at work, then bring it home. Suicide didn't fit his nature in the first place, but *especially* suicide planned in advance. "Uh, I hate to ask this, but where did you find the note that Uncle Will supposedly wrote? I mean the specific location…on the desk…or in his pocket…?"

Dee hugged her arms closer to her body. "I'm not the one who found it. I called 911 when I saw him lying on the floor and it was obvious he was... Anyway, it seemed forever before the ambulance got here, but it couldn't have been more than a few minutes. The paramedics told me to wait in the living room and I knew they believed it was suicide when they came out and started asking questions. Until then I thought it might have been a heart attack."

Her aunt was hovering at the door, still unable to come into the room where her husband had died. It gave Layne a peculiar feeling, too, even if she didn't believe that spirits lingered behind to haunt the living.

"Actually, when the police arrived, I think they said something about finding the note on the printer," Dee murmured. "They gave it to me to read and I couldn't believe what I was seeing."

"Was it in a plastic bag or anything?"

"No."

Layne wasn't an expert on police procedure, but if they hadn't used an evidence bag, they'd probably never considered anything other than suicide. And the police *should* have handled it differently... if Aunt Dee was remembering correctly, the suicide note had been found on a machine that couldn't possibly have printed it. She couldn't explain why Uncle Will hadn't set up the printer, but that probably wasn't important now. All that mattered was the fact that nothing added up.

"Well, I'm going to try to get some sleep," her aunt said. "I'm glad you're spending the night. You've been stretching yourself too thin."

"Don't worry about me." Layne hesitated, glancing at the computer and printer and back to her aunt. "Is the security system turned on?"

"You know I always turn it on before it gets dark."

"Okay. Sleep well."

She listened as Dee's footfalls faded down the hall, barely discernible going up to the master bedroom. Her aunt didn't like admitting it, but Layne knew staying alone in the house bothered her, and having her niece spend the night sometimes helped her sleep.

Layne checked the printer again and tried copying something. It worked perfectly and she tossed the copy on the desk. She'd wanted to believe in Uncle Will because she loved him and thought he was a great guy, but this was tangible evidence.

Her heart raced with both excitement and fear. Nobody was idiotic enough to come back seven months after murdering someone, on the off chance they'd left a clue that the police hadn't found, but she was glad Aunt Dee had a security system, nonetheless.

She pushed the sliding keyboard tray, but it still refused to go fully under the desk. Frustrated, Layne reached under the desk to find which part of the mechanism the cord was catching on. But it wasn't the cord her fingers encountered, it was paper. She pulled out a thin, crumpled folder.

Uncle Will's distinctive handwriting was on a sheet of paper inside.

"Notes for lawyer, if needed," he'd scrawled at the top. Layne's pulse jumped with hope it would contain the information she needed to investigate, but the short amount of text below seemed more like random thoughts than anything else.

We've grown too fast, that's the problem. We need better IT support in the future.

First priority, assure clients they'll be compensated.

Can't believe Peter accused me today. I don't think he's responsible for the thefts, but why is he acting this way? Told him to get off his duff and help find the truth. I'm innocent.

My Darling Dee must stop worrying. The truth will come out.

Wire transfers have a time/date stamp. Can prove I wasn't there, at least some of the nights, just have to get my records and everything else together.

My records?

Layne pulled the keyboard out and searched the sliding tray shelf in the vain hope something had fallen out of the folder, but she didn't find anything else and could have screamed.

What kind of records, and which wire transfers?

These notes might be the last thing Uncle Will had written and the police weren't going to take it seriously without something substantive to go with it. But at least she could discuss the printer issue with them—surely it wouldn't compromise their "open investigation" confidentiality rules to verify where the suicide note was found, and maybe it would make them take another look. In the meantime, she could try to figure out what the "records" were that Uncle Will had referenced. And the "everything else."

Exhilaration replaced the frustration simmering in Layne. She finally had something real to look for— if Uncle Will had believed he could prove his innocence, surely she could, as well.

"HERE YOU GO, MATT," Gillian said on Friday afternoon.

She handed him the copy of the *Puget Sound Babbitt* that he'd requested and hastily exited the office. It didn't take long to learn the reason. Just above the table of contents was the headline: Who Is Peter Davidson of the Eisley Foundation?

Hell.

He flipped the magazine open and began reading.

The article spoke of Peter's marriage to Katrina Eisley, his recent altruism in donating time to his wife's family's charity organization, his investment acumen and his success in private business. It wasn't negative, *exactly,* but it had a tone Matt distrusted.

The author didn't mention the incident at Hudson & Davidson, but Matt knew it could just be the first of several articles, the opening salvo in an attempt to criticize either Peter, or him *through* his stepfather. The press had been quick to question every step Matt had made at the Eisley Foundation.

Or was he just being paranoid? And there was another question...did Layne McGraw and her aunt have anything to do with it? So far Connor's background checks had shown that Layne was exactly what she claimed, a researcher for the regional news magazine, while her aunt was a graphic artist.

It was possible they were simply trying to find out more about what had happened so they could deal with it better. Problem was, it could result in the whole mess being dragged out again in public.

Matt's jaw set.

However much he disliked getting negative press these days, he probably deserved it. Pete didn't. Hell, Pete had given him the job at Hudson & Davidson. And his mother had virtually become a recluse after her divorce from Matt's father, so the media had no business arguing she was a "public figure" and not entitled to her privacy because of it. Not that Matt bought that crap about a person giving up the right to privacy simply by choosing a more public life.

Matt had read the preliminary file Connor had put together on Layne. She had a degree in library science, owned a home in the university district and came from a highly successful family of professionals. No red flags. No reason to think she'd make trouble for the sake of making trouble. Yet that was part of the problem...if Layne didn't have ulterior motives, she might sincerely wonder if her uncle was innocent. It didn't mean she was right, but by stirring everything up, she could cause trouble with the best of intentions.

Frowning, he picked up the phone and dialed Connor.

"Yeah?" the security chief answered.

"It's me. Can you come up to my office?"

"Be right there."

Spinning around in his chair, Matt looked out the window at Lake Union; it was raining, so the view was partially obscured. Despite the weather, he saw a crewing team on the water, rowing toward the docks. He envied them—the effort, the teamwork, the burn of muscles being used, it was cleaner and simpler than changing your ways and running a multibillion-dollar philanthropic foundation.

Even as the thought formed, the door behind him opened. "What's up, Matt?"

Matt turned and slid the copy of the *Babbitt* across the desk. "There's an article in there about my stepfather."

Connor raised an eyebrow. "Full of crap?"

"Not exactly. More like damning with faint praise. I have no idea if Layne McGraw is behind it or not."

"Doubtful. It's unlikely she'd want media attention on her uncle's case."

"I agree." Matt looked down at the magazine, wishing he could get Layne McGraw's voice out of his head…the voice that questioned whether there might be more to the embezzlement case than what everyone believed. Anything was possible. "Connor, what do you know about the thefts at Hudson & Davidson?"

"Not much. Mr. Davidson didn't want me becoming involved with security issues at his company, before or after the thefts."

Matt's nerves tightened. "Why?"

"Ego, most likely. He's wealthy, but it's peanuts compared to Eisley money. Mind if I have a drink?" Without waiting for a response, Connor pressed a button on the wall and two heavy panel doors glided open, revealing the wet bar left from Gordon Eisley's day. He poured himself a finger of whiskey before sitting and planting his feet on the office's nineteenth-century mahogany desk.

Matt smiled. Connor didn't have any reverence for antiques. He'd probably driven Gordon crazy with his offhand ways and strong language. Gordon Eisley had worked hard and made an obscene amount of money, but he believed in a rigid code of how things should be done. He must have tolerated Connor because he had recognized there wasn't anyone better to handle the family's security needs. Not that Matt's grandfather was playing an active role in his business affairs or the foundation these days; he'd finally decided to listen to his doctor and relax.

"I'm getting rid of that bar," Matt commented.

"Too bad, it's the only thing I like in this office. Besides the view." Connor waved his glass as if in a toast. "I hand it to you Yanks—bourbon whiskey is a fine thing the Americans gave the world, and your grandfather stocked the best."

"Bourbon was never my drink, so I'll take your word. Do you have any ideas for dealing with Ms. McGraw?" Matt asked.

"Talk to her. It could be a mistake, but there isn't much else to do without getting heavy-handed."

"Aren't you the one who told me speaking with the press was the same as spitting into the wind? Not that I paid much attention at the time, but even if Ms. McGraw isn't a reporter, she's still connected to the *Babbitt*."

Connor snorted. "When I told you that, you'd just spent three days with a female shark from the worst rag in the business—pillow talk makes for a fool's interview. Just talk to the McGraw woman and find out what she wants."

Matt didn't try to defend himself. He'd met the female "shark" when he was twenty and terminally stupid. He wasn't sure if age bred wisdom, but it certainly taught caution, particularly when it came to women and the paparazzi. Not that he'd cared about racy pictures or being seen as a player back then; his concern had been keeping his grandfather from cutting off his monthly trust-fund checks.

"Maybe *you* should contact Layne," Matt suggested.

"Bad idea. She'll think you're trying to intimidate her. But I'll go meet the aunt. She hasn't seen me before, so she won't recognize the connection to the Eisley family."

"What good will meeting her do?"

Connor's gaze dropped to his bourbon as he shrugged. "You never know."

"Whatever. I'll go see Ms. McGraw."

"Fine. But a word of advice." The security chief swung his feet down to the thick carpet and got up. "Try not to lose your temper with the woman."

"Wow, thanks. I'm glad I have you around—I would never have thought of that."

"Sarcasm is wasted on a hardheaded Irishman," Connor said at the door. "Use irony the next time."

ON SATURDAY MORNING Layne dug a stubborn weed from her garden and tossed it onto the patio. Lately she'd had little time to dig for anything except answers about her uncle, and in the lush Pacific Northwest, ignoring your yard was a mistake. With the rain they received throughout the summer, blackberry brambles and other unwanted plants could invade in an instant.

Nevertheless, she loved having her own place.

Weeds and all.

Usually she could clear her mind while gardening, yet this morning everything kept going through her head. She'd shown Aunt Dee the brief list Uncle Will had written, but beyond identifying her husband's handwriting, Dee didn't have any insights about it. Dee was relieved to have some confirmation of her husband's innocence, but there were still too many unanswered questions for either one of them to relax.

Layne flung another weed over her shoulder and heard a sharp exclamation. Whirling around, she gaped. Matt Hollister was standing on her patio, brushing bits of dirt from his fine suit. Her stomach did a cartwheel.

"Oh, I didn't know you were there," she said.

"I rang the doorbell and nobody answered, but your car was outside, so I came around. That classic Mustang in the driveway belongs to you, right? You should keep it in the garage for safety. Cars like that can be a target."

Layne tensed. "I left it out because I'm going to Carrollton later." *And what business is it of yours, anyway? Planning some vandalism?* she wanted to add, except it would sound rude and challenging. The McGraws and Hudsons probably weren't his favorite people at the moment, and it wouldn't be good to antagonize him further…at least not until she got the information she needed.

"I understand. I wanted to talk to you." Matt held up the latest edition of the *Babbitt* and Layne winced. So much for not antagonizing him.

She stepped off the low retaining wall to the patio below. "I didn't have anything to do with that article. Not directly, at least. Noah Wilkie, the *Babbitt*'s social reporter, overheard part of what my aunt was saying at the gala, so he may have mentioned it to one of the other reporters."

"I see."

"But I'd still like to apologize…and also about my aunt getting so upset. It wasn't like her, but she's been through a lot. And she…" Layne's voice trailed. She was in danger of starting to babble, and she reminded herself of her plan to treat Matt Hollister as a fact to be researched, instead of a sexy guy who turned her brain into a mass of overreacting neurons. Problem was, she tended to babble at the oddest times, anyhow.

"Mrs. Hudson seems like a nice lady."

Layne nodded. "She is. By the way, I appreciated your coming to my uncle's funeral."

MATT RECOGNIZED THE sorrow still shadowing Layne's eyes and sighed. It would be a lot easier to deal with the situation if he could simply see her as a troublemaker, not as a grieving niece.

She wasn't his type, but something about her intrigued him. Her small breasts had tightened in the cool, morning air and their firm imprint under her T-shirt was playing havoc with his pulse. What's more, she didn't seem to be putting on a feminine act of any kind. She certainly hadn't primped or been flustered about her casual appearance.

Matt pushed the thought away. Over the years he'd learned to quickly size up women, and Layne was the sort he avoided—unsophisticated, family oriented and likely to develop expectations about the future.

"If you think William Hudson was innocent, who do you think stole the money?" he asked.

"I don't know, but his death seems awfully convenient. He died before he could even start to defend himself or present his side of things. And his so-called suicide note didn't have a single personal message to his wife. It just said 'I can't face what's coming, I'm sorry,' and that's all. Uncle Will was honorable and decent. It's hard to imagine him living entirely one way and then suddenly doing something so totally out-of-character."

"Actually, some people do." The words came out more stiffly than Matt had intended, perhaps because *he* was doing something out-of-character and was having to fight an uphill battle in the court of public opinion. Nobody wanted to believe that Matthew Hollister could go from wild partygoer to serious director of a philanthropic foundation. Because of it, most people preferred to criticize, rather than rolling their sleeves up and working with him.

But he *was* serious.

Dead serious.

"Look, do you have *any* reason to think your uncle was innocent?" he asked. "The police and D.A. are convinced he was guilty."

A hint of anger flared in Layne's eyes, then she drew a deep breath. "My aunt asked me to look into the charges against Uncle Will and I've been searching, but it's hard to get anywhere without knowing how or when the thefts occurred. All I've been able to piece together is that it has something to do with wire transfers and they probably happened at night. I wanted to talk to Mr. Davidson about it, only he wasn't available, so I got the meeting with you instead. Then a few days ago I discovered something that shows Uncle Will *didn't* kill himself. It won't convince the police, but it's enough for me."

Matt frowned. "What is it?"

"Aunt Dee was told he died of a massive drug overdose. They found a note and declared it a suicide, even though the letter was typed and unsigned."

"That's hardly proof."

"No, but I've done research on suicide. Apparently a note isn't that common, and when there *is* one, it's usually handwritten. On top of which—" she paused "—it was found on the printer in Uncle Will's home office, but that printer doesn't work with his computer."

"The ink cartridge probably just dried out."

Layne shook her head. "That's not what I mean. After his personal belongings were delivered from the company, Aunt Dee locked the office. She never goes in there. The other day I tried to print something on my uncle's computer and discovered the correct print driver wasn't loaded to the system. So why would the note be in the print tray?"

Matt got a cold chill through his stomach. What Layne was saying wasn't conclusive, but it was enough to raise doubts.

"Have you told the police?"

"I spoke to Detective Rivera at the Carrollton Police Department earlier this week. The only thing he'd confirm is that the note *was* found on the printer, but he said that Uncle Will could have brought it from the office and put it there to be sure it was seen quickly."

"It's possible," Matt admitted.

"Anything is possible, but it mostly sounds like he's trying to explain things away so it doesn't look as if the police didn't investigate properly. It's ironic. He claims I'm biased, but they seem far more biased than me. The detective dismissed the printer issue before I even finished explaining. He says I just want the finding of suicide reversed so Aunt Dee can get Uncle Will's life insurance money."

When Matt raised an inquiring eyebrow, she sighed.

"Life insurance policies have suicide clauses. Aunt Dee didn't get a penny and she's about to lose her house. But as much as I want to help her, I wouldn't do anything unethical."

"What about income from Hudson & Davidson?"

"Your stepfather claims they're operating at a loss because of the scandal, so there isn't any income."

"Oh," Matt said uncomfortably.

While the company *had* taken a hit, they'd fully rebounded even before he'd left to run the Eisley Foundation. And even if Peter was directing all profits to himself to repay the personal funds he'd used to restore client accounts, it wasn't the same as operating at a loss. He hadn't legally "loaned" the money to the company, so it shouldn't be claimable as a line item expense.

Surely Layne had misunderstood.

"Aunt Dee won't accept anything from the family," Layne added, frustrated. "The only thing I can do is try to learn what really happened. It isn't just the insurance—clearing Uncle Will's name is awfully important to her. And with what I've found so far, I think I can do it."

Matt had an odd feeling Layne wasn't telling him everything. Not that he blamed her. She'd found something that suggested her uncle had been murdered, and he was connected to one of the people she probably suspected. Hell, maybe she even thought he'd try to protect Peter at all costs.

It was a sobering thought.

He wanted to keep Pete's reputation from being ripped apart for no reason, but he wouldn't protect him from embezzlement and murder charges. Besides, why would his stepfather embezzle? Peter had inherited money from a distant relative before going into business with William Hudson, parlaying it into a sizable personal fortune by investing in the right places. He didn't need to steal from anybody.

His stepfather was a good guy, and he'd given Matt a job at Hudson & Davidson when no one else would consider hiring him. But what if in his haste to save the company, Pete had jumped to conclusions?

And equally as bad, what if Matt had jumped to conclusions himself, wanting to tie things up quickly so he could start his work with the foundation? If William Hudson *was* innocent, it meant a thief and murderer was still out there.

"Where do you plan to go from here?" he asked.

"I'm going to check everything. Every movement, every piece of paper related to the business, public or private. Backgrounds on employees are a possibility…anything I can put my hands on. If Uncle Will *didn't* steal from the company, he was framed for someone else's crime."

"Okay," Matt said slowly. "I'm not sure how much I agree with you, but I'm willing to meet you halfway. I'll help."

Layne blinked, appearing astonished. "You'll what?"

"I'll help."

"I'm not trying to be difficult, but why?"

"I didn't have much contact with your uncle when I worked at Hudson & Davidson, but I liked him. It was a shock when everything came out about the thefts. I don't like to think we missed something when the police were investigating."

"That was their job, not yours."

"Nevertheless, I'm serious about getting involved."

"Then you'll tell me more about the case?" Layne asked eagerly.

The memory of his stepfather asking what he'd told Dorothy Hudson and her niece flashed through Matt's head. Giving Layne information could make things sticky with Peter, but it was one of those "damned if you do and damned if you don't" situations. Besides, the mess obviously wasn't going away. And even if it caused problems between him and Peter, Layne and her aunt were entitled to the truth.

"Yeah, I'll tell you what I know," he said. "It isn't that much, but it might be useful."

Layne's smile flashed and Matt was startled by its brilliance. "Thanks. Oh…by the way, did you have anything to do with how my uncle's belongings were sent over from Hudson & Davidson?"

"I'm not sure who took care of that. Any special reason?"

"Just curious. We can talk out here." Layne gestured to the patio table. "I'll get something to make notes."

As she disappeared into her house, Matt once again got the feeling she was holding something back. But she had a truckload of reasons to be careful, and he'd gotten her to agree—more or less—to let him be involved in her search for answers.

Strangely, hanging around Layne didn't sound as tedious as it ought to, especially with the lingering memory of her bright smile. But that was just because he sympathized with her and her aunt. They were grieving for William Hudson, at the same time trying to find answers about his death. It couldn't be easy.

CHAPTER SIX

LAYNE QUICKLY GRABBED a notebook and pen from her office upstairs, afraid Matt would change his mind. She didn't know what to make of his offer to assist with the investigation, but he was also willing to provide information, and that was exactly what she needed. Yet even as the thought formed, she froze on the staircase and frowned.

Was he hoping to tell his stepfather about what she was doing and what she'd discovered? Even if it was unlikely that Peter Davidson was guilty of embezzling and murder, she hadn't made up her mind about him.

She would have to be very careful of what she said.

Matt wasn't sitting at the patio table when Layne stepped outside, and for a moment she thought he *had* changed his mind. Instead, she found him on the upper slope of her yard, examining the Haida-style totem poles tucked among the trees.

"This is great," he exclaimed. "I looked up and saw mysterious images gazing out at me."

"That's the point." Layne walked up to where he was standing. She was proud of her garden. College friends majoring in landscape architecture had done the yard as a group project, including carving the totem poles. She couldn't have afforded such a fancy landscape job herself, but it had worked out. They'd received top grades and she'd gotten a terrific outdoor space for the cost of materials.

It was nice having her own house. Her parents had established a college fund for each of their children and let them make their own decisions with it. After two years in a dorm, she'd chosen to buy a place, figuring she probably didn't need the funds for graduate school.

"It looks as if there's a small trail around the perimeter of the yard," Matt said. "What's this?" He was examining a low bridge that linked two sides of a small gully made to look like a rocky creek bed.

"The upper section of the yard is an adventure playground for kids. The plan makes great use of a small space. That's a suspension bridge to teach balance and coordination."

"Please don't tell me you have children."

He sounded so horrified that Layne rolled her eyes. It was no secret how Matt Hollister felt about children; he'd mentioned his opinion often enough when being hounded by the press. They'd ask if he was going to settle down with the centerfold or actress he was dating and start a family, and he'd pop off a smart comment about staying a bachelor forever. Then he'd say his idea of commitment was the amount of time it took for two people to drink a magnum of champagne.

"No children," she replied. "But my then-boyfriend and I were talking about starting a family when the yard was being designed. Until he met my sister Steffie."

"I thought her name was Jeannette."

"I have two sisters, Jeannette and Stephanie. They're identical twins. Anyway, Richard fell for her instantly. So he dropped me and started asking her out, but at least I ended up with a yard that's ready for kids." Layne realized she was running off at the mouth again and drew a calming breath.

They returned to the patio and sat at the table. "All right," she said, her pen poised over the pad of paper. "Tell me about what happened at Hudson & Davidson. I'm all ears."

"Not quite," Matt returned. His quick survey of her body made her sharply aware of the grubby condition of her gardening clothes, but she stuck up her chin in defiance. No doubt he was comparing her to Jeannie and she was coming up short.

He's just a fact to be researched, she reminded herself for the umpteenth time.

"Like I said, I don't know that much," he continued. "You're probably aware your uncle managed the accounting division of Hudson & Davidson, while Peter ran the investment side. You're right that the investigation was about wire transfers. The thefts were mostly illegal transfers from client accounts to offshore accounts in the Cayman Islands, all on Thursday evenings when your uncle was known to work late."

Layne tried to keep her face expressionless.

Since when had Uncle Will worked late? He'd always spent every minute possible with Aunt Dee. One of the reasons he hadn't gone career in the navy was because there was a chance he might get stationed someplace where his wife couldn't be with him.

"Is there proof he was at the company the nights in question?"

"No, other than the transfers being made using his keycard, password and access codes. The cyber-crime lab also determined the wire transfers were made from the computer in his office. With all the evidence, they felt it was an open-and-shut case."

"People can hack computers and steal access codes and stuff," Layne murmured. "And other employees must have had keys to the office."

"Of course, but there was no evidence of hacking and your uncle never reported a missing keycard."

The case seemed straightforward, yet Uncle Will's notes had said he could prove he wasn't there when some of the thefts occurred. Layne hadn't bothered telling Detective Rivera about the folder, knowing he would just say Uncle Will was trying to make himself look innocent. Perhaps, but there was something else to consider: William Hudson hadn't been a stupid man, and leaving a conspicuous trail of clues to his door was unbelievably stupid. Didn't anyone think it was odd that the case against him was so clean?

"Last I heard, the police were still searching for the missing money," Matt said.

Layne absently doodled a series of question marks on her pad of paper. Why *hadn't* the funds been found? Money these days was mostly electronic; there should be a trail to follow. And it wasn't something she could hunt for herself since that required subpoenas and search warrants and mad computer skills.

"You said the transfers were all on Thursday nights—do you have any specific dates?" she asked.

"They may have been discussed, but I don't recall any."

Fair enough. It hadn't been a member of his family accused of embezzling, and it would be hard confirming dates from memory, anyhow.

"What about the time frame? Were the wire transfers over a period of weeks or months?"

"They occurred between the end of August last year, and the third week in November, not long before your uncle's sui…uh, before he died."

Layne was glad Matt hadn't called it suicide. After her discoveries in Uncle Will's office, she was convinced that he'd been murdered. But it wasn't just because of the printer question. William Hudson had hated taking medication, same as Aunt Dee; normally you'd have been lucky to find aspirin in their medicine cabinet. Layne could see someone being momentarily overcome by depression and popping pills, but you had to have the pills to pop in the first place. She would have to get the autopsy report to find out what he'd died from—an overdose could be either prescription meds or street drugs.

She also still needed information from the police file since Matt didn't have specific dates, but knowing the embezzling had occurred on Thursday evenings over a three-month period gave her a time frame to look at. Now she could focus on finding something that proved Uncle Will wasn't at the office on one or more Thursday nights during that period.

Matt leaned forward. "I'll go through my personal papers and see if I jotted anything else down about the case. I can let you know anything I find the next time we meet."

"How about emailing the information to me? It would be easiest." Layne scribbled her address on a blank sheet of paper and handed it to him. She added her phone number just in case, though she wasn't really sure why.

"I'd rather discuss it personally."

MATT SAW THE reluctance in Layne's eyes and was grimly amused. She *really* didn't want him involved.

"You know, Peter Davidson ought to have a list of the dates and times of all the thefts he could give me," Layne said slowly.

Matt winced. "I don't think Pete is feeling too cooperative at the moment. I mentioned speaking with you and your aunt at the gala and he's upset that everything is being stirred up again."

"I see."

"I wouldn't read anything into it," Matt added. "Pete feels betrayed and wants to put this in the past."

"How do you think Uncle Will felt when his closest friend refused to believe he was innocent?"

Matt saw temper simmering a second time in Layne's green eyes and was curious what more she'd say if she stopped guarding her tongue. But he didn't get a chance to find out; her angry features became unreadable again. "Sorry, I shouldn't have said that."

"It's okay—I prefer honesty."

"A lot of people say that's what they want, then are outraged when they get it." She checked her watch and stood up. "I need to leave soon. My aunt is expecting me and I have to shower before going."

He got to his feet, as well. "When can we talk again?"

"Call when you have some information and we'll set up a time."

"All right."

Layne determinedly escorted him around the side of the house. She gave new meaning to the old joke, "here's your hat, what's your hurry?"

"Do you have voice mail on this number?" Matt asked as they got to his Mercedes-Benz. He held up the sheet of paper she'd given him, though it hadn't been necessary; Connor had provided phone numbers for both Layne and her aunt, along with a whole lot of other information, including details of Dorothy Hudson's financial problems since her husband's death.

"I have an answering machine. I sometimes forget to check it, but I'll try to remember." She looked at his car and he saw a flicker of admiration in her eyes. "Nice ride. But I wouldn't have pegged you for the candy-apple-red type."

"What did you expect?"

"Black, maybe. Or something in silver."

"My first race car was this color, so I'm partial."

"I also wouldn't have guessed you were the sentimental type. Doesn't a fun car like this make it harder for people to take you seriously as a philanthropist?"

Matt's eyes narrowed. "I don't see why it should. You only need a big sedan if you have kids, and I don't plan to have any. Not everyone believes in the marriage-and-family route."

"Whatever," she said quickly. "If you change your mind about emailing the information, let me know."

"I'm not going to change my mind."

Scowling, he sank into the low seat of the Mercedes-Benz. It wasn't just her comments about his car; having a woman wanting to get rid of him was a new experience. Usually it was the other way around. Not that he had any illusions about being irresistible; his money was a big part of the appeal.

Curiously, his father didn't seem to care how many dollar signs were in his girlfriends' eyes. Spence appeared to accept that his fortune was part of his appeal and enjoyed the wider availability of feminine companionship it provided. Not that all of his wives and lovers were after Hollister money—a few of them, like Matt's own mother, had a good deal of wealth in their own right.

LAYNE SHOWERED AND hurried to Carrollton, but she was tempted to turn around and leave when she saw her mother's Audi in Dee's driveway. She parked reluctantly and let herself into the house.

"Hi, Aunt Dee," she called.

"We're in the living room, Lani."

Steffie was there, too, looking perfectly beautiful as usual. Of her two sisters, Layne got along best with Steffie. Stephanie wasn't as outspoken as Jeannie and was less opinionated about how everyone should live.

Barbara McGraw smiled. "Hello, dear. Dorothy and I were talking last night and she mentioned you were coming over, so we came, too. I wanted to bring this so you can start getting ready." She held out an envelope.

"Ready for what?"

"Well, it occurred to us that we've been assuming you would have the same interest in medicine as your father and me."

Steffie gave Layne an apologetic smile. "Mom has a one-track mind."

"I do *not*," Barbara denied instantly. "Anyhow, Layne, I got to thinking about how you loved to read those *National Geographic* magazines. And the light dawned that we've been pushing you in the wrong direction all these years."

"Oh?" Layne glanced inside the envelope and saw a plane ticket to Albuquerque. "You think I should go to New Mexico?"

"I think you should consider archaeology. Your father made some inquiries and there's a new excavation starting. They may have actually found another lost civilization. He got you officially assigned to the project through the University of New Mexico."

Layne stared in disbelief. "He *what?* I can't—"

"Lani, wouldn't you like some coffee? There's a fresh pot in the kitchen," Dee interrupted.

Layne dropped the envelope and stomped out of the living room, fuming. She loved her mother, but Barbara could be the most insensitive person on the planet.

"I told Mom it was bad idea," Steffie said, following her.

"Bad doesn't begin to describe it. Obviously she's forgotten that I wanted to be an archaeologist when I was ten, but she told me I needed to choose a practical career like podiatry, cardiology or obstetrics."

Her sister sighed. "If you wanted to go into archaeology, why didn't you ignore her and do it?"

"Because I'm interested in everything, not just archaeology, and realized I didn't have to dig in the dirt to satisfy my curiosity. Are Mom and Dad really *that* embarrassed about my job? Their pushing isn't new, but the past few months they've been impossible."

"At the risk of sounding clichéd, it's complicated." Steffie nibbled on a piece of biscotto from the cookie jar. "This thing with Uncle Will has rattled them badly. They worry you'll wake up someday and be dissatisfied with your life."

Layne's temper cooled a few degrees, though she noticed Stephanie hadn't denied how Barbara and Walter felt about her being with the *Babbitt*. "I don't think that's what happened to Uncle Will."

"We don't *know* what happened."

"Maybe." Layne stirred cream into her coffee. She was pretty sure Aunt Dee didn't want anyone in the family to know about the investigation unless proof of her husband's innocence was found. "You're looking especially bright and happy, Stef," she commented instead. "Is something going on?"

"Nothing more than usual," Steffie denied, yet the color in her cheeks deepened. Something was *definitely* going on. "Just remember the folks mean well, even if they have the tact of jackhammers."

Layne knew her mother and father had good intentions, but that didn't stop them from driving her crazy.

It also didn't mean they weren't disappointed she hadn't turned out to be more like the rest of the family.

FIVE HOURS LATER Layne walked into Uncle Will's study, utterly exhausted. Her parents and sister had finally left. Aunt Dee, being an unfailingly gracious hostess, had invited Barbara and Stephanie to dinner. Naturally Layne's father was also called and invited, so he'd driven in from Issaquah. They'd eaten and chatted and laughed with an occasional glance of exasperation in her direction.

"Don't let it get to you, Lani," said Aunt Dee as Layne sank into her uncle's executive chair. "Barbara doesn't mean to upset you—it's just her way. She was appalled when I wanted to study painting in Italy instead of going to college. At the very least she felt I should get a doctorate in art history and teach at the university."

"But you met Uncle Will in Italy."

"And now she probably feels it would be better if we *hadn't* met."

Layne was startled. "Surely not."

"Barbara has her own way of looking at things."

"True enough. Oh, I have news. Matt Hollister came by my house this afternoon."

"Did he want an apology?" Dee leaned against the doorjamb with a chagrined expression. "I don't know what came over me at the gala. I've just been so frustrated with everybody refusing to talk to me, and suddenly I'd had enough."

Layne didn't remind her aunt of the wine she'd consumed that night, which probably had something to do with lowering her inhibitions. "He didn't ask for an apology. He claims he wants to help and gave me some details of the case. The embezzlement was done through illegal wire transfers from client accounts on

Thursday nights, using Uncle Will's passwords when he was working late. I don't get it, why was he working late *any* night?"

"That was when I was driving up to Mount Vernon every week to spend time with your grandmother," Dee explained. "Remember? She wasn't doing well after her gallbladder operation and Will urged me to visit as often as I wanted. I went up every Thursday morning and returned by the time he was home from the office on Friday afternoon. I really don't know what Will was doing those nights, or who he might have been…with."

"Oh." Layne couldn't help noticing the way her aunt broke eye contact and the unhappy line of her lips.

Dear Lord, could she have suspected Uncle Will wasn't at the office because he was having an affair? It seemed impossible.

"I'd get back from Mount Vernon and William would ask how Mother was," Aunt Dee murmured. "I would ask him about his days and he'd say it was fine, and that was that. He didn't talk about his work. Look, if you don't need me for anything, I'm going up to my studio."

"Sure."

When Layne was alone again she flipped through her notebook. Something had been nagging at her since talking to Matt, so she read through the list of everything she'd logged from the boxes sent over by Hudson & Davidson. *Yes,* that was it—a phone message. She extracted a small sheet of yellow paper from the files she'd created; it was a form used by a secretary to pass on phone calls to an executive. Printed at the top was the company logo, and it read "*UR VM bx is full! RD called n wants 2 know if ur coming 2nite.*"

The message showed the month and day, but there was no return phone number or other details, not even who'd taken the call. The texting style was unusual in connection to a dignified firm like Hudson & Davidson, so the author should be easy to identify. Layne hadn't questioned the note when she'd filed the message, thinking RD was Robert Dunnigan—her mom and Aunt Dee's brother—and that they were visiting him together. RD was what Uncle Rob's friends called him. But now, thanks to Matt Hollister, she knew why the police had suspected her uncle and more about how and when the thefts had occurred.

Layne pulled up the calendar function on Uncle Will's computer and checked the date of the call against the prior year. It was a Thursday, not long before everything had fallen apart, and she recalled that Rob had been on medical leave at the time, recovering from injuries he'd gotten from a roadside bomb in the Middle East.

Was that the proof Uncle Will had expected to use? The message *could* have been from Rob, calling to confirm plans to visit. They'd gotten along well, speaking the same language with Uncle Will being former navy and Rob being a naval officer in a special forces unit. And, if Uncle Will could have proved he was visiting his brother-in-law on one of the nights an illegal money transfer occurred, it would have thrown doubt on the original investigation.

Layne was shaking with excitement, but she'd have to wait to email Uncle Rob. Her pay-as-you-go phone didn't have internet access and Aunt Dee had canceled her internet service to save money after Uncle Will died. In any case, it might take Rob a while to call; he was an explosive ordnance disposal specialist and could be deployed anywhere in the world.

She had to be careful or the police would claim she was just making assumptions. But Rob had been staying at a friend's home in Aberdeen, Washington, at the time, and Aberdeen was near enough that Uncle Will could have driven there for an evening.

Yet Aunt Dee didn't seem to know about it.

Why?

And if "RD" was Robert Dunnigan, why hadn't Uncle Rob mentioned William's visit to his sister?

CHAPTER SEVEN

DOROTHY CIRCULATED AROUND the art gallery, chatting with the customers. It was a typical Sunday afternoon, with busy and slow moments. She enjoyed the visitors, even when they weren't knowledgeable about art. When William was alive they'd been so focused on each other and their friends and family, she hadn't felt the need for casual social outlets like the gallery.

Now she welcomed it.

Yet in a lull between customers she began kicking herself for hinting to Layne that William might have been having an affair. Would Lani be hurt and disappointed?

Sometimes Dorothy was so tired of the questions. She wanted to let it go, she just didn't know how to without knowing what had happened. Everything inside her shrank from believing Will had been doing anything wrong. And in the beginning she'd had no doubts—Will was innocent. Period.

But as the weeks had passed, and loneliness took over, it was hard not to start wondering if there had been something that she hadn't seen. Perhaps it was just part of the grieving process, trying to rationalize that what you'd lost hadn't been that great, anyway.

Yet if she *did* discover Will had been having an affair, would it change what they'd shared together? He'd loved her, but for some men, being unable to have a biological child was a huge deal. Was it possible that Will had spent so much energy reassuring her about not having children, he'd suppressed his own feelings? And if he'd looked for comfort elsewhere, did that make her partly responsible?

"Hello. Do you work here?" said a man with a strong Irish brogue, startling Dorothy from her unpleasant thoughts.

"Yes, I do. May I help you?"

"I wondered if you could explain that." He pointed to an abstract painting done by one of the other artists who, in Dorothy's private opinion, was trying too hard to be avant-garde.

"The painter has explained this is an expression of the purity of sexual energy. Cynthia feels sexuality is on a higher plane than other human emotions."

"That's bull crap. Obviously she's never gotten laid."

His blunt, outrageous response was refreshing and Dorothy tried to keep from laughing—she'd often thought the same about Cynthia. "I wouldn't know. Are you more interested in abstract paintings, or other forms? Impressionist, perhaps?"

He shrugged. "Not interested, period. I'm just

looking for a birthday gift to send to my sister back home in Ireland."

It made sense. Dorothy tried not to pigeonhole their patrons based on appearance, but this guy did *not* look like someone who'd ever visited an art gallery. He wore jeans and a blue linen shirt and had a strong build, without a spare ounce. His manner suggested he was quite down-to-earth and confident. At the same time he appeared to be successful, if the fine sports watch on his wrist was any indication.

"What part of Ireland are you from?"

"Dublin, mostly. Early on we lived in Dún Laoghaire, and I was born in Drogheda." His brogue became particularly strong as the Irish names rolled off his tongue. "I came here as an ambitious lad, over thirty-five years ago, though I've lived in other countries, off and on."

"But you still consider Ireland home, though you've spent your adult life in other countries?"

He appeared surprised. "Sometimes, I suppose. But I've done well. Didn't have much interest in the backbreakin' work my father killed himself doing by the time I was seven, at any rate. Now, about this…" He pointed a different painting on the wall. "What does that one say to you?"

Dorothy looked at the canvas. It was another of Cynthia's creations and held even less appeal for her personally. "I have no idea," she said honestly. "A spilled egg yolk, maybe? The artist calls it *Broken Sun in a White Sky*."

The man laughed and leaned forward to read the nametag on her shoulder. "I like you, Dorothy Hudson. My name is Patrick Donovan. Show me something you've done yourself."

Dorothy led him to a couple of her favorite pieces. One was of Mount Rainier, and the other depicted a hawk sitting on a fence post. She did little abstract or expressionist work, unlike many of the artists exhibiting at the gallery. Most of them didn't have a high opinion of her ability, claiming she played up to the tastes of tourists, but her paintings sold well and the owner approved of her for that reason.

"This is more to my sister's taste," Patrick announced. "I'll take the one of the mountain."

"We have many prominent regional artists who are considered quite collectable," Dorothy urged. "You should look around and be sure you've seen all that we offer."

He shook his head. "I know what I want and don't need to go shoppin' around."

The look he gave her wasn't inappropriate, but it made her sharply aware of him as a man. Guilt flashed through her; Will had only been gone since December. It didn't mean anything—she was just lonely, that was all. They'd done everything together and as much as Layne tried to be there for her, it wasn't the same.

"Very well." Dorothy pushed the thought away. "Would you like us to ship it to your sister in Ireland?"

"May as well. But I'll have to return with Alleyne's address. When will you be working here again?"

"Any of us can assist you. Or you can call and provide the address."

"I don't want anyone else. I want you, and I prefer taking care of it in person."

Dorothy occupied herself with taking the painting off the wall. Patrick wasn't flirting—he seemed too plainspoken to flirt, but there was something in his tone and eyes that suggested he found her attractive.

"I'm not scheduled again until Wednesday between two and four in the afternoon," she explained. "Will that make it too late to arrive in time for your sister's birthday?"

"There's enough time."

She calculated the cost of shipping to where his sister lived, and added it to the sale, getting another surprise when he took out his wallet and paid in cash, though she caught sight of several credit cards. It wasn't a problem, just unexpected. The gallery charged high enough prices, they didn't see many cash sales, and shipping out of the country was pricey, as well.

Patrick slid the wallet back into his pocket. "Is there a place to get coffee or tea nearby?" he asked.

"The Seattle area is a coffee capital. We may have more places to drink coffee than anywhere in the world," Dorothy answered wryly. "When you go out of the gallery, turn right and you'll find a shop three doors up the block."

"In that case, will you have a cup with me?" He looked at his watch. "No other customers are here and you should have closed twenty minutes ago."

Startled, Dorothy hurried over and changed the discreet open sign to Closed. Normally the owner or a paid employee also worked at the gallery, especially on a Sunday, but they'd been shorthanded with a summer flu bug making the rounds. Ideally the "artist on duty" got an opportunity to sketch or paint during their stints at the gallery, with the paid attendant answering questions and handling sales.

"How about it?" Patrick queried again.

"It's nice of you, but I have to finish here."

"I'll wait."

Dorothy considered refusing, but she'd enjoyed talking with him. Besides, over the past few months she'd gotten into such a deep rut in her life she could barely see over the top of it. At least having a cup of tea with a stranger would be different, and it *wasn't* as if it was a date. "Dating" sounded funny for someone her age, anyway. Not that she was old, she'd just felt older these days, and she certainly wasn't ready to think about that aspect of her life.

She finished the basic tasks, then locked up and walked with Patrick to the small shop. Muldoon's was more appealing than some of the modern cyber cafés, offering a bakery and a garden area she enjoyed.

Instead of coffee she chose apricot tea and saw that Patrick selected tea, as well, but when the barista asked him what variety, she received a direct look.

"Tea, with none o' the frills. Just put in three bags to make it good and strong and leave room for plenty o' milk." He also ordered a selection of sweets and thrust the basket at Dorothy when they sat at one of the outdoor tables.

"Eat. A breeze would blow you away," he said gruffly.

She ate an apricot thumbprint cookie, unsure of what to say. "What made you decide to get a painting for your sister?" she asked finally.

"Alleyne is full o' fancies."

He seemed to think it was sufficient explanation and Dorothy hid a smile. Did his indifference extend to all the arts, or just painting?

Patrick didn't eat the desserts he'd bought, but he drank his tea in long gulps before ordering another cup. They talked about Ireland and their families—there were three Donovan siblings. Patrick was the eldest. His twin brother and sister, born after his mother married again, were nearly fourteen years younger. The brother lived in Kilkenny with his wife and five kids, while Alleyne had been widowed while still a bride and had never remarried.

Patrick set his cup down. "Did you and your husband have children?"

"No, but one of my nieces was at the house so often it was almost the same as having a daughter. Layne has grown into a wonderful young woman."

Yet a faint pang went through Dorothy. She'd gotten over the regret of not having kids, but now she was having to deal with it again because of her questions about William. Oddly, she would have liked to ask Patrick his opinion about whether being sterile could lead a man to have an affair, only it wasn't the sort of thing you discussed with a stranger.

"What does Layne do?" Patrick asked.

"She works for the *Puget Sound Babbitt* as a researcher."

Unable to resist, Dorothy pulled several pictures from her purse, shuffling the Christmas photo of her sister's family to the bottom. It was a good shot of the rest of the family, but Layne looked out of place among her blond siblings and their tall, confident mother and father—as though a woodland pixie had appeared unexpectedly in the family's midst.

Her favorite picture of Layne had been taken at Seattle's Pike Place Market, holding three long loaves of French bread in her arms and laughing at the camera.

"That's Layne," she said, passing it to Patrick.

"She looks Irish."

"With her dark hair?"

"I have dark hair, too." True enough. His hair was black, shot with a few strands of silver, and his eyes were a piercing blue. "The Irish are not all redheads with green eyes and a belief in leprechauns."

"It never occurred to me that you believed in leprechauns." Dorothy passed him another two pictures. "Those are of Layne's twin sisters and her brother. She's the youngest. And the second one is of Barbara and her husband."

He didn't seem particularly interested in the family photos and asked if she had another of Layne. Dorothy hesitated before showing him the one she always carried of her niece and Will, taken a few months before his death. Will had an arm around Lani's shoulders and their expressions were carefree and happy. It was probably the one she liked best of William, though she wished it didn't hurt so much to look at his face and wonder about everything.

Patrick gazed at the picture for a long moment. "Your husband?"

"Yes."

"I'm sorry for your loss. He looks to be a fine man."

"He was."

Normally Dorothy cringed at expressions of sympathy, but Patrick simply handed the photographs back to her and began talking again about his homeland. Of course, since he didn't know the events surrounding William's death, it wasn't as awkward as it could have been.

It wasn't until her cell phone rang that she realized they'd been chatting for over an hour. "I'd better take this," she murmured as she pulled the phone from her pocket and answered, knowing it had to be Layne.

"Hey, Aunt Dee, it's me."

"Lani, I didn't realize how late it was."

"Not a problem. Did you get held up at the gallery?"

"Uh…something like that." Dorothy shifted uncomfortably, though it wasn't as if she was being unfaithful to William's memory by drinking a cup of tea with a man. "A customer asked me to have tea with him and I lost track of the time."

"Him?"

"Yes. He bought that painting of Mount Rainier you especially liked. I'll be there in a while."

"No rush. I'd offer to start cooking dinner…."

"No," Dorothy said hastily.

Layne laughed. "Don't worry, I'm not going to burn up any of your special pans."

CONNOR TRIED NOT to appear interested as he listened to Dorothy Hudson's side of the conversation with her niece.

For all he knew, Dorothy might be the reason her husband had been an embezzler. She could have pressured him into stealing from his company, wanting a grander lifestyle than the one he could provide through normal means, especially with their debts mounting. Or William Hudson could have done it without her knowledge, aware that she was dissatisfied—she didn't seem the type, but women could be hard to read.

Connor tipped the dregs of his tea down his throat.

Normally at this point he'd be congratulating himself for devising a reasonable excuse for returning to the art gallery, but there hadn't been a real need to come in the first place. What Matt needed to know could be learned through the widow's financial records.

Yet Connor wanted to understand why Dorothy Hudson affected him so much. For days he'd been unable to get her out of his mind. She was beautiful, but it was more than that. The look in her eyes… He sighed. Dorothy could become like Alleyne, lost in her grief and not really living. Perhaps it was foolish to compare them, but sometimes it seemed as if his sister had buried her soul along with her husband.

Connor's mouth tightened. Alleyne would take little help from him. When she'd finally visited Seattle, he'd told her the plane ticket was from frequent flyer miles he would never get around to using. It was true enough; he'd never go to the trouble of using them for himself, but he would for Alleyne.

"I'm so sorry," Dorothy said as she ended the call. "My niece was expecting me. I think she was worried and didn't want to admit it."

Connor shook himself. "That's all right. Is Layne nicknamed Lani, or is this a different niece?"

"It's Layne. Will and I are the only ones who've ever called her Lani. I'd better go—we're supposed to have dinner."

"I understand." He stood and held out his hand. "I'll see you on Wednesday."

Dorothy's hesitation before extending her own hand was so brief that most people wouldn't have noticed. "Yes, Wednesday. Thank you for the tea and pastries."

She hurried away and Connor watched the gentle sway of her hips before heading toward his Jeep. Be-

cause he had parked outside of Dorothy's house for
an extended period the previous Sunday, he'd left the
Jeep three blocks away to avoid the remote possibility she would remember seeing it. He would use another vehicle when he returned.

He also hadn't brought Finnster since he'd used the
rottweiler on his original reconnaissance of the Hudson household. Finn was sulking at home, resentful
of being left behind, though he was allowed to roam
the extensive Eisley estate at will.

Connor muttered a Gaelic curse at how complicated things had become. He'd almost introduced
himself as Connor O'Brian, yet Patrick Donovan was
the name he used undercover. The art of undercover
work was not to lie; his full name was Connor Patrick Donovan O'Brian. What's more, the family had
called him Patrick when he was a boy—it being a
proper saint's name—and Alleyne did have a birthday coming up.

Perhaps he shouldn't return to the art gallery. Dorothy's grief was too new for her to be interested in another man, yet that was partly what bothered him. She
was thin, drawn to a fine edge, the way Alleyne had
been in the months after Liam's accident…. Months
that had dissolved into years. Perhaps it was his guilt
for not doing more for his sister that drew him to
Dorothy Hudson.

LATE SUNDAY EVENING Layne tucked her legs beneath
her and read through the company phone bill that had

accidentally been sent over in the boxes from Hudson & Davidson.

It was big.

She didn't spend that much on local and long distance service in a year. Uncle Will had probably been reviewing the monthly statement around the time he'd died, which is why it had been packed up. But did it mean anything?

Individual phone numbers were shown, some more than once. There were annotations beside most of the entries, though Layne didn't know what they meant. She thought they'd probably used it as a record of billable hours for client services…and hoped the company had lost revenue by misplacing it. Unfortunately, a replacement bill wouldn't have been hard to obtain.

Not nice, Layne thought. But Hudson & Davidson wasn't being nice to Aunt Dee, either. And Layne strongly suspected Peter was trying to bilk Aunt Dee out of her share of the company.

She'd printed a calendar for the year Uncle Will had died and began comparing the dates when calls were made to see if there was a pattern, particularly around any Thursday. The biggest problem was that she didn't know *who* had made the calls, and which numbers, if any, belonged to her uncle's personal clients. It was information she might have been able to get from Matt's stepfather. Unfortunately *that* ship had sailed, particularly now that the *Babbitt* had done an article on the man—Peter was probably even more suspicious than his stepson.

Darn Matt anyhow.

He'd even made her worried about the Mustang, so much so that she'd put it in the garage for the night next to Aunt Dee's Volvo. Sure, she parked in her garage at home, but never at her aunt's house. The neighborhood was upscale and impressive cars could be found in most of the driveways, so why her 1966 Mustang would be a target, she didn't know. Yet Matt's comments, however well intentioned, had made her uneasy.

Now, *Matt's* car would be a target anywhere. And whether he liked it or not, the sporty red Mercedes-Benz belied his fancy suits and supposed newfound propriety. Not that respectable, *responsible* people couldn't drive a red sports car, but few of them had Matt Hollister's reputation to live down, either.

All at once there was a sound in the direction of the kitchen and Layne got up. Yet when she got to the kitchen, everything was quiet and the lights were off except for the LEDs beneath the translucent quartz countertops.

Layne frowned.

Aunt Dee could have gone back to her bedroom, but there'd been no footsteps in the hallway outside the office. Restless, she checked the doors and windows and security system before climbing the stairs to her aunt's studio. During the day the large room was perfectly lit by skylights and the floor-to-ceiling windows that looked out on the wooded canyon below. Moonlight filled the studio now, giving everything a silver gleam.

"Aunt Dee?"

Silence, then a shadow moved near the open door where the art supplies were stored. Layne swallowed, remembering the Cowardly Lion in *The Wizard of Oz* repeating, over and over, that he did, he did, he did believe in spooks. But *she* didn't believe in spooks or ghosts or any of that nonsense.

"Yikes." A shriek escaped her as something warm struck her leg. "JoJo, you rotten cat. Are you trying to scare me to death?"

She lifted the large feline, cuddling him to her chest while a purr boomed from his chest. Layne went back down the stairs with JoJo, heading for Uncle Will's study. Another sound came, but this time Layne recognized footsteps descending from her aunt's bedroom.

"Lani?" Dee called.

"I didn't mean to disturb you, but I was working and thought I heard you get up. It turned out to be JoJo wandering around."

"You didn't wake me. I haven't been able to sleep."

"Thinking about that customer who bought your painting and fed you tea and crumpets?" Layne asked lightly as they walked into the great room. She settled on a couch, still petting JoJo.

Dee sank down on a chair. "It was mostly cookies. And yes, I *have* been thinking about Patrick. A couple of nonsense things are nagging me. He paid cash, for one."

JoJo hooked his paw around Layne's wrist to get her attention and she scratched under his chin. "Some people like to use cash. That doesn't make him a criminal."

"I know, but the total was over twenty-four hundred dollars—I've never handled a cash sale that large at the gallery. How many people carry so much around with them?"

"Maybe it's an Irish thing. Or ego. You said he seemed direct and down-to-earth, but that doesn't mean he's above wanting to carry a bundle of money as a reminder of his success."

"Perhaps."

"Besides, we're probably both going to be uptight about everything for a while. I heard a sound in the house and the next thing you know, I'm searching the place. JoJo nearly gave me a heart attack when he head-butted my leg in the dark."

Dee laughed and visibly relaxed. "You're right. It's just been so long since a man noticed me, I must be looking for reasons to excuse it away."

"They notice, you just don't notice back," Layne assured her.

It was endearing that Aunt Dee always seemed

oblivious to male admiration. The surprising part wasn't that a man had made moves on her; the surprise was that she had actually gone to tea with him.

CHAPTER EIGHT

"HELLO. THIS IS Layne McGraw," said the recorded greeting. "Leave a message after the beep and I'll get back to you. Thanks and have a great day."

The beep sounded in Matt's ear. "Hi, this is Matt Hollister. I don't have more information about the thefts, but I have a little on your uncle's schedule during that period. Please call and we'll set a time to meet." He recited his home, cell and private phone number at the office.

Restless, he got up and walked toward his step-father's office, hoping Peter was in. Pete was still spending the majority of his time at Hudson & Davidson. It would be helpful when the company sold and he had time to provide recommendations on the foundation's administrative budget.

The Eisley Foundation paid its employees well, but Matt wanted to keep a careful rein on other expenses. It was one thing for his grandfather to spend money freely on redecorating or creating a relaxation waterfall in the employee solarium; it was another for *him* to be extravagant. The press loved to point a finger with the attitude of "What else could you expect from that Hollister fellow?"

Hell, not one, but *two* pictures of him at the gala had been printed in the newspaper, the first with Jeannette McGraw, and another with the reigning Miss Seattle beauty queen. The coy captions had suggested he was more at home at a party than an office, even going so far as to ask, "Is he already bored with philanthropy?"

A part of Matt didn't care about public opinion, but there were things he wanted to accomplish at the foundation—especially getting top people for the ALS research—and leading researchers *did* care who they were associated with. In particular, Matt wanted Remy Saunders to head up the project.

Remy Saunders was known as a synthesizer, someone who could take differing points of view and come up with revolutionary new concepts and directions for research. While Remy was considered a radical in certain circles, Matt had done enough of his own research to decide he wanted someone willing to be unconventional. Better yet, Dr. Saunders had an interest in ALS and was concluding his current study on heart disease, so hiring him wouldn't affect another project somewhere else.

Matt just had to convince Remy that he was serious about a long-term, well-funded research project, and would stay at the foundation to see it through. Remy's concern was understandable. If Matt left, another director might decide to end ALS research in favor of something else.

"What brings you here?" Peter said as Matt walked through the open door of the financial office suite.

"Mostly stretching my legs." The interior hallways of each floor were popular for anyone wanting a quick walk as a break. "I apologize for not making it to dinner the other night."

"You're always welcome, son. You don't need an invitation."

"I know, but I've been busy studying the foundation's projects and getting to know people. It keeps me pretty busy."

"Mmm, yes. Have you heard more from Dorothy Hudson and her niece?"

Matt shifted uncomfortably. "Layne and I have spoken."

"Is she listening to reason?"

Matt almost told him what Layne had revealed about her uncle's home computer and printer, then stopped, recalling what she'd said about hacking computers and stealing access codes. Who would have been in a better position to get into William Hudson's company office and obtain copies of his keycard and access codes than Peter himself?

The thought shocked Matt. He didn't believe his stepfather was capable of embezzling and framing his business partner for the crime, did he?

"Layne seems sensible," he said noncommittally. "Did you know her as a child?"

"Not really—we only met a couple of times. William and Dorothy adored her. What did you two talk about?"

"We mostly discussed the landscaping in her backyard. It's very appealing."

"Good, keep it that way. Don't tell her a damn thing."

Matt hiked an eyebrow. He was an adult and he'd tell Layne any damn thing he thought was best to tell her.

Peter must have read something in his stepson's expression, because he flushed. "Sorry, I know you'll use your judgment. I just hate having this mess stirred up, especially now that I have an offer to buy Hudson & Davidson. The last thing I need is the scandal going public again."

"I doubt Layne and her aunt want that, either."

"Yes, of course." Peter brushed a speck of dust from the shiny surface of his desk. "I hope it stays that way."

Matt gave him a tight smile, said goodbye, then headed downstairs to see Connor.

"Good morning," he said, walking in to find the security chief cleaning his firearm. "Planning to use that soon?"

"You never know." Connor smoothly reassembled the revolver. "How did your meeting with the niece go?"

"So-so. How about your meeting with the aunt?"

If anything, Connor's face became even more impassive. "It went. I bought one of Dorothy Hudson's paintings to smooth the way. Mrs. Hudson is very charming. I take it her niece is *not*."

"It isn't a question of charm," Matt felt compelled to say. "Ms. McGraw is determined to carry on her investigation and I offered to help. I gave her details of the case as a sign of good faith."

"Can't think of any reason she shouldn't have them. The police wouldn't have told you anything confidential."

Matt agreed, which made Peter's reluctance to have Layne and her aunt know what happened seem even odder. *Was* Peter responsible for the authorities refusing to give information to them? Everything his stepfather had said about protecting Mrs. Hudson and wanting to keep the scandal quiet to shield the company's value seemed reasonable, but it didn't sit comfortably with Matt. On the other hand, it sounded as though Dorothy could use her share of the proceeds if Peter sold Hudson & Davidson, so the higher the sales price, the better.

"Connor, how would you feel if a friend and business partner was caught stealing from your company?"

"I'm not a good person to ask. I've never cared enough about anybody beyond my mother and sister and brother for something like that to matter."

Matt knew that wasn't true.

He'd only seen Connor drunk once—the night word had come that Grady Eagan had died. After consuming enough bourbon to make most men comatose, Connor had begun talking about his stepfather and sister and a few of the security operations he'd run in his clouded past, including the very first, when they'd lost a hostage. Apparently he still felt responsible for the young woman's death, though he couldn't have prevented it.

"I forgot to mention that your operating expenses should go on the family account," Matt said. "Don't charge them to the foundation."

"The painting is a birthday present for my sister, so I'm payin' for it myself. Alleyne is angry when I send a money order, even returned the last one sayin' some fool thing about not taking charity. It's a female point of view—how else can I be sure she gets what she needs? She'll be amazed about the painting, but will like that it isn't money."

"Amazed?"

"Art isn't practical."

The statement didn't surprise Matt. Connor had a pragmatic point of view—if it wasn't something to eat, wear, sleep on or shoot bullets with, he did without. Still, it sounded as if he'd devised a good excuse to explain his presence at the gallery—one that shouldn't arouse suspicion.

"What do you think about Mrs. Hudson? Her niece tells me she won't let her family pitch in, though she's in debt, so it's unlikely she has a few million dollars hidden in a mattress."

For the first time Matt could remember, Connor seemed ill at ease. "Still working on my report," he said. "I'm goin' back to see her today. The gallery is shipping the painting to Alleyne and I said I'd have to return with her address."

"Good. I'm trying to reach Layne to set up another meeting."

"Does she trust you?"

"Not in the slightest. She's polite, but I think my stepfather is probably on her list of suspects and I'm tainted by association. She'll realize sooner or later that Peter didn't do anything wrong," Matt said, trying to inject confidence into the words.

While it was possible that his stepfather *had* been involved in the embezzlement scheme, Peter would have to be a master criminal to have escaped the scrutiny of the district attorney's office. A few weeks ago Matt wouldn't have questioned his innocence—and shouldn't now—but the things Layne had told him were troubling, including the part about the supposed loss Hudson & Davidson was operating under. How could Peter be so cavalier about Dorothy's financial situation? Was his pocketbook hurting, as well?

Surely not. When it got right down to it, Matt knew his stepfather much better than he knew Layne McGraw or her aunt. There wasn't a scrap of evidence to show Peter was connected to the embezzling. Hell, he'd paid back the stolen money with interest and had cooperated fully with the authorities. And while it was possible Peter wasn't treating William Hudson's widow as well as he should be, his sense of betrayal had gone deep.

Matt wanted to understand, but aside from Terry, he didn't have many friends. And he wasn't even that close to his siblings from his father's various marriages, though he was trying to get to know them better. Few of S. S. Hollister's children had faith in any sort of relationship after watching Spence run through wives.

Aaron was the only one of Matt's siblings who had even bothered *getting* married. The wedding in California had been a small affair, but Matt had to admit that if you were going to take the plunge, doing it with a long-legged redhead like Skylar wasn't a bad way to go. The real question was whether the marriage would last.

Connor glanced at his watch and dropped his feet to the ground. "Hell, I have to be going. Mrs. Hudson is working the two to four shift this afternoon at the art gallery."

"Good luck."

"I'm Irish, I don't need luck."

"According to my father, you can never be too rich or too lucky."

"I've always appreciated Spence's originality."

Matt left, chuckling.

ON SATURDAY MATT parked in front of Layne's house at noon, a full hour earlier than they'd agreed. It wasn't that he suspected she wouldn't be there, but she hadn't sounded thrilled about him coming over, suggesting instead that they meet at the foundation later in the afternoon.

In college his business professors had taught that people usually preferred their own turf in power negotiations. Layne either didn't understand negotiation strategy or wanted to keep her house out of the mix regardless of the advantage of being on her home ground.

The doorbell was the loud, old-fashioned kind that sounded like real metal chimes. Matt waited a minute, and was about to ring again when Layne opened the door. She was wearing snug green shorts and a T-shirt, liberally dusted with something white, and her expression was harried.

"Oh…hi." A thud and the sound of breaking glass came from behind her and she cursed beneath her breath. "Damn, I hope that isn't what I think."

She turned and hurried away, leaving the front door open. Matt promptly followed. He found Layne in the kitchen at the back, staring at a bowl on the floor, broken into numerous pieces.

"What was it?" he asked.

"Pistachio cake. It's supposed to be a no-fail recipe that turns out absolutely wonderful. I was going to bring it to dinner with my family tonight." She made the family meal sound like being thrown into an alligator pit.

"You don't sound excited about going."

"I'm just busy. We always get together the second

Sunday of the month, but my sister Stephanie has an announcement to make."

"Oh." Matt bent and began picking up pieces of glass, covered with batter.

"Don't do that," Layne protested. "You'll get it on your clothes and I'm already a mess."

He watched as she efficiently scooped glass and spilled batter into a large dustpan. Then using a huge wad of damp paper towel, she cleaned splatters from the cabinets and finished by wiping up the floor.

She *was* a mess, but it was cute and he liked that she didn't fuss and fume about it.

"What are you doing here so early?" Layne asked, putting away the cleaning supplies.

"I had an idea for the investigation and wanted to discuss it right away. Are you going to try baking something else?"

"I'll just pick something up from the store. It's what I usually do, anyhow. But my mom 'suggested' I try to do something special."

"What's the big deal?"

"In my family you're supposed to do everything well. They're embarrassed that I can barely boil water. What's the idea you rushed over to tell me?"

"Maybe you've thought of it, too, but how about going through your uncle's credit card statements? That way you could see if any purchases were made on the days he supposedly took money from his clients' accounts—the purchases would probably have been after work. The credit card company tracks where the purchases were made and when. There's probably even a time stamp the police could get if needed."

LAYNE SCRUBBED HER sticky fingers at the sink, thinking about Matt's suggestion. Actually, it wasn't a bad idea. She turned around and her appraisal of him became more speculative.

She'd already planned to go through Uncle Will's personal and financial records to see what she could learn, so Matt's ideas weren't revolutionary, but he'd obviously put thought into the matter. It was more than she would have expected, despite what he'd said about wanting to be sure he hadn't missed anything while working at Hudson & Davidson.

Maybe he was also concerned about his mother. If Peter *was* somehow involved, it would mean Katrina was married to a not-very-nice person. If Layne had been in his shoes, she'd want to know who was carving a roast with her mom every Sunday, and all the days in between, as well.

"I haven't gotten to Uncle Will's personal records yet," Layne said. "They're packed up. Uh…in storage." It was true, they were stored in the house, but she didn't want to be too specific about where potential evidence might be located.

"Okay. You know, there's something I don't understand in all of this." Matt sounded genuinely puzzled. "Why didn't your uncle offer Mrs. Hudson as an alibi for the nights the thefts occurred?"

"I talked to Aunt Dee about it the other day. At the time, Aunt Dee was spending Thursday nights with my grandmother up in Mount Vernon—she'd leave Thursday morning and return Friday afternoon. Uncle Will probably decided he might as well work while she was gone."

"That explains why he was at the office some evenings. I'd heard it was out-of-character for him."

"He was devoted to Aunt Dee. Normally they did everything together." Layne didn't intend to admit to Matt Hollister that her aunt had worries about an affair. Besides, once she heard from Uncle Rob, she might be able to dismiss the possibility altogether *and* get an alibi for Uncle Will.

"In that case, when we look at the credit card statement, we should also check your aunt and uncle's home phone bills to see if any calls were made on the evenings when illegal money transfers were made. If your aunt was out of town, logically, Mr. Hudson would have made them."

Slick the way Matt had gone from saying "you" to "we" in nothing flat.

"Uh…maybe. But I'll need Aunt Dee's permission to let you see any of the records."

"I understand."

Layne began putting away baking supplies and filling the dishwasher. What had made her think she could make a cake? Regina had claimed it was foolproof, so she'd talked herself into trying it. Granted, it might have come out if she hadn't put the bowl too near the edge and gone to answer the doorbell, but something else was just as likely to have happened. The last time she'd baked—a pie from the grocery freezer case—she'd nearly burned the house down.

Matt glanced around the breakfast area and kitchen. "From what I've seen of it, this is a really nice place."

"Thanks."

She loved her late-nineteenth-century home. The kitchen hadn't been redone since the art deco period, but the prior owners had kept it in perfect condition. As for the rest of the house, the hardwood floors were still pristine and the windows had the original leaded beveled glass. Fortunately the bathrooms had gotten an update before she'd bought it, so that hadn't needed doing. The only way she'd been able to afford the place, even using her college fund, was because the housing market had taken a tremendous crash and prices fell.

"Mom and Dad are appalled by the kitchen," she said. "But that's because they're really into modern. They got me new appliances as a housewarming gift and it drove them crazy when I wanted everything in a retro style, especially in that light turquoise color."

"The same shade as your car."

"Yup. And I've been getting reproductions of cookware from the 1920s and '30s because they look so great in here. It almost makes me wish I could cook like Aunt Dee."

"Maybe someday you'll get better."

Layne shrugged. "I'm not holding my breath. My sisters got all the talent—they can both cook as if they'd gone to Le Cordon Bleu School in Paris. It has to be genetic. When Jeannie was only thirteen she made *pâté de canard en croûte* from Julia Child's French cookbook. She must have repeated the name a thousand times—I've never forgotten it."

"What is that?"

"Basically it's a boned duck that's stuffed and baked in a pastry shell. And of course, it came out absolutely flawless." Layne could still remember the golden perfection of Jeannette's pastry crust, and her own conviction that she'd rather eat hot dogs than spend that much time in the kitchen. Of course, she was only ten at the time and had loved hot dogs.

"Uh…I've never cared for duck."

"Me, either. I'll take chicken any day. You said you have some info on my uncle's schedule?"

"Yes." He pulled an envelope from his pocket. "By the way, my security staff is available in case we need them to do background checks or something."

"I'm a researcher—I can take care of that myself."

"They could save us time. Don't worry—my security chief is an expert at getting information, along with his staff."

"Is he the same security chief who did a background investigation on Peter when he courted your mother?"

Matt's eyes widened. "How did you know a background check was done on my stepfather?"

"I didn't." Layne tried to keep from looking smug. "But I've always figured that people with serious money investigate everyone they come in contact with."

Like me, she nearly added.

Matt had undoubtedly had her checked out, but she didn't think she had any deep dark secrets to uncover.

Let's see...at six she'd shimmied up a telephone pole, accidentally setting off a fire alarm—the fire department hadn't been amused. She'd kissed Billy Chalmers behind the library while cutting eighth grade science class, hardly a felony except to her parents. But it wasn't the kissing that had bothered them, it was her cutting class. And as a college freshman she had gone skinny-dipping in chilly Lake Washington at midnight with a group of friends, only to be caught by the police. The officers had politely asked them to choose a more private location the next time.

Nobody was going to care about *those* offences, and while she had her share of faults, they hadn't resulted in her getting arrested, thrown out of college or fired.

"Say, I'm hungry. How about you?" Matt asked. Without waiting for an answer he took out his phone. "I'll order lunch. What kind of food do you like?"

She regarded him for a long minute. Eating together implied a closer bond than she'd like. Still, it didn't necessarily mean he had ulterior motives, and getting close to Matt was no more likely than her getting to ride on a space shuttle.

"I like anything that doesn't move on its own or is illegal." Layne tossed him the phonebook. "Look for places in the university district that deliver."

He grinned and started flipping through the pages.

LATER THAT EVENING Layne returned from her parents' home in Issaquah filled with a curious mix of happiness and melancholy.

Steffie had announced she was engaged and her fiancé, Owen Fitzsimmons, seemed to be a terrific guy. Only Jeannie had appeared out of sorts following the big announcement—maybe she'd expected to be the first McGraw daughter to get married.

Probably to someone like Matthew Hollister, Layne thought.

But even if Matt and Jeannie did start dating, a long-term relationship wasn't likely. Matt had made it clear that his feelings about marriage and children hadn't changed from his partying days.

Yet she frowned as she arrived home.

While her sister could be an opinionated pain in the ass, Layne didn't want her getting hurt and Matt Hollister was a heartbreak waiting to happen. But surely Jeannie would have said if she was seeing him, so it must be okay.

Layne locked the garage and waved to her neighbor who was watering his flower beds.

"Hi, Sanjiv."

He waved back. "Hey, Layne. Sorry you're having

trouble with your cable connection again. We finally got ours straightened out."

"My cable?"

"We saw the repairman go into your backyard. I didn't know the company worked so late on Saturdays."

Layne's stomach did a slow flip-flop. "I'm not having trouble. Was there a company logo on his uniform?"

Sanjiv turned off the water. "I think so, but I didn't see him that well. Maybe he got the wrong house."

"It wouldn't be the first time. How long ago did he leave?"

"Two hours, give or take."

"Thanks. I'll check into it."

Layne walked back to the front of her house and regarded it unhappily, though there were legitimate reasons a cable repairman could have been there.

She climbed the steps to the porch, giving herself a lecture about being a strong, independent woman, able to handle anything.

Liar.

Right now she wished somebody was with her— even Matt Hollister would be a comfort, being at least ten inches taller and sixty pounds heavier than her.

Bending over, she saw scratches on the dead bolt, but couldn't swear they were new. And it was locked—she turned the knob and shook the door to be sure. Swallowing, she went around to the backyard. The growth was so heavy on the upper slope of the yard, she couldn't tell if anyone was there, but the rest of the garden was empty.

She checked the locks on the rear door and saw more scratches—marks that could mean anything. And it was secure, the same as in front. It was possible someone had tried to get in, but who would break into a house and lock it *up* again?

Nevertheless, chills went down Layne's back as she turned the key in the dead bolt and stepped into the mud porch, half expecting to see the place ransacked. Cell phone in hand, she searched each room, even peering under her four-poster bed, but the windows were fastened and nothing was out of place.

Hmm. Layne sank onto a chair by the phone and willed her heart to stop racing. She was just reaching for the handset to contact the cable company when it rang.

The caller ID display showed "Hudson, Wm." The phone company still hadn't updated the listing…or else Aunt Dee hadn't asked them to. It was curious the small ways you tried to keep someone alive. Layne touched her throat; ever since the funeral she'd been wearing the tanzanite and diamond pendant that Uncle Will and Aunt Dee had given her for Christmas two years ago. She just couldn't take it off.

Layne pressed the talk button on the receiver. "Uh, hi, Aunt Dee. How are you feeling—do you need me to come over?"

Dee hadn't come to the family dinner because of

a migraine, though Steffie had called and put her on speakerphone when announcing the engagement.

"I'm better. I just want to see how *you're* doing."

For a moment Layne flashed on the supposed cable repairman and the scratches she'd found on the locks, then shook her head. Aunt Dee didn't know about that; she must be referring to Steffie's engagement and how Layne felt about it. It *was* vaguely depressing to see other people getting something she couldn't seem to find, but she didn't begrudge Steffie's happiness.

"I'm all right. Owen is a nice guy and he should fit right in—he can probably even cope with Mom and Dad."

"Is that a compliment?"

"More or less. I'm sure they'd prefer he was a doctor or lawyer instead of a high school teacher turned writer, but they didn't say anything. It's probably easier for them since his last nine books have hit the *New York Times'* bestseller list."

"I enjoy his work."

"Me, too. Look, you'd better set the security system and sleep the rest of that migraine off," Layne urged, wanting to be assured that her aunt was safe.

"Why have you started asking about my security system?"

"No reason," she said hastily. "Except that paranoia we talked about."

"Okay. You be careful, too."

"I will. Good night."

When she was off, Layne dialed the cable company.

"There *was* a report of cable outage on your street, and on the street behind you," the operator assured. "Not for a specific address, but we got a call from a gardening service, admitting they might have damaged some lines in that area. Our repairman could have entered your yard while investigating. Have you checked your television and internet connection?"

"No, but I will. Thanks." Relief filled Layne as she disconnected. Jeez, she *was* getting paranoid. And she really *didn't* think a thief and murderer would come around months later, just to be sure they'd covered their tracks.

Still…

She thought about the documents she was reviewing at Aunt Dee's house. So far most weren't significant, but maybe she should scan them and put anything that seemed promising in a safe deposit box. She could even keep a copy on a portable hard drive in her filing cabinet at the *Babbitt*.

It might be overkill. After all, Aunt Dee had a security system, and while Dee believed she'd sensed William in the house, the spirit of a loved one, whether real or imagined, wasn't the same as a criminal. On the other hand, there was no harm in being extra careful.

CHAPTER NINE

"GOOD MORNING, DOTTIE."

Dorothy spun and saw Patrick Donovan. Her heart gave a small jump of pleasure. "My name isn't Dottie and I'll thank you not to call me that."

"Dot, then."

She pressed her lips together in an attempt to keep from smiling. Her regular Friday shift at the gallery had gone by without Patrick appearing and she'd been unreasonably disappointed. It was ridiculous to feel that way—on Wednesday he'd given her his sister's address, so he no longer had any cause to come.

Of course, he *had* stayed on Wednesday. He'd taken her to Muldoon's Coffee and Tea Shop again, saying something about supporting a fellow Irishman. She'd razzed him for assuming the owner was male, which led to debates about the value of art and science and a range of other subjects. His opinions were interesting, even if she didn't agree with them. And he'd asked when she was working again at the gallery, making her think he would return. Then when he hadn't…

"Has your sister received the painting?" she asked. It had only been six days since the gallery had sent the package and international shipping could be slow, but Patrick had paid for the fastest courier service available.

"That she did. Emailed last night to scold her hard-headed brother for spending money on frivolity."

"*Frivolity?* Her word or yours?" Dorothy wasn't bothered that Patrick didn't appreciate art—she'd gotten the impression that it was hard for him to see a need for something without a practical purpose.

"Mine," he said with a wry grin. "Alleyne loved the painting. She visited a few years back and said it reminded her more of the grand old mountain than any photo she'd taken. Told me to come and tell you."

He'd only returned because of his sister? Mild disappointment filled her, yet it was just as well. Dee wasn't prepared to consider anything except friendship with a man.

"That was thoughtful of her."

Patrick smiled gravely. "I was grateful for the excuse. Would you care to drink tea with me after you're finished here, or are you tired of my company?"

"No, I've enjoy our talks."

"Good." He planted himself on a chair, looking thoroughly out of place, and Dorothy was conscious of his gaze as she walked about, talking with visitors. They were still shorthanded due to illness, but the owner was back today and handling the sales. The artist stints at the gallery were more for show than anything. It was only lately that they'd been helping out more.

Dorothy didn't mind the extra shifts. The customers tended to be a varied group—ranging from art connoisseurs to casual tourists in flip-flops. And they were a distraction she'd needed from less pleasant considerations.

In a quieter moment she smiled at Patrick. "Wouldn't you be more comfortable waiting at Muldoon's?"

"Not particularly. Have you brought any other paintings in for display? Thought I'd take a look."

"One. I'm doing illustrations for a children's book and haven't had much time for anything else."

Patrick stood and she took him across the room to where her latest work was hanging. Since he had little use for art, she figured he would see even less value in this one. It showed the remains of Mount St. Helens and Spirit Lake after the volcanic eruption in 1980, but in faint hints of color and brush strokes, she'd superimposed an image of the mountain and lake in its former glory. She had seen it as a girl before the violent upheaval, and the stark contrast still haunted her.

Patrick looked at the painting for a long minute. "You've a keen eye for sorrow. Are you certain you're not Irish?"

In an odd way, she knew it was a compliment.

"No Irish ancestors that I know of. Mostly French, Swedish and Welsh."

"Is your shift over?"

She glanced at the clock. "Yes, and Patille is here to take my place. I'll let Sherman know I'm going."

When she was done they walked down the street and she sat at their "usual" table in the garden seating area while Patrick went inside. As he'd done the previous times, he got a basket of baked goods, which he set in front of her, along with her cup.

"You act as if I'm starving to death," she commented, choosing a lemon scone.

"I don't hold with women being so skinny it isn't healthy."

"I'm healthy."

Patrick just shrugged. "My sister faded to near a shadow after her husband died. Wouldn't care to see it happening again to anyone. You're pale and underweight."

Dorothy blinked at the frank reply. "I eat enough. You needn't be concerned."

"About you or my sister?" He lifted the tea bags from his cup and poured milk into the dark liquid. "Alleyne refuses to let us do for her."

"I understand how she feels."

"Do you? Do you also know how it hurts the family to see her going without?"

"Maybe she needs to feel independent," Dorothy asserted, somewhat annoyed.

Patrick shrugged. "Independence doesn't heat the house or feed the stomach. She's too stubborn for her own good."

Dorothy wasn't sure if she should leave, argue with him or change the subject altogether. He couldn't possibly know anything about her situation, yet it almost seemed as if he wasn't *just* talking about his sister.

She gestured to his cup, deciding to change the subject. "I've noticed you like your tea as strong as coffee. Is that an Irish preference?"

"My mother brewed it that way when I was growing up. Never could abide the sugar she favors, though."

"How about whiskey or brandy? My father said nothing took the chill off better than a mug of tea laced with whiskey."

Patrick's eyes gleamed. "Now there's a man I would have liked. But how did he raise such a delicate lady of a daughter?"

"Lady? Delicate? That's nonsense." Yet she smiled, even as she scoffed. Her father would have liked Patrick, too. Brian Dunnigan had fought in World War II and been a man's man—decisive, direct and keen on the outdoors. After returning home from the war, he'd determinedly put aside his dark memories of combat and focused his attention on getting an education, and later on raising a family when a girl twenty-two years his junior convinced him to marry her.

Dorothy knew her mother wasn't sorry for her choice, though she was spending her senior years alone because of the age difference—Adele celebrated her memories and didn't waste time with regrets. It would be nice to follow her example, but it wasn't that easy…suicide wasn't the same as passing peacefully in bed at the age of ninety-six.

THE WEATHER TURNED hot on Tuesday and by Wednesday, Layne was miserable. Usually it cooled off in the evenings around the Puget Sound, but every few summers they had periods when it stayed muggy and warm all night long.

The doorbell rang while Layne stood in front of her open refrigerator, fanning cool air onto her skin. She reluctantly left the small oasis and went to answer.

"Oh," she said, startled to see Matt on the porch.

He lifted two bags. "I hope you haven't eaten."

"No." Puzzled but curious, she stepped to one side.

Matt headed for the kitchen and put one of the bags inside the freezer. "Four pints of ice cream," he explained over his shoulder. The second bag he put on the counter.

Layne's nose twitched. It smelled like garlic and peanuts and was making her mouth water, though she hadn't been hungry because of the heat.

"What's this?" she asked.

"Pad thai. You mentioned liking practically everything."

She should politely kick him out, but she loved pad thai and the containers were from one of Seattle's best restaurants.

"I brought the background checks on the employees your aunt remembered," Matt announced as they settled on the couch in front of her electric fan. She'd given him the names the last time they'd talked, almost as an afterthought.

"That didn't take long."

He forked up a mouthful of noodles and chicken. "I'm not sure where Connor learned all his skills and wouldn't dare ask him, but he's good."

"Wouldn't dare?"

"There are some things you *know* aren't a smart idea to ask. Connor has connections everywhere."

Matt had talked her cell phone number out of her and had called each day since, discussing the case as if they were the best of friends and cohorts. He took an envelope from his pocket and dropped it on her coffee table. "Here they are. Actually, Connor's still checking one of the names. Do you know how many Henry Browns are listed in the area?"

"Quite a few, I'm sure."

"Yeah, he's going to send someone out to verify which one works for Hudson & Davidson."

"No," Layne said hastily. "I don't want anyone getting *more* uptight about me calling. I've only talked to a few of the employees, but apparently word has already gotten around that I'm asking questions. They don't like it any better than your stepfather."

"Then I'll tell Connor to back off."

Relieved, she stretched her bare feet toward the electric fan. Perspiration trickled down between her breasts and she would have taken off her shorts and T-shirt if Matt hadn't been there. Lord, she hated hot weather; she was miserable, yet he looked cool and unwrinkled.

It was revolting.

And sexy.

Layne squirmed. Being attracted to Matt was both dumb and futile. He'd shown no signs of reciprocating—which wasn't surprising considering he'd already met Jeannie—but he was also *Matt Hollister,* an avowed bachelor. She wasn't a kid—she didn't want a brief, meaningless affair. She wanted something real and lasting. Besides, she couldn't compete with the women from his past, much less the ones he was meeting now.

"How is your aunt doing?" Matt asked after he'd polished off his pad thai. "You were worried that she could lose her house."

Layne winced. Her mouth *really* ran away with itself around Matt. "Things are about the same. She works awfully hard. I can't tell you how often I find her working in her studio in the middle of the night when I stay over. Some of that may be insomnia, but not all."

"Studio?"

"She mostly does commercial art. She doesn't enjoy it, but there isn't much choice. While she sells a few paintings every month, it isn't enough to live on. Uncle Will admired her talent so much. He'd be appalled that she's spending her time on greeting cards and the like."

"It should help when Peter sells the company. He told me he has a good offer."

"Yeah, well, we'll see." Layne pressed her lips

together to keep from saying more. Matt must not know his stepfather was trying to keep virtually all the proceeds from the sale of Hudson & Davidson, and probably wouldn't believe it if she told him. She poked at the pad thai with her fork, then set the container on her broad coffee table.

She wanted to scream, but it wasn't Matt's fault that his stepfather was a louse. And it was nice that he seemed concerned about Aunt Dee—maybe he wasn't as shallow as she'd believed.

Damn.

It was hard enough being sexually turned on by Matt, she didn't want to *like* him.

She dropped her head backward so the breeze from the fan could have better access to her neck. There was so much to do. The mountain of papers to go through seemed endless, and waiting for Uncle Rob to call was putting her on edge. But the thing bothering her the most was waiting for the autopsy report—Aunt Dee had requested a copy, but who knew what was holding it up, or if they were going to send it at all. They could have deliberately lost the request in bureaucratic red tape or be withholding it for another reason.

The secrecy alone seemed questionable—if no one had anything to hide, why were they so uptight about providing information? Layne knew enough about police procedure to realize some details were always withheld so a suspect's story could be cross-checked, but if they truly believed William Hudson was their embezzler, what was the problem? Moreover, the Carrollton Police and the D.A.'s office weren't just withholding some details; they'd hardly told her anything.

It was exactly the sort of thing that turned a perfectly normal person into a conspiracy theorist.

MATT FELT LIKE a voyeur as he watched Layne from the corner of his eye. She was short, definitely *not* curvy, and looked fourteen with her pink toenails and hair pulled high in a ponytail. It didn't make sense that she was affecting him so much. Yet even though her bust was smaller than he preferred, he had a strong urge to see *beneath* the thin fabric clinging to her damp skin.

The faint scent of warm peaches rose, tickling his nose, and he restrained a groan.

Maybe he was having trouble with his libido because it was easier than thinking about Peter and wondering what was going on with Hudson & Davidson. He was getting better at reading Layne, and he knew something was up from the tension in her body when he'd asked about the sale of the company. But surely Peter was handling it ethically. Hell, his stepfather was now the Chief Financial Officer of the Eisley Foundation. He'd damn well *better* be doing the right thing.

"Uh…how about some ice cream?" Matt suggested, putting his empty food container on the coffee table, as well.

"Sure. You said you got four pints. Do you always go overboard like that?"

"It's Ben & Jerry's Cherry Garcia. You can't go overboard with Cherry Garcia."

Layne raised an eyebrow at him. "I wouldn't have pegged you as the cherry ice-cream type."

"Oh, yeah?"

"Yeah. I'd have expected something more...I don't know, *sophisticated,* like...kiwi and passion-fruit gelato with kirsch. What *is* kirsch, anyway?"

"It's brandy made from cherries, so you're partly right. And in my opinion, it's great with Cherry Garcia ice cream."

"I'll have to take your word for it—I'm not much of a drinker. I prefer soda water." Layne got up and returned a few minutes later with two bowls of ice cream.

"So, what was your sister's big news at the family dinner on Saturday?" Matt asked, dipping his spoon into the creamy concoction.

"She's getting married."

He choked and nearly inhaled a large chunk of cherry. Layne thumped him on the back as he coughed.

"You *did* say it was your other sister making the announcement, not Jeannette, right?" he asked, recalling the prowling gleam in Jeannette McGraw's eyes only a few weeks before.

"Yeah, Stephanie is engaged to Owen Fitzsimmons, the author. I didn't know they'd met, but apparently Steffie operated on his grandfather and one thing led to another. She's a neurosurgeon."

"Jeannette didn't mention that," Matt murmured, trying to recall what Layne's sister had said about her family at the gala. Not much, actually. Other than commenting that her parents were doctors, she'd mostly wanted to ensure he didn't have any interest in Layne.

"Steffie is brilliant. She went through medical school and her training in record time. And my brother, Jeremy, is running for Congress next year. Obviously *he* didn't go into the medical field, but my parents are okay with it."

Matt ate another bite of ice cream. "So when can we go through your uncle's credit card statements?"

"With so much going on I haven't had a chance to talk to Aunt Dee about it. But I've been thinking. I know Mr. Davidson doesn't want me investigating, but I need to talk to more employees. You never know what piece of information they could tell me that would be important. So I'd like to ask him for a full employee list."

"Pete feels the case is closed."

"Yeah, but—"

"Layne, my stepfather didn't want me to tell you *anything*," Matt said bluntly. "I did it because I believed it was right."

She blinked. "Oh."

"I can try getting Pete to agree to a meeting, but even if he sees you, I don't think he'll cooperate. You'll probably just be wasting your time."

"It's worth a shot."

Though Matt knew he was going to regret it, he nodded reluctantly. "Okay, I'll talk to him in the morning and ask if he'll meet with you."

"I'm willing to come whenever he's available. My work hours are pretty flexible," Layne said eagerly. "I met Mr. Davidson a couple of times when I was visiting my aunt and uncle, but I don't remember him that well. In the meantime, I'll keep calling the employees my aunt remembers, along with the names the ones I've talked to have given me."

Terrific.

Matt spared a brief, longing thought for the period in his life when all he'd worried about was having fun. He wouldn't go back to those days and didn't regret giving them up, yet it *had* been so much easier to drink a piña colada on a beach than be an adult with real responsibilities.

LAYNE DRESSED CAREFULLY for her meeting with Peter Davidson the next afternoon. She didn't have a high opinion of the man, but it wouldn't do any good to offend him by seeming too casual.

Matt had called that morning arranging for them to get together in his penthouse on the top floor of the Eisley Foundation building. He was waiting in the foyer when she arrived and took her up in his private elevator.

"Peter sent a text message that he'll be delayed a

few minutes," Matt explained as he escorted her into the living room.

Though Layne figured the "delay" was a power strategy, she didn't mind. It gave her time to gape at the view, which was even more spectacular than the one from Matt's office. As for the rest of what she could see of the penthouse, it was rather cold and stark. The large room had an open industrial look with the original brickwork and old iron pipes left exposed. The furniture was black leather, and a handful of metal sculptures provided focal points.

"Have a seat." Matt motioned to one of the chairs.

Layne sat down, her pulse speeding up when she heard the restrained chime of the private elevator. What would it be like to have an elevator opening into your home? Matt had used a special key and code to operate it, so he had privacy if he wanted, but it still seemed weird.

"Hello?" called a voice.

"Come in, Peter." Matt walked toward the partition screening the elevator and an older man appeared around it. They shook hands and Layne watched, trying to discern as much as possible from Peter Davidson's face.

He was handsome, startlingly so, with light brown hair that was silvery at the temples. His tall, athletic build reminded her of a tennis player—a game he'd have plenty of time to play once he sold Hudson & Davidson. It also wouldn't hurt that he was married to the daughter of an obscenely wealthy man.

As for whether he was the real villain, stealing from the company and then killing her uncle to pin it on him…? It was most likely that Peter had simply taken the expedient route of assuming Uncle Will's guilt and brushing everything under the carpet, but who knew?

The two men turned and Peter's tight smile faded as he stepped toward her.

"Ms. McGraw," he said coolly, extending his arm.

"Mr. Davidson." Layne had an impulse to wipe her hand after their fingers touched. She felt an instant dislike for her uncle's business partner, though she was willing to acknowledge she was already biased. The only good thing she had to say was that Peter hadn't claimed it was a pleasure meeting her.

She looked closer and saw that the expression in his eyes wasn't cold…it was furious.

"I wanted to ask if you would give me a full list of employees who were working at Hudson & Davidson seven months ago. Particularly from the accounting division," she said without preamble, figuring there wasn't much hope of calming him down.

"Why, so you can make more trouble?"

"I'm not trying to make trouble. I'm just trying to find the truth."

Peter's eyes narrowed. "We know the truth."

"Actually, the only thing *I* know for sure is that my uncle was accused of a crime and died before he could defend himself," Layne countered, trying to keep from losing her temper.

From the corner of her eye she saw Matt sink onto a bar stool with a resigned expression. He probably expected her to blow up and make everything worse.

"The people who matter know what happened."

"The people who *matter?*" she repeated in disbelief.

"Yes. The district attorney, the police and myself. Or are you forgetting that I'm the one who had to clean up the mess William made? And now you're asking questions and making *more* problems for me to handle. The only reason I took this meeting was to tell you to stop. William's assistant phoned me several days ago, saying you'd spoken to her. We've finally found some peace, and now you're stirring things up again. He was guilty, plain and simple. Accept it and move on."

"If you're so sure of the evidence, why won't you let the Carrollton Police Department and the D.A.'s office talk to anyone?" The query was a stab in the dark; Layne didn't know for certain that her uncle's business partner was behind the bureaucratic stonewalling though it seemed likely. Her research had revealed that Peter was not only friends with the D.A., but a major contributor to his last two reelection campaigns. The D.A. was probably happy to do him a favor, especially if it helped keep a large company like Hudson & Davidson from going out of business.

Peter crossed his arms over his chest and planted his feet like a bulldog. "I've tried to keep the details out of public view to save the company, my reputation and what's left of William's good name. It's the least I can do for his wife."

"The least you could have done was to stand by your friend when he told you he was innocent," Layne said quietly. "The way he would have stood by you. And maybe if you'd tried to find the truth, we wouldn't be here today."

She got up and walked to the elevator, feeling curiously calm. Matt had explained you could exit without the special key, so she pushed the button and the door swooshed open.

Nothing had been accomplished, but her dislike for Peter Davidson had turned into outright loathing.

CHAPTER TEN

MATT HAD NEVER seen his stepfather so angry. He rested an elbow on the breakfast bar, watching Peter pace the long length of the living room.

"How can you help that woman?" Peter demanded. "I couldn't believe it when you said you'd told her about the case."

Matt thought about how "that woman" had handled herself. Hell, didn't Peter realize how badly he'd come off in comparison?

"I told her because nothing I know is confidential and because she just wants answers. Look, I may not have been at Hudson & Davidson for long, but I *was* there when this all happened. To be honest, I'm worried we could have missed something. Layne has uncovered information that suggests William Hudson didn't kill himself."

"That's impossible," Peter scoffed. "There was more than enough evidence to convict him. That's why he committed suicide—he couldn't face any of us, or a prison sentence."

"I still think it merits a second look," Matt insisted.

"Go ahead and look. I'm done with it." Peter sank

onto a chair, rubbing the back of his neck. "It was a nightmare the way William took advantage of our friendship. We were once as close as brothers, and then he nearly took me down with him. And don't forget, he put your plans for taking over the foundation at risk, too."

"I don't think Grandfather would blame me for another man's mistakes."

"Perhaps. But William played roulette with all of our futures. To think he's the one who used to talk about integrity and honor as if it was a religion."

Matt leaned forward. "I didn't know him that well."

"I'm sure you would have liked him, everyone did. He was crazy about his wife. Optimistic. Intelligent." Peter smiled grimly. "He had a helluva sense of humor, too. I miss the friendship, even if I can't forgive him for what he did."

And Layne can't forgive you for abandoning her uncle, Matt added silently. As for the optimism Peter had described in his partner, that didn't fit with a man who would kill himself without offering a stronger defense than, "I'm not guilty."

"Before I met your mother, I was a seven-days-a-week workaholic," his stepfather murmured. "But while William would put in a hard day, he usually didn't stay late or come in on weekends. That's what was so strange about him starting to work Thursday evenings."

"I can explain that—Mrs. Hudson was spending Thursday nights with her mother. He was staying late because his wife was out of town."

"Oh." Something flickered in Peter's eyes, but was gone so fast, Matt couldn't read it.

"It must have been annoying all those years when you *were* working such long hours, and he wasn't," Matt commented casually.

"Not really. I would have done the same if Shelley had been alive. Hudson & Davidson wouldn't have grown as much, but it wouldn't have mattered, either."

"Shelley?"

His stepfather's face seemed to age instantly. "My first wife. She died in a car crash shortly before our baby was due. I didn't mind that William wasn't putting in the long hours…but I envied him. William and Dorothy had each other, and though they couldn't have children, I knew Layne was becoming like a daughter. He had what I'd lost until I met your mother. I'm fortunate to have both of you now."

A headache pulsed in Matt's temples. While he recalled his mother telling him that Peter was a widower, he hadn't truly considered what it meant. Something like that must change a person. He'd seen how divorce affected people, but death? *That* was what Dorothy Hudson was dealing with now, and if his stepfather had gone through it himself, why did he have so little compassion?

"I don't know, maybe I should have…" Peter's voice trailed off and he stared out the window at Lake Union, clenching his fists.

Matt wondered if his stepfather was questioning how he'd handled things with Layne, or the way he had responded to the supposed embezzlement by William Hudson.

He thought back to the morning the police had shown up at Hudson & Davidson and the silence and shock in everyone's eyes. William Hudson's suicide had been an even bigger bombshell.

Layne was right—her uncle's death *had* been convenient. And if William Hudson was innocent, it meant Matt had been part of a system that had destroyed a man's reputation and let a thief and murderer get away.

"I never heard how much of the money was found," Matt said slowly.

"None of it. The D.A.'s office says it was moved from one international account to another until it became impossible to track." His stepfather cleared his throat. "Look, I wish you hadn't gotten caught up in this, son, but I understand your wanting to be sure things weren't missed. I apologize for getting angry today."

"It's a touchy subject for everyone," Matt said, getting up. "I'd better go back to work."

"Yes, of course."

They went down in the elevator together. Matt felt he owed a certain loyalty to Peter for giving him the job at Hudson & Davidson, but at the moment he wasn't terribly impressed with his stepfather. On the other hand, he'd known Peter a whole lot longer than Layne McGraw, and he didn't have any clear reasons to distrust him.

THAT EVENING LAYNE sat on her living room sofa, clutching a pint of Ben & Jerry's Cherry Garcia ice cream. The stuff was *good*. She'd never had it before the previous night, and had been pleased to discover it contained fudge flakes, along with generous chunks of cherries.

Damn.

She didn't need expensive tastes *or* such sinfully rich ones, either.

Layne dug out a spoonful of ice cream and ate it down, unable to stop thinking about her encounter with Peter Davidson. How could Uncle Will have been friends with a man like that? He was *awful*.

The door chimes rang and she considered just sitting there, stuffing herself with Cherry Garcia and feeling depressed, but when they rang again, she sighed and got up.

It was Matt.

He looked at the half-empty pint of Ben & Jerry's in her hand and held up a grocery bag. "I brought reinforcements."

Layne dropped onto the couch again as he disappeared into the kitchen. She heard the freezer door open and close before he reappeared with a spoon of his own. He sat next to her and dipped it into the pint she held.

"I apologize for Peter," he said after a moment.

"You warned me." She ate another bite of ice cream.

"But I didn't think he'd lose his temper."

She recalled Peter Davidson's handsome face,

dark with self-righteous fury. You'd think he'd start to question if he could have made a mistake—most reasonable people would have gone through a self-questioning period. Naturally there was still the possibility Mr. Davidson had been embezzling himself in order to get control of the company, but it seemed awfully complicated and Machiavellian.

"Here."

Still depressed, Layne shoved what was left of the ice cream at Matt and rested her head on the couch. She had little recollection of her uncle's partner from childhood; he'd looked slightly familiar and that was all. But surely he had *some* qualities to recommend him, or he and Uncle Will wouldn't have become friends in the first place.

"Hey." Matt ate the last few bites before tossing the empty ice cream carton aside and tugging a lock of her hair. "It's okay. We'll keep looking."

That was nice. He could be encouraging her to give up, instead of urging her on. It wasn't necessary—she had every intention of continuing—but it was nice to get a pep talk.

She glanced at him.

The last, lingering rays from the sun were coming through the windows, refracted into a thousand rainbows and flashes of light by the beveled glass in her windows. They played across his face and athletic body and she sighed. He really was *very* attractive.

Matt leaned closer and kissed her with unmistakable expertise. Layne's stomach flipped. His kiss deepened as she responded, coaxing and gentle and demanding at the same moment. They slid down, along the cushions, and she ran the arch of her foot along his leg.

Mmm. He was wearing blue jeans and the sensation of hard, denim-covered muscles pressing against her bare thigh sent lust streaking through her veins. For a guy who was famous for partying late every night, he was in awfully good condition.

"Do you run or what?" she muttered between kisses.

"What?"

"To stay in shape."

"The Eisley Building has a fitness facility for the employees. I use it after everyone has gone home."

His hand eased under the hem of her shorts and cupped her bottom while the other unsnapped the waistband and eased the zipper downward. Not to be outdone, Layne pulled on the shirt tails tucked into his jeans and put her fingers on his back.

Matt pushed her shirt upward and gazed at her breasts for a moment. She rarely wore a bra at home, and the fleeting thought went through her head that she was probably half the size of the lovers he'd had in the past. But before she could think of covering herself, he stroked one of her nipples, then drew it into his mouth, teasing the tip with his tongue.

Each of her breasts received equal attention and Layne's abdomen clenched and unclenched as she arched upward. She couldn't remember the last time she'd felt so outrageously aroused; Matt appeared to know exactly what he should do to drive her insane.

He kissed her again so deeply that she tasted the sweet flavor of cherry ice cream, then began playing with her hair, seemingly fascinated by its thick length. Her legs moved restlessly.

All at once Matt broke free. He rested his weight on his arms and stared down at her. "I'm sorry. I didn't come here to have sex with you. That was the last thing on my mind."

Layne's blood cooled instantly. "Oh?"

"I feel bad about today. You've become a friend and I wanted to make you feel better, except now I've made things worse."

Wasn't that great? He'd brought ice cream and given her a pity kiss as if she was a twelve-year-old. "I don't need you to make me feel better," she said, pushing him away.

"Don't be angry."

"Why would I be angry?"

"I'm not sure, but you looked pissed."

"I realize it's a cliché—but if you don't understand without being told, you never will." She squirmed away, yanking her shirt into place as Matt sat up and watched warily. It wasn't as if she'd actually *wanted* to have sex with him, but she knew enough about male behavior to know that they didn't usually just call a halt once things had gone a certain distance. At least not when they were truly aroused.

Jeez.

If she'd been low before, now she was positively depressed.

Having Matt call her a friend was probably a compliment, but it was a reminder that *all* her romances turned into friendships. She was an expert at being a buddy; she was even still buddies with Richard, the guy she'd once expected to marry.

When was she going to meet the right man who'd adore her, and not go gaga over Jeannie or Stephanie? It wasn't that she wanted it to be Matt Hollister, but she was tired of being treated like every guy's kid sister.

Determined not to let Matt know that he'd dented her ego, she collected the spoons they'd used and the empty ice cream container, taking them into the kitchen.

If she was honest, the way she felt was only partly about the kiss. It was also about her family and how they were trying to put themselves back together.

"Layne?" Matt stood in the doorway.

She pasted a smile on her mouth. "Never mind. I'm just tired and the hot weather is getting to me."

"It's cooler today."

Layne wiped her hands on a towel. "Cooler is relative. I like needing a quilt to stay warm at night."

"You wouldn't enjoy Jamaica, then."

"Jamaica?"

"One of my favorite places. I went to boarding school in New England and then attended Harvard, so I headed for warm tropical breezes as soon as I got control of my trust fund."

Not just tropical breezes—wild parties, adult beverages with little umbrellas and women in bikinis, Layne added silently. According to the stories, Matt had partied all over the world, but he'd been partial to places like the Caribbean and Hawaii and Fiji.

"But you still traded tropical breezes for Washington rain."

"There wasn't much choice with the Eisley Foundation located in Seattle. Look, I know you're upset, but I don't know what I did and I'm not good at games."

Lord, men could be so dense.

"It isn't a game, and it isn't you, it's…it's all this stuff dragging on about Uncle Will," Layne said, squaring her shoulders and mentally crossing her fingers, even though it was partly true. "You can't understand what it was like growing up with three gorgeous, gifted siblings. No matter what I tried, they'd always done it better. But it was okay when I was with Aunt Dee and Uncle Will. They weren't disappointed that I hadn't turned out as smart and pretty and talented as everyone else. They just loved me."

"Surely your parents love you, too."

"Of course they do. But they still want me to be something I'm not. When I have children, I want them to be kids first, and not just future doctors and lawyers and business professionals in training. Even now my parents push constantly, trying to get me to go back to school and get a doctorate."

Matt frowned. "I've never even thought about how I'd raise a child since I don't plan to get married."

"Well, I want what my aunt and uncle shared. They lived for each other, and what they did for a living was less important than what they had together. Except now she's alone and it's awful for her." Layne gulped to keep from crying.

"I'm lucky, I guess. I haven't lost anyone who mattered that much to me." Despite Matt's words, a spasm of pain crossed his face.

"It was hard when my grandfather died a few years ago, but I wasn't close to him the way I was close to my uncle." Her breath caught again and the ache in her chest seemed unbearable. "And I'm so afraid that I may have to go back and tell Aunt Dee that her husband wasn't everything she always believed."

"BUT YOU HAVE proof that he didn't kill himself," Matt said helplessly.

He wanted to comfort Layne, but he'd screwed up once already that evening and didn't want to make things worse. Besides, while he was far from a paragon of virtue, he'd never taken advantage of a distraught woman and didn't intend to start.

It was clear that Layne McGraw was a hell of a lot more complicated than the women he'd associated with in the past. That alone should send him racing out the door, but he'd offered to help with the investigation. The new Matthew Hollister was no longer irresponsible and couldn't back down from that offer.

Layne flipped on the overhead light. "The police won't accept my proof, remember?"

"You said they didn't want to see it as proof because it might mean they accused the wrong person." Matt understood how the authorities felt—things would be easier if William Hudson was proved to be the embezzler…easier for everyone except Dorothy Hudson and her niece.

"They're probably worried about a lawsuit."

"So let's talk about what comes next," Matt suggested. "Did the employees you've spoken with have anything interesting to say?"

"I've reached several, including Emma Farnon, who was Uncle Will's administrative assistant. Emma retired shortly after his death and doesn't recall specific dates Uncle Will planned to spend the evening at the office. I asked if payroll records would show when she worked late with him, but apparently he was the only company executive who didn't expect their assistant to put in overtime."

"Peter said he was surprised when William began staying on Thursdays. I explained about your grandmother's illness."

Layne wrinkled her nose. "If Mr. Davidson didn't know about it, they must not have been talking much at the time. I'm sure Uncle Will would have mentioned her trips to Mount Vernon at the office. Someone may have realized he wouldn't have an alibi, whether he was at work or not, and framed him."

"Could be."

Matt rubbed his chin. His body still ached and the memory of Layne's responsive breasts was guaranteed to keep him awake for hours. They might be small, but they were very pretty—round, with large, rosy nipples that hardened instantly at a touch...he restrained a groan.

He didn't believe in exploiting an emotional situation any more than he would consider having an affair with a woman like Layne. Hell, she'd just talked about the kind of marriage she hoped to have and the kids she wanted to raise.

Marriage might work for some people, but it didn't work for the Hollisters.

That didn't mean he couldn't deal with Layne on a friendly basis; not everything had to be about sex. Besides, his good times hadn't always been about women; they were about skirting the edge—going faster, longer and better. He'd raced everything from cars to yachts to airplanes. He'd gone skydiving, hang gliding, parasailing and cliff diving. Hell, he'd even paid megabucks to see the rusting wreck of the RMS *Titanic* at the bottom of the Atlantic.

"By the way, when are you going to let me see your aunt again and help review records?" he asked.

"Soon. I've mentioned you to Aunt Dee but haven't told her everything."

"You think she'll be angry?"

"No, but she'll worry. I'll speak to her Saturday, though. Are you available?"

"Just let me know when it's a good time and I'll come right over. I don't have any plans."

It was true. His only plans were going over more reports in his office. Living above the Eisley Foundation made it easy to take care of any needed tasks. He supposed it could become tiresome to live in the same place he worked, but right now it helped to keep him focused.

And he wasn't a homebody, anyhow.

ON FRIDAY AFTERNOON Connor parked the blue Bronco he was using near the art gallery and tapped his fingers on the steering wheel, staring at the expensive storefront.

He'd boxed himself into a corner by unnecessarily using his middle names with Dorothy and not telling her about his connection to the Eisley family. But then, she wouldn't have gone to tea with him the first day, either, if she'd known everything.

What did he want from her?

Sex wasn't likely, however much her beauty compelled him.

Absolution?

The word popped into Connor's head and sat uneasily in his brain. There was little softness in the solitary life he'd chosen, and he was often haunted by ghosts of the innocents who couldn't be saved and the missed opportunities to right another wrong. Yet he'd never really been there for his own family in Ireland. They hardly knew him any longer.

With that unpalatable thought, Connor climbed out and crossed the street. Dorothy came through the door as he approached and he forced a smile.

"Finished already, Dot?"

The nickname made her smile. "I've worked extra lately, so one of the other artists came in early to take my place."

"How about a walk before having our tea?"

She nodded and they headed toward the waterfront by silent accord. The art gallery was in Ballard, Seattle's trendy historic district, and while Connor wasn't disposed to appreciating the fine points of architecture and design, the area was attractive...just like the second painting he'd purchased. Dorothy didn't know that he'd sent one of his men to buy the one she'd painted of Mount St. Helens. It was now hanging in his office.

Hell, he felt like a damned fool.

Beauty was transient—what was the point when someone would just come along and destroy it sooner or later? He'd spent most of his life avoiding useless nonsense, yet even *he* could see that Dot had talent.

The breeze was creating whitecaps on the water and he glanced down. "Cold? It was warmer down here yesterday."

"I like it this way. Lani and I both hate it when the temperature gets too high."

"Then the heat we've had the past few days must have made you both miserable."

"The humidity is the worst part."

He grinned. "You don't know humidity until you've been in hundred degree temperatures with pouring down rain. The air is so thick you have to chew it before breathing."

"Ouch." Dorothy grimaced and then laughed. "You've traveled a lot, haven't you?"

"A fair amount. You?"

"Some. My husband was stationed in Guam when he was in the navy. I loved it and the people were wonderful to us."

"You likely think the people are wonderful everywhere, but that hasn't been my experience. There's a lot of evil out there, waiting to destroy something, often just because it's there."

"It must be awful not being able to have faith in people."

Hell.

Dorothy was a gentle woman who would never understand his rough childhood or the life he'd led since leaving Ireland. Despite what had happened to her husband, she wanted to believe the best in everyone, while he generally thought the worst. She'd been sheltered by the people who loved her, while he'd seen what they could do. Yet Connor felt an impulse to protect her, as well.

Heaven alone knew how she would react when she discovered he'd been lying to her.

"Who do you have faith in, Dot?" he asked, his voice rough. He was attracted to her. But even if this were a normal situation, she'd only been a widow for a few months.

"My family."

"Especially Lani, right?"

"Yes, but I've been leaning on her too much since losing Will. I have to stop."

"It's only been a few months, woman," Connor growled, exasperated. "And you've said your husband was a second father to her. Surely it's all right to let Lani be a comfort."

"She has a life of her own."

"Has she complained?"

"She wouldn't, but that doesn't make it right."

"Right?" He made a disgusted sound. "If Alleyne had let the family do for her when her husband died, she might not be such a lonely, prickly soul now."

Dot set her chin stubbornly. "You don't understand."

Damn the woman. She *was* just like Alleyne. Matt had mentioned Dot's refusal to let the McGraws ease her financial problems, which was his sister all over again. And it had nothing to do with independence; it was that damned Irish and American pride. They should compare notes on how to drive their families crazy.

Or was Alleyne punishing herself?

Connor's eyes narrowed at the thought. His sister's husband had taken a second job so they could get a house of their own; he'd died when he'd run a stop sign and been broadsided by a lorry in the middle of the night. No one was quite sure whether he'd fallen asleep at the wheel, or if he'd just missed the sign.

Could Alleyne still feel responsible after all these years? At the funeral she'd said "it's my fault" over and over, though Liam had taken the second job over her objections.

Perhaps Dorothy was tormenting herself because she hadn't been there when her husband died. Connor gazed at the choppy water and tried to measure the things he knew about the day William Hudson killed himself. It was possible a woman like Dorothy would be haunted by the idea that she could have stopped the tragedy, just by being there. Then again, he might be projecting Alleyne's feelings onto Dot.

The answers weren't clear, and no one would accuse Connor of being overly astute when it came to feminine sensibilities.

In the meantime, he was just borrowing time. And it wouldn't be long before the whole thing came crashing down on his fool head.

CHAPTER ELEVEN

"THERE'S SOMETHING I need to tell you," Layne said to her aunt on Saturday morning.

"What's that, dear?" Dee asked absently. She sat at the kitchen counter, studying storyboards for the children's fantasy book she was illustrating.

"Well, you know how Matt Hollister came by my house and gave me information and said he wanted to help me look for answers about Uncle Will?"

"You mentioned that he's been helping with your inquiries."

"Yes, and he's also had some good ideas…and, uh…well, he arranged for me to meet with Peter Davidson a couple of days ago."

Dee looked up. "You didn't tell me *that*."

"It happened quickly. And besides, you've been distracted by your new friend. Patrick sounds nice."

"He *is*," her aunt admitted. "Though in a different way than William. It's quite innocent. We walk part of the time, and talk."

"And he feeds you tea and crumpets," Layne teased, pouring herself a cup of coffee.

"Actually, there *were* crumpets in the pastries he got yesterday. He doesn't eat them himself—he claims I need the calories and that I remind him of his sister who lost too much weight after her husband died."

"You *are* too thin."

Dee shrugged. "I forget to eat, that's all. At first I thought Patrick was interested in me as a woman and it made me uncomfortable. But after I told him about William dying last December, it became more companionable. Supposedly his sister never got over her husband's death, so I think he has an absurd notion that I need to be rescued."

"Then you no longer think there's anything odd about him?"

"The large cash transaction seemed peculiar, but I suppose everyone handles their money differently. I haven't seen Patrick pay with plastic, even once. But tell me about the meeting with Peter."

"It didn't go anywhere. I don't like him *at all*."

"You don't?" Her aunt looked surprised. "William usually brought in the big clients—you know how personable he was—but Peter dealt with them effectively."

"You mean Uncle Will was the rainmaker for the firm?"

"If that's how you want to put it, but Peter was particularly brilliant with investments. Will used to say he brought clients into the firm and Peter kept them there. What did he do to upset you?"

Layne sipped her coffee, not wanting to repeat a word Mr. Davidson had said. Yet it really wasn't so much the words, it was the *way* he'd spoken. "I just didn't like him, and he refuses to help, though I got him to admit he's behind the police and D.A. refusing to give us information. I don't think it was specifically to keep us from learning anything. He claims he's trying to keep everything quiet to save the company and everyone's reputations."

"But you like Matthew Hollister?"

Layne hesitated. She wasn't sure what she felt about Matt, other than cautious. He'd turned her on in an instant and then promptly smacked her ego with that comment about sex with her being the "last thing" on his mind.

"He's not too bad," Layne said finally. After all, it wasn't as if Matt could help how he felt. "But I'll never forgive him for introducing me to Cherry Garcia ice cream."

Aunt Dee smiled. "When did he do that?"

"He brought dinner earlier this week, with Ben & Jerry's for dessert. That stuff is sinful. At any rate, he wants to come over today and help go through more of Uncle Will's papers. I told him you'd have to agree."

DOROTHY SAW AN odd expression on Layne's face and prayed she wasn't getting personally involved with Matthew Hollister. Working with him was all right, but he wasn't the sort of man she wanted for her niece.

As for Peter?

Dorothy didn't know what to think. They'd all been such good friends once. When he'd called to tell them about Shelley's accident, they had immediately flown to Hawaii to be with him. But after Peter took twenty-year retirement from the navy and moved to Seattle...things were different. *He* was different. William had said to give it time, but nothing was ever the same.

She glanced down at the storyboards. Illustrating children's books had its ups and downs and this one was particularly challenging.

A mental picture of brown sugar cake rose in Dorothy's mind, with whipped frosting and a caramelized filling. Cooking was so much easier than trying to paint someone else's vision, and she *had* worked until 4:00 a.m. the night before on the illustrations. She could take a break.

"You're welcome to invite Mr. Hollister over," she murmured, going into the kitchen. "If nothing else, I should apologize for the way I behaved at the gala."

"Okay." Layne took out her cell phone and dialed. "Hey, Matt, it's me," she said after a moment. "What...oh, stop complaining, I *prefer* this kind of phone. It's mostly for emergencies and I hardly use any minutes...well, yeah, more lately with you calling so much."

Layne didn't say anything for several seconds, then she rolled her eyes.

"Absolutely *not*....yeah...do you want to come over this afternoon and look at some of the records...?"

Apparently the answer was yes, because Layne gave directions to the house and agreed on a time before saying goodbye.

"There," she said. "He's coming."

"What was the bit about the phone?"

"Matt thinks I should have a regular cell phone so my caller ID comes up on his phone. The one I have now is the kind you buy at a convenience store. Is it all right if we use the dining room? I'd rather not have him in the office too much."

"It's fine. I'm planning to work in my studio later, but I'm going to make a cake first."

"Stressed?"

"A bit. Nothing is resolved, and then there's Patrick. I enjoy him, but I don't know what he actually wants, and I'm not ready for anything except friendship."

"I don't think *men* know what they want, so what hope do we have of figuring it out?" Layne swallowed the last of her coffee. "Uh…Aunt Dee, I keep thinking about that evening you hinted Uncle Will might have been…well, with someone else on the nights the thefts occurred. What made you think that?"

Dorothy's stomach rolled. "There were signs that made me start wondering. It was nothing definitive."

"What signs?"

"Little things. Sometimes I would call in the evening from Mount Vernon and couldn't reach him—not at the office or at the house and his cell phone would be turned off. Or I'd come into his home office and he'd get off a call with a rushed goodbye. It doesn't sound like much, but it wasn't like him."

"Neither was having an affair."

"I know. There isn't any proof, and besides, it was probably nothing—at the time I didn't think much of it. It was only later I began wondering."

Layne gave her a hug. "I'm sure it *was* nothing. I don't think Uncle Will knew other women existed after meeting you."

Dorothy smiled, wishing her niece could keep the certainty of youth.

"If it's okay, we'd like to go through your last year's credit card statements and phone bills," Layne added after a moment. "I still don't know the dates of the thefts, but we can record all charges or calls made on a Thursday."

"Oh. All right," Dorothy agreed, albeit reluctantly. She didn't have anything to hide—the police had combed their finances, trying to show unexplained income. It was the *current* records she didn't want her niece to see; it would be even more obvious how the bills had fallen behind, and Layne wanted to help so badly.

Patrick's annoying comment went through her head about how it had hurt his family to see Alleyne going without help.

Shut up, she thought crossly.

Her decisions were none of his business, and she had to learn independence. She shouldn't have let William take care of everything—it had not only left her vulnerable, it hadn't been fair to him. And it would be all too easy to let Lani fill that role.

MATT'S PHONE BEGAN ringing as he drove out of the parking garage under the Eisley Building early that afternoon. It was his mother and he hit a button on the steering wheel to answer. "Hello, Mom."

"Sweetheart, you've been so busy, we haven't talked lately."

Matt grinned wryly, not bothering to point out that they *rarely* talked, no matter how busy he was. He'd always adored his mother, but between him being away at boarding school during most of his childhood and the way she seemed to live in an ivory tower, they weren't close.

Katrina had withdrawn from public life during her separation from Spence, and even if nobody would admit it, she'd become agoraphobic after the divorce. She'd hated the frenzied attention from the media— the nasty speculation and the posed picture of her in her wedding dress published in various print media, shown side-by-side with ones of Spence, whooping it up in Las Vegas with busty showgirls. Matt often wondered how all of their lives would have turned out if his grandparents had gotten Katrina help, instead of catering to her illness.

"I'll try to get over more often, Mom."

"It's all right, but I wanted you to know that Father is so pleased with how you're handling the foundation, he and Mother are going to Europe for an extended vacation."

"I'm glad he approves."

Matt had become better acquainted with Gordon since returning to Seattle, often consulting with him about the various programs. While he was taking the Eisley Foundation in a new direction, he didn't want to undo his grandfather's legacy. They'd had a couple of disputes on policy, but Gordon had ultimately agreed it was Matt's job to make the decisions now.

"I'm proud of you, too," she added.

"Thanks." Yet another flash of wry humor hit Matt. His mother probably hadn't expected to ever claim she was proud of something he'd done.

"The truth is, I've always felt guilty for not becoming involved in the foundation," Katrina said unexpectedly. "Father hoped I would, but the work involves being in the public eye and I just… Anyway, it's wonderful you decided to come back."

"I wanted to do it." He pulled into the flow of vehicles on the road around Lake Union and dodged a bare-headed motorcyclist weaving in and out through traffic with reckless disregard.

"Yes…oh, the other phone is ringing," Katrina told him hastily. "Come to dinner anytime. Bye."

Matt frowned thoughtfully. While he was still trying to make up his mind about Peter in light of what he'd learned over the past weeks, he couldn't deny that Katrina seemed happier now. Before meeting Peter she'd only attended a few private parties, which was where they'd met, otherwise rarely leaving the Eisley grounds. She still didn't enjoy going out in public, but she was traveling a little and becoming more confident. The marriage had helped, but Peter had also gotten her on medication and talking to a counselor. Despite Matt's skepticism about the relationship lasting, he was grateful to his stepfather for the changes.

LAYNE'S CLASSIC MUSTANG wasn't in Mrs. Hudson's driveway when Matt arrived, yet as soon as he pulled in and got out, the front door opened.

"You're right on time," Layne called.

"You sound surprised."

"You got to my house an hour early last Saturday. What happened to being fashionably late like the rest of the rich and famous?"

"I believe in setting my own fashion trends."

She led him inside and Matt sniffed the air appreciatively; it smelled like a bakery he'd once visited in New Orleans, redolent with vanilla and pralines. In the kitchen he saw Dorothy Hudson putting the final touches on a cake that could have been made by a master pastry chef.

"Hello, Mrs. Hudson."

"Please, it's Dee." Dorothy gave him a strained smile and deftly dropped a final sugar-crusted pecan on top of the cake. She dusted her fingers and extended her hand. "I'm so sorry for the way I behaved at the mayor's gala. I hope Layne told you it wasn't like me."

"There's no need to apologize, I would have done the same in your shoes." Once again Matt was struck by Dorothy Hudson's timeless beauty. No wonder Connor was so taken with her and making every excuse to visit, though he had zero reason to do so.

"That's very gracious."

"It's the truth. I admit to being angry that evening, but I've had time to see things in a new light. And I also…" He stopped, wondering how much he should say. "It's long overdue, but I want to express my sympathy for your loss."

Dorothy nodded and he saw her swallow convulsively. "Thank you." She put the cake into the large double-sided refrigerator before looking at him again. "Layne mentioned you'd be working in the dining room. There's coffee in the pot and food in the fridge if you get hungry. I'll be in my studio if you need anything."

Layne scooped a large ginger tabby into her arms and scratched its neck. "Aunt Dee offers food when she can't think of anything else to say."

"It's a shame you're too old to spank, young lady," Dorothy scolded.

"Except you never believed in spanking children." Layne kissed her aunt and whispered something that made her smile.

"All right, all right. Get busy and I'll see you later." Still holding the cat, Layne circled around into the dining room and Matt saw a stack of paper on the otherwise pristine walnut table. "I brought out some of Aunt Dee and Uncle Will's phone bills and other stuff to go through."

"Yeah. Uh, about your aunt…she didn't ask me anything. Isn't she curious?"

"Of course she's curious. It's just hard for her to talk about it with someone she doesn't know."

"Yeah, but Peter is married to my mother. Doesn't she have any concerns about my involvement? No matter what, I'd want to discuss it."

"Oh, please, you're a guy. Besides, you've never…." All at once Layne shot a look in the direction Dorothy Hudson had gone, then put the cat on the floor. She pulled him in the opposite direction, into a bedroom at the end of the hall.

"Okay, what have I 'never' done?"

"You've never lost someone you loved that much." She dropped onto the end of the bed and heaved a sigh. "Try to understand. Without Uncle Will, it's as if half of her is gone. She's been trying to make sense of it, but how can she? Everything fell apart and nobody will give her answers. And…"

"And what?" Matt prompted.

"She knows no matter what answers we find, they won't bring him back. He was the love of her life."

Matt sat next to Layne. "You don't really believe in that 'love of your life' thing, do you? Practically everyone I know who's gotten married for love is divorced and hates their ex-spouse."

"What about the Eisleys?"

"My grandparents married because they were friends, not out of a grand passion. In a way, they lead separate lives. That's probably why they're happy."

"Maybe you don't know the right people. My grandmother Adele and granddad Brian were deeply in love, and my folks are, too, even if it isn't the same as what my aunt and uncle had together."

"Your parents sound like a classic power couple."

"They are. They just don't know what to make of me. Mom and Dad try, but they're so capable and practical and everything falls into place for them... then I came along. I'm the kid that didn't get a doctorate and go into a prestigious career."

"They should be proud you're helping your aunt."

Layne smiled and Matt wondered if she realized how amazing she looked when she let that smile go with no holds barred.

"They don't know what I'm doing, but thanks. Anyhow, I just wanted you to understand about Aunt Dee. She's trying to keep her head above water in more ways than one, and it isn't easy."

LAYNE STOOD AND looked at Matt. Since she slept often at Aunt Dee's, she kept clothing and other personal things in the room, and it was going be hard not to think about Matt Hollister sitting on the bed when she was trying to sleep. Even when she'd disliked him, she'd still acknowledged he was sexy—a woman would have to be dead not to recognize his appeal, and it had been a while since she'd had a serious relationship.

"Let's get busy," she said. "We can look for credit card purchases on Thursdays, as well as phone calls from the house. It helps knowing the thefts were on Thursdays, though I still need the specific dates of the wire transfers. As a last resort, I'll hire a lawyer to throw out impressive legal mumbo jumbo to get things moving with the authorities."

Matt stood up and stretched. "You haven't asked me to intervene with the police or the D.A. Any special reason?"

Layne had considered asking, but if the roadblocks in getting information stemmed from Peter Davidson's political influence, Matt could get into trouble trying to overstep his stepfather. Besides, would the police pay any attention, anyway? Matt was new to respectability and probably didn't have as much clout with the authorities.

"I'm going to try myself again, and if that doesn't do any good, maybe you can give it a shot," she said finally.

"How about me giving it a shot right away?"

She hesitated. "It might make Peter angrier."

The frustration on Matt's face became intense. "Layne, you want answers because you loved your uncle and are worried about your aunt. I want them because I was an executive at Hudson & Davidson when the embezzling occurred. My grandfather has entrusted billions of charity dollars to me at the foundation. I need to know if I've made mistakes that can't be fixed, so I don't give a rat's ass how Peter is going to react."

Whoa.

He hadn't quite said he was suspicious of Peter, but the implication was obvious…he was running the Eisley Foundation and his stepfather was now its CFO. Then there was the little matter of Peter being married to Katrina Eisley.

"All right," she said hastily. "But I still want to try again. I'll let you know if I don't have any luck."

"Good, that's…"

All at once Matt's attention was caught by a framed photo on the high dresser. He went over and stared at the images of Aunt Dee and Uncle Will looking at each other, with Layne as a five-year-old in pigtails, leaning against their legs.

"That was taken right after Uncle Will left the navy and they'd moved back to the Seattle area," Layne explained. "They tried not to play favorites with us kids, but the others were older and busy being over-achievers. My parents were happy for me to spend most of my time with Aunt Dee, especially with my brother, Jeremy, competing in track meets all over the place."

"That's right, he's a runner. I remember the name from the coverage at the Olympics ten or twelve years ago," Matt said distractedly, tapping his finger on the photograph. "From your uncle's expression I'm guessing they were newlyweds when this was taken."

"Actually they'd been married for several years. Uncle Will always had that goofy look around Aunt Dee. But Aunt Dee was the same with him, so it equaled out."

Matt picked up the photo and stared into the image. "They're the reason you believe in fairy-tale love and happily ever after. You must realize it's a fantasy, Layne."

"Even if it *is,* what's the harm? Don't you have fantasies?"

"I've already chased my fantasies. Some were more fun than others."

Layne took the picture and set it back on the dresser. "You know, your old life doesn't sound that great," she murmured. "Everyone needs dreams we can never really attain."

"You must have studied philosophy in college."

"Actually, that's something I learned from Uncle Will. He used to say we should dream for things that are unrealistic, because that's how the impossible happens."

"I SHOW A CALL ON May 14 at 7:27 p.m.," Matt said an hour later as he scanned through one of the phone bills.

Layne marked it on her calendar grid and in the database she'd created.

"Any idea whose number that might be?" he asked absently.

"It's my grandmother Adele up in Mount Vernon.

She's had the same number since before I was born, though I think the area code changed at some point."

"She's the grandmother your aunt was visiting every Thursday, so this could be your uncle calling to make sure she arrived safely. If one of the thefts occurred on the fourteenth, this could show that he wasn't at the office at the time."

"Yeah."

She took the phone bill he'd finished reviewing, sorted through the pages to be sure they were all there, then put it in the feeder of her document scanner. None of the material she'd brought out to work on with Matt was irreplaceable—though the bills would be a pain to get copies of—but she'd decided to make electronic copies, anyway. This way she could study them at home, as well as at Aunt Dee's, and take the more valuable stuff to the safe deposit box she'd rented.

"You've gone through a lot of documents, but I'm not sure how much is pertinent," Matt said, starting on another month.

"Me, either, but you never know what will be helpful."

Matt was frowning as he read. "It's too bad these bills don't list local calls."

"The data must be available. But unless I can sweet-talk the phone company into cooperating— which is unlikely—the case would have to be re-opened and a subpoena or something issued to get it."

His frowned deepened. "You also said you've been

going over your uncle's papers from his company. But why would important evidence be dumped into boxes and allowed to leave the building?"

"I don't know—it's just a possibility. Remember, they got Al Capone on tax evasion."

Matt shrugged. "What does Al Capone have to do with your uncle's case?"

"It's just that there could be more than one way to accomplish something. The government wanted Capone off the streets of Chicago and they got him convicted, even if it wasn't for murder and bootlegging. The police were looking for proof of Uncle Will's guilt, not his innocence, so I might find something in Uncle Will's office records that indirectly leads to the truth."

"I SUPPOSE."

Matt swallowed the last of his coffee. Despite his questions, he was impressed with the way Layne had organized her search. But he still suspected she was keeping part of the information from him, and he'd noticed they weren't working in her uncle's home office. From what Layne had said, William Hudson's home office had sat there all these months, relatively untouched.

The reason for keeping him out could be emotional, or based on suspicion of his motives and what he might tell Peter.

As for her aunt's house…

Matt's gaze swept what he could see of the home.

He could detect Mrs. Hudson's artistic eye in the decor—few knickknacks except for strategically placed art glass and photos, lots of wood, rich color and a balance of natural textures. It was warm and inviting, unlike the Eisley mansion or his penthouse.

Another smile threatened as Matt recalled Layne's expression when she first set eyes on his penthouse. He had to admit, the stark interior was off-putting; the only recommendation was the view.

Layne neatly annotated the phone bills they'd been reviewing in her log and filed them in a cardboard banker's box. She was obviously still feeling her way around the best way to organize the information, but he was pretty sure she could quickly lay her hands on any piece of paper she'd touched.

Watch out, Peter, he thought. Layne wasn't a push-over and she wasn't letting this rest. His stepfather would have been better off helping than trying to stop her.

"Uh…did they send any client files with the rest of the things sent from Hudson & Davidson?" he asked.

"As far as I can tell there's nothing from the official files, though I've found some client information—basically, they boxed and sent all of Uncle Will's private records to Aunt Dee. I'm sure he never intended them to leave his office at the firm. Not that there were account numbers or anything, but I've seen things that *I* wouldn't want floating around."

Matt winced.

Violation of client privacy.

Not good.

They'd reached the end of the documents Layne had set out and he looked at her. "Is there anything else?"

"Uh…I guess we could start on another box sent over from Hudson & Davidson."

He stood up. "Let's go."

Layne didn't seem too happy about it, but she took him into an attractive study filled with books and furnished in rich cherrywood furniture. The only discordant note was a stack of boxes along one wall. Matt grabbed one and set it on the desk, cutting the tape on the lid and opening the flaps. The scent of mold instantly rose in the air.

"What the hell?" he exclaimed.

Layne looked inside and made a face. "From the blue and gold foil sticker on the bag, I think that used to be a sandwich. Uncle Will had a standing order for a vegetarian hoagie from the Blue Ribbon deli. Maybe it was delivered the day he died and he didn't eat it. Or the day after."

"But why is it in *here?*" Matt demanded.

"That's how everything came. Glass in picture frames was broken, things were crushed…there was even a dirty coffee cup. Apparently it was half-full and they just dumped it in with the rest, coffee and all."

"*That's* why you asked if I'd had anything to do with how his belongings were packed."

"Yeah. Let's take it outside," Layne said, going to the French doors and flinging them open.

Matt carried the box to the far end of the yard and put it on a bench. Layne was quiet as they gingerly sorted the contents. There were a few books, including one she'd apparently given William, and tears streaked down her face as she flipped through the pages before storing it in a plastic bag. They found three plaques honoring William Hudson from the Carrollton Chamber of Commerce, the brass somewhat corroded from contact with the moldy sandwich.

They didn't find anything that seemed pertinent to William's case, yet a thought kept pounding in Matt's head…there was something vindictive about putting a rotting sandwich into a box with personal books and tributes, then sealing it with yards of tape.

"I'm sorry," Matt said after they'd dumped the box in a garbage can. "This should never have been allowed to happen."

Layne shook her head. "It wasn't your fault. But please don't tell my aunt about it. She doesn't know. I've had some of the things repaired and will store anything that's beyond help in case she ever asks."

Matt sighed. There were dark smudges beneath Layne's eyes and her thick, silky hair seemed to overwhelm her pale face. She'd lost weight since the first time they'd met in Matt's office and he clenched his fingers into a fist. He was no Galahad and Layne wouldn't appreciate him trying to rescue her in the first place. But for the first time in his life, he was wondering what it would be like to be someone a woman like Layne could rely on.

And it scared the hell out of him.

CHAPTER TWELVE

THE CELL PHONE ringing on Matt's bedside table dragged him slowly from sleep. He read the display on the clock and groaned. It was 2:00 a.m. Once he'd stayed up that late every night, but not any longer.

"Uh…yeah?" he answered.

"Don't tell me you were asleep, son," cried Spence's energetic voice. "We're winding down here, but it's still the top of the evening in Seattle."

"Dad, you forget I'm a working guy now. I no longer party until five or six every morning."

"How dreary."

"Where are you, anyway?" Matt asked, yawning. In the background he heard steel drums, clinking glasses, and the chatter of a party.

"Jamaica. Can't beat the Caribbean."

"That explains the music." Matt's eyelids drifted down as he recalled the beaches and warm, crystalline waters of Montego Bay and the scantily clad women who swam in them.

Would Layne ever go topless? She had a hang-up about her appearance compared to her well-endowed sisters, but she'd be delicious in island gear and she really needed a break from investigating… Matt's eyes popped open.

No.

Layne would slap him if she knew how thoroughly he'd envisioned her with sun-kissed skin and no tan lines. She might not be generously endowed, but there was something appealing about her trim lines. He needed to remember Layne's fairy-tale faith in marriage and that "love of your life" nonsense. The most he could offer was a week in Fiji or Montego Bay, and while he'd never wanted to spend an entire week with any woman before, she'd still see it as an insult.

Matt shook himself. "Why are you calling, Dad?"

"It's been a while and I wanted to say hi. Brought Delia down for a little sailing."

Delia?

"Is that a boat, or one of your girlfriends? Oh, God, it isn't a new wife, is it?"

Spence chuckled. There wasn't much that bothered him. "Nope, just someone I met on a layover in Chicago. Lovely girl. Wants to be an author. No stamina though, went to bed hours ago."

"She'd better be over eighteen," Matt warned.

"Twenty-four and just got her graduate degree. A Fulbright scholar. Stacked, with mile-long legs. I keep telling her she could make a fortune in Vegas."

"I'm sure she appreciates the career advice."

Matt didn't know how Spence did it—a beautiful, twenty-four-year-old Fulbright scholar, thirty-plus years his junior?

He got up and wandered into the living room. The lights of the city were sparkling on the skyline above the dark expanse of Lake Union.

"Maybe you should have her talk to April and Tamlyn's mother. Or is Ginny no longer performing in Las Vegas?" he asked, knowing perfectly well that his former-showgirl ex-stepmother was living comfortably on her divorce settlement in Barcelona. Ginny hadn't kicked her legs on stage since giving birth to his twin sisters.

"I wouldn't know."

Actually, Spence probably *didn't* know. Once his children reached eighteen and he was no longer dealing with support issues, he tried to forget his ex-wives.

"I miss you, son," Spence said unexpectedly. "We used to see each other more often before you re-formed."

"You could come to Seattle for a visit."

"Nope. I gave Seattle to your mom and kept the rest of the world. How is she, anyway?" he asked carelessly.

"We don't discuss her, remember?"

One of the forbidden subjects between S. S. Hollister and his children was their mothers. His charm was legendary, but his relationships with ex-wives were toxic. It was largely due to his casual attitude toward marital fidelity; Spence adored falling in love and thought a pregnant woman was radiant, but found the domesticity of actually being married and raising a child an unbearable slog.

Matt didn't want to hurt women the way his father had hurt them. *Don't make promises you won't keep.* It was a lesson Spence had inadvertently taught over the years, just by being an optimist who always thought that *this* time he would stay in love forever.

Forever was a fantasy, no matter what Layne said.

"Ah well, just thought I'd ask, son. Have you heard you're going to be an uncle? Aaron and Skylar are having a baby."

"I heard. Aaron and I *do* talk now and then. But I'm already an uncle—Karin, his stepdaughter, is my niece, too. Aaron is crazy about her."

"That he is. I'm having a trust fund set up for them both. Hope the baby is another girl and she gets her mama's red hair and sass. That gal is a real looker."

Matt pressed a finger to his temple, a hint of irritation rising inside of him. "Skylar is your *daughter-in-law,* Dad. Your *only* daughter-in-law. Not a potential girlfriend."

"That isn't what I meant." Spence sounded genuinely indignant. "I want all of my children to be happy."

Maybe. But he also wasn't willing to be a real father. Most of the time he wasn't even around.

"Fine. I don't hear calypso any longer, the party must be over."

"Guess so. Let me know when you get tired of being good and we'll throw a bash of our own down here. Bye, son."

Matt tossed the phone on the couch, disgusted. It

was just like Spence to wake him up in the middle of the night, chat about nothing and then go off to an untroubled sleep after a night of unbridled partying.

Hmm, Montego Bay.

Warm tropical breezes, sailing, brilliant sunsets… They were a far cry from meetings, reports and cold northwest rain. Matt knew he'd be a hypocrite to deny there was a seductive appeal to his old life. But if he went back to it, he'd throw away his chance to do something that actually mattered.

ON SUNDAY AFTERNOON Dorothy finished her shift at the art gallery later, with no sign of Patrick.

She got into her Volvo and sat for a long minute. More often these days, she heard Will in the house, walking up and down the hall, catching echoes of his laughter and low voice. She felt him lie down next to her in bed and smelled the pipe tobacco he used to smoke. Maybe it *was* her imagination, but she looked forward to it. The hints of his presence were never quite tangible, yet reassuring in their way…and a reminder that she hadn't cleared his name yet.

A rap on the car window made her jump.

Patrick was leaning down, peering in, and she hit the button to lower the glass.

"You were a million miles away, Dot," he said, smiling. "I was delayed, something came up and I couldn't get away. Do you have time for tea?"

Dorothy checked her watch. "I can't, I have a contract deadline coming up."

"When is your next shift at the gallery?"

"Not until Friday afternoon. That's my regular day. I usually don't work several times a week, but they've been shorthanded. If you're free on Friday we can go…that is, I'm sure I'll be done with my project by then," she said.

"I'll be here. Promptly. Even if I have to shoot someone."

"That's drastic. Why don't you just set the alarm on your watch and tell whoever that you have a prior commitment?"

"Right, less paperwork that way."

Dorothy waved as she drove off, wondering if she *would* see Patrick again. She wasn't being coy, she just needed space to think. Meeting him right now wasn't the best timing in the world. But then, life didn't happen in neat little packages, and it certainly didn't happen when it was convenient.

LAYNE WAITED IN the Carrollton Police Station on Tuesday afternoon, watching officers and other employees pass back and forth as if she didn't exist. The chief detective who'd worked on Uncle Will's case had finally agreed to talk to her, but so far she hadn't been taken to his desk—he probably hoped she'd just give up if he waited long enough.

"Ms. McGraw?" a man finally said and she looked up.

"Yes. Are you Detective Rivera?"

He nodded. "Come with me. I have a small conference room reserved where we can talk."

The "small conference room" reminded Layne of the places in television shows where the cops questioned suspects and there was even a mirror on the wall that she suspected was one-way.

Layne sat down and took her notebook from her purse.

"That won't be needed," said the detective. "I don't have information to give you. Our files are confidential, but I wanted to speak with you directly after all the calls from you and your aunt."

"My uncle believed he could prove his innocence. I just need to know when the illegal wire transfers occurred in order to *look* for that proof. Surely it isn't too much to ask."

Rivera rubbed his forehead. "I speak with families every day who don't believe their loved ones could be guilty of a crime. Possibly the most difficult aspect of my job is seeing the expression in people's eyes and knowing their faith was put in the wrong person."

Layne's jaw tightened. "My faith in Uncle Will aside, haven't you ever had a case where you considered the evidence to be overwhelming, only to discover things weren't what they appeared?"

"Of course, but it's extremely rare."

"And can you honestly say that it isn't suspicious

to find a suicide note on a printer that couldn't have printed it?"

"All right, I'll admit that seems…questionable."
Hallelujah.
She'd finally made an inch of progress.

"I never met your uncle," the detective murmured after a moment. "I was on the investigative team from the start, but didn't become team leader until a few days after he committed suicide. As a matter of fact, I'm the only officer left in this precinct who *was* on the team."

Layne's stomach swooped and rolled. "Were you at the house the night…the night he was found in his office?"

"Yes."

It was difficult to think about. Aunt Dee had waited to call the family until after the police were gone and she was alone. Layne had gotten there first and the house had seemed unbearably silent, as if in shock along with the rest of them.

"About the autopsy report…" she started to say, only to have Detective Rivera shake his head.

"I don't control those records."

"Surely you have a copy."

"As I explained, the police records are not available. Please, there's nothing more to discuss and I'm late for my son's birthday party." He stood, indicating the discussion was over.

She'd known it wasn't a good sign when he arrived

without a file and brought her to a stark, empty room. But curiously, Layne didn't dislike the detective the way she'd expected.

"I'm not giving up."

The detective gave her an unexpected smile. "I'd be surprised if you did. And believe it or not, I wish you luck."

Yet before Layne got to the door, he cleared his throat. "Er...Ms. McGraw, I was just wondering if you know what kind of printer paper Mr. Hudson used in his home office."

"I'm not sure, probably standard twenty-pound all-purpose paper. Oh, wait a minute, I have a sample."

She took out a sheet she'd grabbed the other day to make a shopping list. It hadn't escaped her notice that while Detective Rivera wasn't willing to provide information, he felt free to ask *her* a question.

Rivera fingered the paper. "You're right, it appears to be twenty-pound bond. That's also what they use at Hudson & Davidson."

Her eyes narrowed. He'd just wanted to confirm the paper from each location was the same?

Now *that* was annoying.

"I never claimed they were different," Layne said crisply. *"Good afternoon."*

OUTSIDE THE POLICE station Layne dropped into her Mustang and tapped the steering wheel. She'd been working with Matt on Uncle Will's records since Saturday, and an odd companionship had grown between them.

He was also having his security staff get the phone numbers of the new employee names that Emma Farnon and other Hudson & Davidson employees had given her. Emma seemed nice enough, even though she'd contacted Peter Davidson to tell him that Layne was asking questions. And despite the accusations against Uncle Will, Emma had fond memories of him as her boss.

Squaring her chin, Layne took out her cell phone and dialed Matt.

"Hey. What's up?" he answered.

She blinked. "How did you know it was me?"

"Easy, I added your number to my contacts so your name will show up. Though I still think you need a regular cell phone. Is there a problem?"

"I just got done meeting with Detective Rivera at the Carrollton Police Station. He was nice, but it's a no-go on telling me anything from the file. So if you want to talk to him, go ahead."

"I remember Rivera—he was in charge of the investigation, right?"

"Yeah, part of the time."

"It sounds as if he annoyed you."

"Good guess."

Layne hadn't wanted Matt to contact the police department or the D.A.'s office, but it now seemed clear she wouldn't get anything from them without help. A lawyer *might* be able to do something, only she'd rather avoid official channels at the moment.

"I'll call him as soon as we get off," Matt said.

"He mentioned being late to his son's birthday party, so I don't think he's there."

"Tomorrow, then."

"Okay. Thanks." Layne got off the phone and pulled into traffic. Aunt Dee wasn't expecting her, so she decided to drive home and try getting a good night's sleep.

Layne parked in her garage and locked it, shivering as she regarded her lovely Victorian. She hadn't slept well since discovering the scratches on her door locks.

Perhaps she should get an alarm system, Layne thought as she checked both the front and back doors and surveyed the exterior of the house for any obvious problems.

Hmm, nothing.

Just the creepy feeling she kept getting that something wasn't right. And that she was being watched.

She went inside and phoned the cable company again. "I just need information," she said when she reached the repair department and had given them her address. "I'm trying to find out when your repair guy was in my neighborhood on June 16th, either in the late afternoon or evening. I understand you got a call about damaged cable lines."

"Let's see…the call was logged at 6:22 p.m., and our repair specialist was contacted at 6:37 p.m. He was on another site and my records don't show when he arrived in your area. Are you lodging a complaint?"

"No, just checking."

Layne's creepy feeling grew. According to Sanjiv, the repair "specialist" had arrived no later than six. A cable repairman never showed up to fix a problem *before* it was actually reported. Sanjiv could have been wrong about the time, but what if he wasn't?

Reluctantly, Layne dialed the police nonemergency number. They couldn't do anything, but at least they could check the house and give her a little more peace of mind.

ON WEDNESDAY MORNING Connor stared at the painting on his office wall and scowled, making his second in command let out a low whistle.

"What in bloody hell has you in a mood?" asked Riley Flannigan.

"Nothing." Connor used the tone he employed when he didn't want questions, but Riley simply appeared bored and half asleep. It was an act he excelled at—few people would guess that beneath his nonchalance he was a martial arts expert with lethal skills.

"Your 'nothing' has everyone in duck-and-cover mode."

"I notice you're still sitting there."

Riley yawned. "I don't have anything to worry about—I'm a better shot. I'm not the one who blew my last session at the shooting range. In that last set we each fired off six rounds—mine were perfectly placed, but one of yours was half a centimeter off-center."

Connor's eyes narrowed. "It was perfect, the ventilation system simply turned on and shifted the target."

"You should have compensated."

"Go to hell." Connor was tempted to kick the other man's ass into next week, but that would just prove Riley's point.

And in all honesty, he wasn't in the best of moods. Connor thought back, recalling his brief conversation with Dorothy on Sunday. Nothing in her manner had suggested she was suspicious of him. Nevertheless, as Matt became increasingly involved in the investigation with Layne, the risk that Dorothy would discover he hadn't been truthful with her was also greater.

And the damned part of it was that he could have told her his real name, though revealing his connection to Matt would have been trickier. But he'd spent so much of his life in half truths and concealed identities, it was hard to break the habit.

Finnster was asleep in the corner, lying on his side, an occasional low grunt coming from him, accompanied by a faint twitch. What did a dog dream about, anyhow? Racing through fields, eating meaty bones…being petted and spoiled by two women while ignoring a primary command? Connor was trying to be philosophical about that part. He'd run Finn through a vigorous set of exercises since then and he had performed perfectly.

Riley stood up. "It's a shame the princess and her hubby cancelled their trip to California. I wouldn't have minded a cushy assignment for a week or two."

"Stop calling her the princess," Connor ordered, annoyed. Katrina Eisley Davidson had her problems, but she wasn't arrogant or a pain in the ass. Riley just had a hang-up about beautiful women with money, no matter what their age.

Riley simply yawned again.

Connor considered pushing the issue, but it wouldn't do any good. He didn't pick his people for their willingness to agree with him; he picked hardheaded, skilled operatives who made up their own minds and were happy to tell anyone to go to hell, including their boss.

"Get out of here," he muttered.

"I'm already gone."

Riley sauntered out and Connor looked at the report his team had compiled on Emma Farnon. A number of Hudson & Davidson employees had retired or taken other positions in the past few months and Matt wanted each of them investigated for unexplained financial windfalls.

Matt seemed to think there was compelling evidence that William Hudson could have been murdered. It *was* curious that Hudson had committed suicide so quickly, but some men couldn't face ruin. And it wouldn't have been easy for William to look into Dorothy's eyes and realize he'd destroyed the life they'd shared.

Connor looked again at the painting of Spirit Lake below the shattered ruin of Mount St. Helens. He wasn't one to look for hidden meanings in physical objects, yet he wondered at the eerie images superimposed on the canvas of the mountain and lake before the volcanic eruption. Had Dorothy let her imagination take flight, or was there a message in the images... perhaps one about her life?

But which was more real to her—the pretty vision before ruin and devastation, or the reality of death and scandal? He got up and looked at the canvas, suddenly spotting a clump of lupine blooming on one of the gray slopes...renewal in the midst of devastation. Was that a third possibility?

Impatient with the questions, and most of all with himself, Connor grabbed the report on the Farnon woman to take to Matt, along with the contact information he'd obtained on additional Hudson & Davidson employees. He was old enough to know better than to develop feelings for anyone, much less an artistic widow devoted to the memory of her husband.

And he was smart enough to know that using a false name had doomed any friendship from the start... which might be precisely why he'd done it.

THAT NIGHT LAYNE sat on the bed with her laptop, so jumpy she had trouble concentrating, and she kept getting up and looking out the windows to see if any-one was hanging around.

The police had come the night before, searched the house and backyard and promised to increase their presence in the neighborhood for a few days. While they were sympathetic, it was also clear they thought she was overreacting.

The phone on the bedside table rang and Layne's heart jumped. She grabbed the receiver, hoping it was Uncle Rob. He had called a couple days before and left a message, so she'd sent him another email, giving him her work hours and asking him to phone again, no matter what the hour.

"Uncle Rob?"

"No, it's me," Matt said. "I thought it would be all right to call since your lights are on."

"You're outside my house?"

"I'm parked in your driveway. I have that updated list of addresses and phone numbers. Connor gave it to me this afternoon, but I was in the middle of a negotiation and couldn't get away earlier."

Layne got up and went to the front bedroom win-dow and scowled. Matt's red Mercedes-Benz was in her driveway; she should have heard him arrive—practically every *other* car driving down the street had gotten her attention.

"I'll be right there."

She ran downstairs and opened the door when she saw Matt coming up the walkway. He looked triumphant and to her surprise, gave her a swift, very thorough kiss.

"Uh…what was that for?"

"Ever hear of Remy Saunders?"

"Can't say that I have."

"Well, he's a leading medical researcher and has signed a contract to head a new project on amyotrophic lateral sclerosis. I took him to a late dinner and then dropped him at the airport."

"ALS? That's a dreadful disease."

A flicker of emotion darkened Matt's expression. "Yes. And usually fatal in two to five years. There are exceptions, like the physicist Stephen Hawking, but not many."

"A friend's great uncle died of ALS a few years ago. It's weird—apparently several members of his high school graduating class have had ALS, too."

"Really?" Matt looked genuinely interested. "How many in the class?"

"I don't know, but it couldn't have been that many. He grew up in small California town."

"Can you get the details? We're interested in disease clusters to help look for common factors."

"I'll talk to Annette and find out anything she knows."

"Appreciate it." Matt held up an envelope. "Here's the information on the employee names that Emma Farnon gave you."

Layne took out the pages. The information was in a bold, no-frills font, which fit the little she knew about Matt's security chief. She wasn't looking forward to making the calls—from her conversations with Emma and the others, she knew the embezzlement case was a touchy subject.

"Thanks. It's too late to call anyone now, but I'll start tomorrow." Layne glanced at Matt. "You look tired. Was it that exhausting getting a research director to sign a contract?"

"No, but my dad called again last night at two in the morning."

"Again?"

"Yeah. He phoned Saturday night, too. Or rather, Sunday morning as his party was ending in Jamaica. His kind of party doesn't end until after the sun is up."

"But it's nice, isn't it, that he wants to talk?"

Matt shrugged. "Dad only calls when he wants something. In this case, when his twenty-four-year-old girlfriend goes to bed before he does. He gets bored easily."

"Twenty-four?"

"Yeah, and a Fulbright scholar."

"Wow."

"Yeah. I've never been sure how he does it. One minute he's talking to a woman while waiting for a flight, the next she's off to Rio or Montego Bay or the Mediterranean with him."

Layne raised an eyebrow. "You've never picked up a woman that quickly?"

"Not exactly. And we're talking about my father,

the aging Lothario with more ex-wives than he can count. I don't think it's just his money attracting them, though he's paid out several fortunes in divorce settlements."

"I understand he's charming and attractive."

"Looking for an introduction so you can be the next ex-Mrs. S. S. Hollister?"

"Me? I'd need to grow five inches and several bra sizes to appeal to your father. Being blonde, blue-eyed and drop-dead beautiful wouldn't hurt, either. Do you want some ice cream?"

Matt's faint scowl disappeared. "What do you think?"

They went into the kitchen and she took bowls from the cupboard, while he got a carton from the freezer. She'd done her best to ignore the remaining pints of Cherry Garcia in the house, but it hadn't been easy. At stressful moments they positively called her name.

Matt spooned out generous portions and they sat at the kitchen table.

"I called the Carrollton police station several times today," he said after swallowing a bite of ice cream. "Detective Rivera is working a homicide, at least that's what the dispatcher says, but I'll keep trying to reach him. What about your idea of consulting an attorney?"

"I'm not ready to go that route yet." Layne licked her spoon methodically and suddenly became aware of Matt's attentive gaze. She was too old to blush, but she felt warm. Worse, did he think she was trying to be provocative? Trying to act that way would make her feel ridiculous and he'd probably just roll his eyes.

"I'm glad you don't want to meet my dad," he said. "I've already had two stepmothers younger than me. It's weird, even though I don't see his wives that often. Not that any of his marriages last—Spence divorced one of his wives before anyone in the family met her."

Layne dug out a chunk of fudge from her ice cream and ate it. "It doesn't matter, I'm not his type."

"Spence doesn't have a type."

She snickered. "If you think that, you're blind. His women are all tall, long-legged and well endowed. He likes them bright, but will tolerate dumb-as-a-fence-post if they're gorgeous, eager and built like a *Playboy* magazine centerfold. Right?"

Matt groaned.

"That's your type, too," she added.

"Certainly *not*." Now he sounded annoyed. "If I have a 'type,' it's intelligent women with a nice laugh and zero interest in getting married and having children."

"Who are also supermodels."

"How would you know?"

Layne tucked a leg beneath her. "I looked you up online. My favorite photo is of you in the hot tub, holding the champagne flute."

"Oh, dear *God*. Can't anybody let me live that down? I'm more than a guy in a Jacuzzi."

Matt looked grumpy, so she dumped the remainder of her Cherry Garcia into his bowl. Luckily the prospect of more ice cream seemed to brighten his mood. It was strange having this half friendship with Matt Hollister. He was the guy you read about in tabloids, not someone you ate ice cream with in your kitchen. It just went to prove she was the original buddy magnet, though she was sure that once they'd finished their investigation, she'd never see him again.

"I'm not a PR expert, but I wouldn't let anyone know those photos and stories bother you," Layne said thoughtfully. "Show a sense of humor about your old reputation and use it to get people to listen to what you're doing now, like the ALS research project."

"A sense of humor, huh?"

"Why not? You seem to be hoping everyone will forget about the constant women and parties and extreme sports, but I don't think it's working."

"You may be right."

Looking sinfully handsome, he ate the ice cream she'd given him, and Layne squirmed at the traitorous heat in her abdomen. If she wasn't careful, she could fall under the Hollister spell herself, and that would be a disaster. It wasn't just that Matt was opposed to marriage and fatherhood—it would be like falling for the prince in a movie. Cinderella might get her Prince Charming, but women like Layne McGraw didn't.

"So…you were really excited about this Remy Saunders guy agreeing to head the ALS project. What's so special about him?" she asked as a distraction.

"Remy thinks independently. He explores radical ideas without discounting traditional research. You never know where an answer will be found to a problem. I've read about high school science projects that have resulted in amazing discoveries."

"Me, too. Maybe it's because kids haven't learned that certain things aren't supposed to be possible. It could almost make someone reconsider having children."

Lord, her mouth had a wild and free life of its own.

Matt glared. "Don't you start that. My grandmother is making noises about great-grandchildren. I told her to adopt an exhibit at the zoo and leave me alone."

"It's hard to dandle a lone wolf on your knee."

"She isn't the dandling type."

"Yeah, and you take after a laughing hyena so much more." Layne tried to keep sounding tongue-in-cheek, but having him mentally leap from her to his grandmother was another blow to her feminine ego. "Um… how about offering an annual scholarship for the best high school science projects on ALS?"

Matt brightened. "I'll mention it to Remy the next time we talk." He put his bowl on the table and stretched, sending another twinge of awareness through Layne. "I'd better get going. I have appointments early in the morning."

"Okay."

Layne locked the door behind him and wished her body was more cooperative. Wanting to rip Matt's clothes off wasn't conducive to getting anything done, and he'd just think she was pathetic if she tried it.

CHAPTER THIRTEEN

LAYNE'S CELL PHONE rang the next afternoon in the middle of a meeting with Carl Abernathy and the rest of the staff. She winced as Carl's eyebrows shot upward. One of his rules was no cell phones in meetings.

"Sorry," she said, fumbling as she turned it off.

"No, please, don't let us interrupt your social life."

"It's not… Sorry," she apologized again. Layne had gotten a good enough look at the display to know it was Matt calling, and while she was dying of curiosity, talking to him would have to wait. It must be about something good. Matt didn't call her during work hours, probably for fear that someone at the *Babbitt* might discover she was in contact with him.

It wasn't impossible. Layne glanced across the table at Noah Wilkie. He'd love to hear what Matt had said the previous night about his father—S. S. Hollister didn't live in the Seattle area, but he was always good for filler copy since one of his ex-wives lived here. And farther down the table sat Karl Withers, their medical writer—he'd practically kill for an inside scoop about a new Eisley Foundation research project.

After the meeting, Annette Wade handed her a sheet of paper. "It's the information you asked for about my great-uncle," she explained. "It's where he went to high school in California, also the dates he served in the air force and the reserves."

"Thanks."

"Any special reason you asked?"

"Oh, just some research on ALS," Layne said guiltily. "I want to see if your great uncle's high school class has been identified as a disease cluster."

"What do you think about Phillip getting married next month?" Regina asked, coming up behind them. "Isn't it great?"

Phillip Stanton was the *Babbitt*'s obituary writer and had announced he was engaged at the prior week's meeting.

"Mmm, yes," Annette agreed dreamily. She wrote the nuptials column for the *Babbitt* and was the worst romantic. "Layne, Regina and I are throwing an office wedding shower for Phil and his fiancée. Will you help us shop for it?"

"Sure, when are you going?"

"We need more information from Phil before we can make plans," Regina said practically. "You know, where they're going to register, when his fiancée will be available to come to a wedding shower…that kind of thing."

"By the way, my sister is getting married, too," Layne told them. "Stephanie is engaged to Owen Fitzsimmons."

"Oh my God," Annette exclaimed. "The author? Is he just as handsome in person as on his book covers?"

"More."

Regina fanned herself. "He's delicious. I met him once at a book signing. Have they set a date yet?"

"Next May." Layne dropped the information from Annette into her purse. "Owen has a book tour this fall, and Steffie says she wants a spring wedding, anyhow."

"She's the nice one, isn't she?" asked Annette.

Layne squirmed. She loved both of her sisters and they were both nice people at heart, but it hadn't kept her from regularly complaining to her friends about Jeannie. "They're both okay. Jeannie just can't help interfering—she has that big-sister-knows-best attitude when it comes to me."

"I'm never doing a column on *her* wedding. I bet she'll be the worst bridezilla."

Layne suspected the same thing, but didn't want to admit it. Annette was popular with brides and received dozens of wedding invitations weekly, from Centralia to Bellingham. If a wedding received Annette's stamp of approval she wrote beautifully about it, getting just the right pictures and making it sound like a magical event.

"I'll let you know when I have a firm date for Steffie's wedding," Layne assured her friend. "But they said something about a small ceremony, so I'm not sure it's something you'll be interested in covering."

"That's what most couples say, then it turns into a three-ring circus," Regina scoffed.

Layne bit her lip so she wouldn't smile. Both Regina and Annette were romantics, but Regina tried to hide it, being ambitious to become a big-name reporter. Layne checked the clock on the wall. "Quitting time," she pointed out brightly. "I'll see you guys tomorrow."

She gathered her belongings and headed for the parking lot. Once inside her Mustang, she turned her phone back on and called Matt.

"Hey, it's me," she said, still breathless. "I was in the middle of a meeting when you called. What's up?"

"I just talked with Detective Rivera. He's willing to see us Saturday morning at eight—he implied he might have something he'll let you read, but didn't promise copies or anything."

"It's better than nothing."

They agreed to meet at her house and drive to the station together. Layne was thrilled at Matt's success in getting the detective to see her again. Maybe he had more political clout than she'd thought.

LAYNE RACED OUT to her car after nine that evening, so excited she could hardly stand it. She drove to her aunt's house, wanting to tell her the news in person. She called out as she let herself in and turned off the security system, resetting it behind her—the peculiar events at her own house were making her very careful.

"Hey, Aunt Dee, it's me."

"I'm in the kitchen. What are you doing here so late?"

"It isn't that late—it's still light outside. But never mind that, I'm filled with information." Layne grinned. "Uncle Rob just called. I didn't tell you, but I found a phone message in the boxes sent over from Hudson & Davidson. It was in texting short-hand and indicated that an 'RD' asked if Uncle Will was coming that night. I thought it might have been from Uncle Rob."

Aunt Dee's face had gone white and Layne hastily guided her to one of the bar stools at the counter, real-izing she'd been too abrupt. "It's okay. I mean, it may not help the investigation, but you'll like what he said."

"You didn't tell him that I wondered whether Will-iam was having an affair, did you?"

"No, of course not. That's between us. I just men-tioned that I was trying to establish if Uncle Will had an alibi for any of the nights a theft occurred, and that I'd found a phone message suggesting he might have gone to Aberdeen while Rob was staying there with a friend."

"Did he?"

Layne nodded. "Yup. They talked often on the phone and Uncle Will went to Aberdeen to visit sev-eral times while you were in Mount Vernon with Grandma Adele. Unfortunately Uncle Rob can't ver-ify the dates, but it was always on Thursday nights when you were out of town."

"Wait, Lani, back up," Dee said. "Why wouldn't William tell me he was visiting my brother?"

"It's complicated. You know how Uncle Rob was hurt in that roadside bombing?"

"Of course. He almost died."

"Well, he was having a rough time recovering, but with the family worrying about Grandma Adele, he didn't want anyone to know and worry about him, as well. Uncle Rob wasn't specific, but I'm guessing he's had post-traumatic stress and being able to talk to Uncle Will helped him deal with it."

"That makes sense," Dorothy said slowly. "William was former navy, so they had a common language."

"Exactly." Layne took her aunt's hand. "It didn't occur to Uncle Rob to tell you about it after everything happened. He said it was almost funny the way Uncle Will would get off the phone whenever you came around. Apparently he was trying to respect Uncle Rob's wishes, but he was such a lousy liar and thought if you realized he was talking to your brother, you'd want to know why."

Some of the tension in Dee's face began to ease. "You're right. It sounds silly now."

"I've been thinking about how easy it is to read meaning into things after the fact," Layne said. "I'll never forget my neighbor swearing her dog predicted that big earthquake we had a few years ago. She said Ranger was leaping at the fence and barking, which meant he *knew* a big quake was on the way and was trying to warn her."

"And you told her that Ranger had leaped at the fence and barked every day since you moved in, so unless he was predicting earthquakes in China and Guatemala and Timbuktu, he was no more psychic than your pet rock."

"Yeah, I should have been more diplomatic."

"But I see your point." Aunt Dee yawned. "You know, I may actually be able to sleep tonight. Stay and we'll have waffles in the morning before you go to work."

"Deal."

An hour later Layne crawled into bed in the room at the end of the hall and smiled happily. If she accomplished nothing else with her investigation, she'd taken *one* weight off Aunt Dee.

Layne snuggled deeper into her pillow. She'd enjoyed talking to Uncle Rob. He rarely made it home for the holidays or other visits. He was the youngest of Grandma Adele and Granddad Brian's children. Grandma Adele had figured her family was done after Aunt Dee was born, but nine years later, when she was in her forties and Granddad in his sixties, she'd gotten pregnant. According to Aunt Dee, Granddad had taken it in stride, the way he'd taken everything.

Turning on her side, Layne drew her feet up, remembering how she and Matt had sat on the end of the bed and talked. He was different than she would have expected a playboy to be. At least he had a good sense of humor and seemed to care about people.

And he'd gotten Detective Rivera to agree to another meeting and was going with her to the police station.

Layne yawned and closed her eyes.

She wasn't going to let Matt Hollister keep her awake. Not tonight. Not when she'd been able to give Aunt Dee good news for the first time.

On Saturday morning Layne parked the Mustang near the police station. She was tense and Matt pulled her arm through his as they walked out of the lot. The police station was in the back of the city's administrative center—all very modern and lacking in charm. Obviously Carrollton didn't believe in spending money on architectural frills for their official buildings.

They didn't have a chance to give their names at the front desk; an unsmiling Detective Rivera was waiting and he immediately took them upstairs to a private room—one without a mirror this time.

He shut the door and drew a deep breath. "Ms. McGraw, I'm not breaking any laws, but I'd appreciate your keeping this meeting confidential."

Layne blinked. "Of course."

Rivera pulled an envelope from inside his coat and fingered it for a minute. "I don't enjoy political pressure," he said surprisingly. "But I can honestly say that I believed your uncle was guilty when my superiors insisted on disbanding my team. The only question mark was the missing money. It was never clear to me that William Hudson had sufficient computer skills to make money vanish that way, while other employees at the firm undoubtedly did. Several worked in the computer industry prior to being employed at Hudson & Davidson."

Layne sat down in one of the chairs. "But that wasn't enough for you to keep looking."

"The evidence against Mr. Hudson was compelling and the D.A.'s office was satisfied. They felt it was a waste of public funds to continue. After all, the man who everyone believed responsible for the thefts was…"

"Dead," she finished flatly.

"His suicide did appear to be an admission of guilt. But what you said about the printer and the suicide note got me thinking." Rivera opened the envelope he held and took out a picture. "Please take a look. This is a shot taken the night William Hudson died."

Layne braced herself, but it was simply a photo of Uncle Will's bookshelf with the printer in the middle. A sheet of paper with a few lines of print was visible in the tray, oriented as if it had just been deposited by the mechanism.

She handed the photograph to Matt.

"You told Layne that her uncle could have put the note on the printer to be seen easily," he said, examining it closely. "But the print on the note is upside down to someone walking up to the printer."

"Exactly. And then I recalled thinking there was something unusual about the paper, so I checked the file. The report indicates it was probably sixteen pound—"

"That's why you asked me what kind of paper Uncle Will used," Layne interrupted, looking at the detective with renewed respect.

"Yes. And since Hudson & Davidson uses the same paper as Mr. Hudson did in his home office, where was that note printed? Sixteen-pound bond isn't common."

"Does this mean you're going to start investigating again?" Matt asked. There were lines of strain around his mouth, and his gray eyes were so dark, they seemed black.

The detective sighed. "Not officially. I spoke to the D.A.'s office and they still don't feel it's sufficient to warrant a new investigation."

"That's outrageous," Matt exploded, slapping the photo down on the table. "If William Hudson didn't kill himself, he was murdered."

"Take it easy. They simply need more to back it up. I'm hoping Ms. McGraw may be able to find something else to show her uncle was innocent. Even if it's circumstantial, I'm willing to push the D.A. again."

"You mean you want her to do *your* job."

Layne put her hand on Matt's arm, hoping to calm him down. "Detective Rivera, I'll keep searching and may already have something to alibi Uncle Will, but having more information would make it easier. Mr. Hollister has explained the outlines of the case, but if you could tell me the dates and times the illegal transfers occurred, I'll have a better chance of getting the necessary proof."

"I figured as much." The detective held out the envelope in his hand. "I believe what you need is in here."

Layne took it, hardly daring to breathe for fear he'd change his mind. "Thank you."

"Don't thank me. A copy of the autopsy report is also in there—they aren't pleasant to read, especially for the family. Your best bet are the dates the transfers occurred. If you can demonstrate your uncle was somewhere else, the D.A.'s office will *have* to reopen the case."

"That's what I'm hoping." She put the envelope in her canvas purse and zipped it shut. "I won't tell anyone where this came from, Detective Rivera."

"Thank you. As I said, I'm not breaking any laws, but nobody above me wants this case dragged out again."

THEY SHOOK HANDS with the detective and hurried back to the Mustang. As soon as the doors were shut, Layne grabbed the envelope from her purse, ripped it open and began reading. Matt resigned himself to a wait and watched her shifting emotions, his own gut churning.

Damn.

A single tear slid down her cheek.

He concentrated on his breathing, wanting to rip the papers from her hands. A second tear followed. Then another until there were too many to count.

"Layne..." Matt said helplessly.

She wiped her cheeks, but the tears kept falling and Matt finally leaned across the hand brake to pull her into his arms as she wept.

A shudder came from deep within him. Layne had been closer to her uncle than Matt had ever been to anyone, even his mother. Her grief was wrenching to see.

Matt eased the sheaf of papers from Layne's fingers and glanced outside the Mustang. Fortunately they were parked in a less traveled part of the lot and didn't have any curious onlookers to deal with.

He closed his eyes momentarily. Peter was asking questions, trying to find out where the investigation was going, and Matt had found himself avoiding the inquiries, or making ambiguous responses that didn't reveal anything useful. And he still needed to ask Layne about the proposed sale of Hudson & Davidson to be sure it wasn't being mishandled.

After a long time Layne's tears slowed and she tipped her head back. Matt handed her a tissue. "I think that's been coming for a while."

Layne nodded and let out a shuddering sigh. "It's almost like going through it again."

Her arm was looped around his neck for support and he looked down at her face. Unlike some women when they cried, Layne wasn't red-eyed and puffy; she looked like a lovely, sad little pixie. It stirred an annoyingly impractical chivalry in him—he was quite certain Layne wasn't the type of woman who waited around to be rescued, and he was hardly the man she'd count on for it, regardless.

Still…he dipped his head to kiss her, unsure if he was being insensitive or not. It took a moment for Layne to respond, but her arm finally tightened on his neck, drawing him closer.

"That's nice," Matt whispered before deepening the kiss, an ache growing around his heart. He shifted, trying to get better access to the small swell of her breasts, and his elbow sharply rapped the dashboard.

Crap.

Matt lifted his head and gazed into Layne's face.

"We're in a Mustang," he muttered.

"A classic Mustang," she corrected with forced brightness. "I'll bet you wanted to make out in a nifty car like this when you were sixteen."

"It's nifty all right, but a sixteen-year-old boy is mostly obsessed about making out, not where it happens. And broad daylight, a block from the police station, isn't the place I would have picked back then, no matter what."

"Oh. Yeah."

They untangled themselves and were finally standing on the asphalt, flushed and breathless. Matt's groin throbbed, but it was just as well they'd been in her small Mustang—it would have been easy to forget himself in the moment.

Layne leaned inside to collect the papers Detective Rivera had given her. "Here." She handed him the keys. "Why don't you drive?"

"Not if you're going to start reading that thing again," Matt said bluntly.

"I'll read it again another time. I just…" She shrugged.

Matt took the keys. It was flattering that Layne trusted him with her car, and as long as she wasn't going pull out the autopsy report again, he would enjoy taking the wheel. After all, he'd driven a wide variety of vehicles, but never a 1966 Mustang.

WHEN THEY WERE on the road, Layne drew a calming breath. It had been an emotional moment and having Matt put the brakes on was understandable. And it was just as well he hadn't wanted to continue; she'd been upset and people made bad decisions at times like that.

She looked up. "Uh…go left here."

The town of Carrollton lay northeast of the university district and she preferred taking the back roads. She directed Matt through several turns, retracing the route they'd taken earlier that morning. The Seattle area was beautiful and there were little hidden wild areas that could take you by surprise. Yet as they made another turn, she saw Matt frowning.

"Is something wrong?"

"I don't want to make you nervous, but the same car has been behind us for ten minutes and we've taken several different roads. Is this a common route to the University of Washington?"

"Not that I know of—it's just my favorite way." Layne twisted to look out the back window and saw a dark gray, nondescript SUV behind them. The sight of the driver gave her a shiver. She thought it was a man, but despite the warm summer day, he was wearing a heavy overcoat, a hat pulled down close to his eyes and sunglasses. "Uh…go right at the next—"

Even as she spoke, the SUV suddenly swung into the opposite lane, roared up and turned sharply against them. She gasped and the impact threw her against the door as they veered toward the ravine at the side of the road. The sound of screeching tires filled her ears and she instinctively pressed her foot to the floor as if hitting the brake.

Matt turned the steering wheel into the skid and she couldn't breathe as he worked to bring the Mustang under control. It seemed like forever but could only have been a few seconds before they were motionless at the side of the road.

He looked at her.

"Thank you for not screaming."

Layne swallowed. "Thank you for keeping us out of the ravine." She unbuckled her seat belt and tried to get her pulse under control.

"I raced cars for a while. It helped."

Right. She remembered he had a history with extreme sports, including race-car driving.

"Are you okay?"

"Fine, just a little shaken up," Layne deliberately

didn't touch her right collarbone; he'd want to check it and she couldn't handle a platonic inspection of her body at the moment. "How about you?"

"I've gotten worse falling out of bed."

"With or without company?" She tried to sound flip to cover the way she was shaking from head to toe.

"I wouldn't have been getting out of bed if I had company."

Layne glanced around. She'd never see this stretch of road in the same way again—she'd loved it, driven it hundreds of times in her little turquoise car, and now…she sighed. It was hard to comprehend that someone had attempted to kill them, or at least had tried to cause a serious accident. And they might have succeeded if it hadn't been for Matt's expertise.

"I don't suppose anyone is *really* pissed at you…a former girlfriend, maybe?" she asked hopefully.

"Not that I know of. I think you may have rattled somebody with your investigation."

Yup.

That's what she thought, too.

Layne pressed a hand to her abdomen. The sun was shining, the air scented with growing things and someone had just tried to kill them.

"I'd better call the police. Or sheriff's office, rather, since I think we're outside any town limits." Layne pulled her phone from her purse, dialing 911 and talking to the dispatcher as calmly as she could manage.

They promised to send an officer within the hour. When she was done she glanced at Matt. "Not that they can do much. The license plate was covered, though it happened so fast, I couldn't have gotten the number anyway."

"We'll have to let Detective Rivera know what happened."

He got out and walked around to open her door. The gentlemanly act almost made her smile until she saw the crumpled rear fender.

"Dammit."

"Hey, it can be fixed."

"That's not the point. Uncle Will and Aunt Dee gave me this car. How *dare* anyone damage it or try to intimidate me out of investigating? *No way* they're getting away with murder and theft. I'm finding who-ever's responsible and putting them in jail where they belong. And I hope they rot there *forever.*"

She kicked a spray of gravel toward the ravine and glared in the direction the SUV had disappeared.

MATT MARVELED AS Layne stalked up and down the side of the road, cursing a blue streak. Most of the women he knew would be a basket case after an at-tack like this one, but not Layne McGraw. She might be pint-sized, but inside, she was a six-foot Amazon with a steel backbone.

The possibilities with a woman like that were… exhilarating.

Annoyed with himself, Matt pushed the thought away. He had much more serious concerns than hot sex with an unsuitable partner—somebody had just tried to kill them. Layne's classic Mustang, with its turquoise color, was highly distinctive, and they were on her favorite back route to her home from Carrollton. It had made her an easy target.

Too easy.

A chill of anger and fear went through him. An SUV had followed them until reaching a deserted stretch of road next to a deep creek gorge, then the driver had tried to force them into it.

Keeping an eye on her, he pulled out his cell phone.

"What?" Connor answered on the first ring.

"Meet me at Layne McGraw's house. Someone just tried to run us off the road in her Mustang."

"Injuries?"

"Mostly to her temper—if the guy was here she'd take him apart with her bare hands. The Mustang was a gift from the Hudsons and she's taking the damage personally."

"Attempted vehicular homicide *is* personal."

A shriek of fury came from Layne as she stopped and surveyed the crumpled fender again, followed by another string of curses and threats. In any other circumstance, Matt would have grinned. She had a remarkable command of the English language.

"I heard that," Connor said casually. "She's in a fine mood."

"Yeah. Sparks are flying. We're waiting for the

sheriff to arrive and take a report. Then we'll head for her house. I want a team on both Layne and her aunt around the clock."

"Fine, but I'll send Riley to meet you instead of coming myself."

Grim amusement filled Matt. "That's right, I forgot you've been courting Mrs. Hudson. You wouldn't want Layne to put two and two together and realize her aunt's new Irish friend is actually my security chief."

"I'm *not* courting Dorothy Hudson," Connor growled. "She just lost her husband in December, for God's sake."

"Then why *are* you seeing her? You gave me the final background check on Layne and Mrs. Hudson ages ago."

"None of your damned business. Is the Mustang drivable?"

"Yeah, but I want an expert to do the restoration for Layne. In the meantime she'll need something safe to drive."

"I'll take care of it. Ms. McGraw likes dogs, so I'll tell Riley to bring his German shepherd to stay inside with her. We'll talk later."

Matt barely blinked as the call disconnected abruptly—when Connor was done talking, he was done. He pulled up another number he'd programmed into the phone and dialed the Carrollton Police Station, asking for Detective Rivera, saying it was urgent. When the detective came on, Matt quickly explained what had happened.

"You're sure it wasn't an accident?"

"Positive. They followed us for a long distance, through numerous turns, and Layne says the license plate was covered."

"Could be gang related. We've had cases where a vehicle was singled out for no apparent reason."

"You don't seriously believe that's the explanation?" Matt asked drily. "It's no secret that Layne is looking into what happened with her uncle. She's called a number of the employees who worked with Mr. Hudson, and some of them already knew she'd been asking questions. I think someone is worried about what she may uncover."

"It's possible. Are you requesting police protection?"

Matt restrained a laugh. He liked the detective and thought Layne felt the same, but her overall opinion of the Carrollton Police Department wasn't high. Anyway, there might be jurisdictional issues since she didn't live or work in Carrollton.

"I have my own security staff, Detective Rivera. My people will be looking after Ms. McGraw. I just thought you should know what happened."

"Thanks. Ask the officer taking the incident report to send me a copy."

A few minutes later a vehicle came down the road, lights flashing. Matt watched Layne lift her chin as it pulled in behind the Mustang.

She was really something.

Her parents must be blind if they were disappointed in the woman she'd become.

CHAPTER FOURTEEN

LAYNE'S COLLARBONE ACHED as she watched the deputy sheriff measure the skid marks on the road and take pictures. Then he used a knife to scrape gray paint from the dented fender of the Mustang into an evidence bag.

The sound of metal on metal made Layne wince.

Both Matt and the deputy had tried to get her to wait in the patrol car, but she'd refused. When they were finally finished, Matt drove to her house and her mouth tightened as she saw a tow truck in front of it.

"You didn't," she said.

"No, I didn't. My security chief probably ordered it, thinking you'd want your car fixed as soon as possible."

"Yes, but I'll have to make an insurance claim and get estimates and all sorts of stuff. And in the meantime, I have to get to work and the supermarket and everywhere else."

"I'm sure that's taken care of, too."

Layne spotted a sporty-looking Volvo and her eyes narrowed. "I'm going to ignore the tow truck and that expensive status car in my driveway."

"Volvos are *really* safe."

"I know. That's why Uncle Will always got one for Aunt Dee to drive. But I'll rent whatever car is covered by the insurance company."

Matt released a heavy sigh. "Do you know how difficult you are?"

"I believe in taking care of myself."

"Call it whatever you want, but think about using the Volvo. It's not a big deal—we have a fleet of vehicles to use when needed. Besides, you said the Hudsons gave you the Mustang. Think how much it would upset your aunt to see the dented fender. This way you can just say you had car trouble."

"I have to tell Aunt Dee. She'll be more upset if she finds out on her own."

"It still would be better for her to hear about the damage than to see it and imagine what happened. So just use the damned Volvo," he said with obvious frustration.

It was true about Aunt Dee, but that still didn't mean she could accept. From what Layne knew about his former lifestyle, she suspected Matt had been surrounded by people so rich they didn't think about who was paying for what. She also guessed there had been a good number along for the free ride. Matt might be used to that, she wasn't.

Anyway, accepting that kind of favor from Matt was a slippery slope. Layne wasn't sure what was at the bottom of that slope, but she believed in being self-reliant.

She got out of the Mustang, ready to continue

the argument, when a tall man stepped from a blue Dodge Dakota parked on the street. He was darkly attractive and nodded to her as he approached.

"Hello, Miss McGraw, I'm Riley Flannigan, part of the Eisley security team. The chief asked me to come over. He mentioned you were upset about your Mustang getting hit."

"Yeah, I lost my temper and used language that should make me blush."

Riley Flannigan gave her a lazy grin. "That's all right, I'm a man who appreciates feisty women, but I'm sorry about your car."

"Not as sorry as the person responsible will be when they're caught, I assure you."

"Like I said, feisty."

She laughed and his grin widened.

MATT WAS UNACCOUNTABLY annoyed at Riley's not-so-subtle efforts to be charming, and even more irritated when he saw the subtle shift in the security operative's stance at the sight of Layne's brightest smile. It was the one that took over her entire face and Matt had only seen it a couple of times himself.

"Layne, Mr. Flannigan is going to be on the team watching your house," he interjected. "There's another team assigned to your aunt. They'll make sure she doesn't see them until you've had a chance to let her know they're there."

"It's okay to have them watching Aunt Dee's house, but I don't need anyone watching me."

"Let's talk about it," urged Riley. "We're on staff, so it isn't as if Matt will be paying extra to have us here. Besides, how else can I get to know you?"

Matt snorted and Layne hit him with her elbow, probably the way she'd try to put her big brother in his place.

Hell.

She couldn't possibly like Riley, could she?

"Mr. Flannigan won't be coming inside, he'll be located in a van on the street," Matt said, but no one paid any attention.

Just then a large German shepherd jumped through the window of Riley's truck and padded over to where they were standing. Toto ignored Matt's outstretched hand and planted his butt at Layne's feet, looking at her expectantly.

"What a beauty," she exclaimed, kneeling to rub his ears and run her fingers through the thick fur around his neck. "Is he yours, Riley?"

"Yeah, but sometimes I think Toto owns me. Especially when I haul his fifty-pound sacks of food into the house."

"Toto?" Layne tipped her head back and smiled again, full force, and Riley crouched next to her, ostensibly to pat Toto's flanks.

"Yup. As a scruffy puppy he looked like Toto in *The Wizard of Oz,* so I went with it. Who'd have guessed he'd turn into this?"

"You mean other than him being part German shepherd and part horse?"

A chuckle came from the security expert and Matt gritted his teeth. He wasn't paying Riley to flirt, and why hadn't he been this pleasant to Tamlyn when she'd come to visit in the spring? Riley had gone all rock-jawed and secret-service-style impassive with Tamlyn.

"By the way, would you consider keeping Toto inside with you?" Riley asked Layne. "He wouldn't be any trouble and I always keep a sack of food in the truck for him, so his meals are covered."

Layne lifted an eyebrow. "I haven't said yes to you guarding the house."

"Yeah, but Matt will insist we spend the night out here whether you agree or not."

Layne gave Matt a cool look while he glared at Riley. Since when was he the fall guy? Of course, Riley was just trying to jolly her into accepting the inevitable, but *still*.

"How about it?" Riley wheedled. "It would be a huge favor if you keep Toto—the security van is too small for a dog his size to be comfortable."

Toto put a paw on her knee and let out an eager yip.

Layne's smile brightened to megawatt candescence. "How can I resist an appeal like that?"

The warm approval in Riley's eyes made Matt's jaw clench. Layne had never treated *him* with the same sweet, flirty manner. Of course, it was best that she didn't see him in a romantic way, but it was annoying nevertheless.

"Come on." Matt helped Layne to her feet. "Let's

talk inside while Mr. Flannigan gets Toto's food and leaves it on the porch, before getting settled in the van with the rest of the team."

"I'll see you later," Riley assured Layne as she walked up the steps to her porch.

"Great." She unlocked her front door and Toto slid into the house ahead of her. "Riley seems nice," she commented to Matt.

"Only when he wants to be. Look, I've been intending to ask you about the sale of Hudson & Davidson. I got the impression there's more to it than what you said."

Layne sank onto the couch and tossed the envelope from Detective Rivera onto the coffee table. "Mr. Davidson claims that Aunt Dee's share of the sale is zero, though he's willing to give her twenty-five thousand as a token gesture. He sent her a letter citing things like the calculated damage to his good name and what he'd put out to replace the embezzled money, plus interest. He states that because of Uncle Will, the company's worth dropped to a fraction of its former valuation following the scandal, and since he's personally responsible for any restored value, the increase isn't 'accruable' to her. He wants her to sign a separate agreement to that effect."

"Your aunt needs to consult a lawyer."

"Except his note tells her she needs to agree to his terms if she doesn't want the whole thing getting stirred up again. He claims it will cost her thousands in legal fees and that she'll just sully Uncle Will's reputation more. Not to mention crashing the value of the company a second time so she *still* won't get anything."

Matt's gut churned. Depending on how the letter was worded, his stepfather could be arrested for blackmail—emotional blackmail for monetary gain was still blackmail. But even if it was legal, his actions weren't right.

Damn it all. *This* was the man who Matt had chosen as financial director of the Eisley Foundation... and the man who was married to his mother.

"Aunt Dee says Mr. Davidson is getting impatient now that he has an offer on the company," Layne added. "If I prove Uncle Will is innocent she'll feel free to fight him, but with everything dragging on, it's getting hard to put him off."

"Does your aunt have a copy of the sales agreement and the other document he wants her to sign?"

"I'll have to ask. Probably."

"Good. I want to go over them if she'll let me."

"Why not ask your stepfather for copies?"

"I don't want Peter to know I'm looking at it," Matt told her. He wanted to know *exactly* what his stepfather was up to without any attempt to clean it up or put a positive spin on the situation.

"Okay. I'll ask Aunt Dee." Layne's eyes were closed.

"I'll get out of here and let you rest. Call if there's anything you need."

"Besides a security van outside my house?"

"Uh, yeah, besides that."

Matt checked the porch and saw a bag of dog food next to the door. He put it on the coffee table and said goodbye, though he wasn't sure Layne was awake. She had to be exhausted after everything that had happened.

CONNOR DROVE TOWARD CARROLLTON, but before arriving in Dorothy Hudson's peaceful neighborhood, he called the team watching the house.

Gavin Weis picked up the call. "Yeah?"

"It's me. I'll be there in a few minutes. Are you parked up the block? This is strictly covert until notified."

"We're north, on the opposite side of the street, one house down. You can pull in directly behind us without being in line of sight for the Hudson household."

Connor turned onto Dot's street. "How have you covered the backyard?"

"The place backs onto a canyon, with a wooded slope down to a creek. It's unlikely anyone would approach from that direction, but we were able to install cameras while Mrs. Hudson was away. Someone will be watching from the van, and two others will watch the street, with a fourth to spell the rest. If she goes out, half the team will follow."

"You'll have to tag team in two vehicles for now. Mrs. Hudson's niece will decide the best time to inform her that she's under protection."

"Gotcha."

Connor stopped behind the surveillance van. "I'm coming in. Don't shoot," he announced and turned off the phone.

"Hey," Gavin said as Connor opened the door and stepped in. Shandra Mason waved vaguely. She was wearing a pair of earphones, her gaze fixed on a monitor, split into four images. Ed Nelson lay on a bunk over the driver and passenger seat, reading.

A pot of coffee sat by the compact sink and Connor poured himself a cup. "I want a video conference with the other team," he ordered. A moment later an interior picture of the van assigned to Layne McGraw's house appeared.

Riley was nearest the video camera, his feet up and a cowboy hat tipped over his eyes.

"Wake up, Flannigan," Connor ordered.

"I'm awake," Riley replied without moving a muscle. "What's the chance of something happening? You didn't give me much except that someone tried to run Matthew and his passenger into a ravine. I presume they were after the lovely Ms. McGraw, rather than Matt."

"As far as we know, that's the situation." Connor paused, debating how much to say. "Both the aunt and her niece are potentially at risk. It could be a murder someone hopes to keep covered up."

Riley lifted his hat and looked directly into the camera, a wintry expression in his eyes. "They'd better hope I'm not around if they try something."

Connor smiled a brief, humorless smile. "Same here. Now brief me on the setup there."

LAYNE WOKE A few hours later, stiff and sore. It was mostly from her awkward position on the couch, but getting slammed around in the Mustang hadn't helped any.

At least her aunt wasn't expecting an update on the trip to the police station and wouldn't have to be told about the Mustang right away. Layne hadn't wanted to raise her hopes again, so she'd kept it quiet that they were meeting Detective Rivera. She *would* tell Dee everything, and would also have to ask about the paperwork on the sale of Hudson & Davidson, but it could wait for another day.

An unexpected yip from Toto made Layne jump; she'd forgotten about the German shepherd. "Poor boy, you're probably thirsty."

Groaning at her uncooperative body, Layne got up and filled a large bowl with water. Toto lapped a small amount and then she let him outside. He hurriedly did his business in the front yard and returned, settling quietly on the floor by the couch, ears high and alert.

In all honesty, Layne felt relieved that Matt's security people were watching the house. She wanted to believe that there was nothing suspicious about the cable repairman and that no one had tried to get inside, yet there was a part of her that kept wondering.

She looked down at Toto. There were tons of things

to do, but she hadn't slept well lately. Surely it would be all right if she crawled into bed for another nap.

"Toto, will you wake me up if you need to go outside again?"

He let out a small yip.

"That sounds like yes to me." Layne climbed the stairs and dropped onto her bed with an exhausted sigh.

MATT WAS WORKING at his office in the late afternoon when a reminder popped onto his computer about having lunch the next day with his mother and stepfather.

He frowned.

With everything going on he didn't have time to play "let's pretend we're a normal family," and he especially didn't want to do it with Peter. Quickly he sent an email to his stepfather's address—his mother didn't use computers—apologizing that he couldn't make it. But not five minutes after he'd sent the message, his private line rang and the caller ID showed it was Peter.

Matt lifted the receiver. "Yes, Pete?"

"Son, I just got your message. Are you sure you can't come tomorrow? I hope it isn't because of that business with William's niece."

Matt thought about Layne's face when she'd looked at her damaged Mustang, along with the concern he felt for her safety.

"Actually, it is. Layne and I were nearly run off the road this morning, and it wasn't an accident."

"That's terrible." Peter sounded appalled. "Are you all right?"

"*We're* fine, just some bruises," Matt said, his irritation growing. Peter didn't get it. Layne and her investigation weren't the problem and he couldn't pretend her away. She was just doing what the police and D.A. and the rest of them should have done back in December when everything had blown up in their faces.

Yet in a way, Matt knew he was mostly angry with himself. He'd been so focused on getting out of Hudson & Davidson and taking over the Eisley Foundation, there was no way to be sure he hadn't missed something he should have seen.

"Er, yes…naturally I'm glad Ms. McGraw is all right, as well," Peter assured him hastily.

"I expect to spend the day with her working on the case," Matt said. "Besides, I'd be lousy company for Mother with so much on my mind."

"She wouldn't care, but I'll explain."

"Thanks. I'll probably see you on Wednesday or Thursday, unless you won't be in this week at all?"

"No, I'll be there."

Matt got off quickly, scowling. He'd liked his stepfather a whole lot better before meeting Layne.

Two hours later Matt was in the penthouse, working through a new stack of reports, when the intercom from his private parking garage buzzed.

"It's me again," Peter said through the speaker. "Do you have a minute?"

Matt gritted his teeth. His stepfather was the last person he wanted to see, but it wouldn't be tactful to send him away. "Sure, I was in the middle of paperwork and could use a breather." He got up to ring Peter in.

A few minutes later his stepfather was sitting on the couch, looking distinctly uncomfortable. Curiously, he handed over a bag from a store called the Carrollton Reader.

"I can't give Layne an employee roster—it wouldn't be legal. But I thought she might like to have the Hudson & Davidson Employee Cookbook. It's being sold in local bookstores to raise money for the employees' charity drive."

Matt almost laughed. It was so simple. Nobody had to release an employee roster; the employees had done it themselves. He remembered getting emails, asking for contributions to the cookbook. Their goal had been one hundred percent staff participation. He'd gone to his grandmother for a recipe to submit.

"Thanks."

"While I don't enjoy having the mess being aired again, the things Layne said…" Peter shrugged. "I suppose she made me somewhat ashamed of myself. The outcome wouldn't have changed, but perhaps I should have supported William more than I did."

Glad to hear you're keeping an open mind, Matt

thought wryly as he glanced through the cookbook. "I'll get this to her."

He'd also get a second copy for Connor to pull out names and do background checks, but Peter didn't need to know that.

"Good, good." Peter cleared his throat and got up. "I hope we'll see you soon at the house, son."

"I'll try." Matt walked his stepfather to the elevator and said good-night, then returned to the report he'd been studying. But it was difficult to concentrate and he finally dropped the folder and stared out the window.

His stepfather probably hadn't done more than rush to judgment about his friend, but what if there was more to the story? The things Layne had told him about Peter's note to Dorothy were disturbing. Hopefully she'd misunderstood, because if his mother hadn't been able to deal with the media storm following her divorce, it would be even worse having a husband on trial for blackmailing his friend's widow.

DOROTHY PACED THE floor of her studio, wishing she could focus on her art instead of the nagging voice inside her head. Layne hadn't called all day. It was highly unusual and made Dorothy feel even guiltier *because* it was unusual. Ever since Will's death, Layne had been even more attentive.

It had to stop.

Has she complained?

The memory of Patrick's casual question was annoying. He was concerned about his sister back in Ireland, which was understandable, but Alleyne's situation wasn't the same. Alleyne had been a young bride when she was widowed, she hadn't spent twenty-nine years letting her husband shoulder all the responsibilities.

Patrick might see her a certain way because of his sister, but it was making Dorothy think. Will, the eternal optimist, would have told her to stop fussing about things she couldn't change. And maybe she should. Will was gone. She could find a thousand reasons to feel guilty, perhaps mostly because she was alive and he wasn't, but it was too late to fix anything.

And what Patrick had said about Will being a second father to Lani also deserved thought. Layne *was* behaving like a grieving daughter. Pushing her away wouldn't be right, either. She'd come to the house almost as often when Will was alive, and had helped out, especially when either of them was ill.

Sighing, Dorothy took out her phone and called her niece. "Hello?" Layne answered after three rings, sounding groggy.

"Oh, dear, were you asleep?"

"Not really. I should have called earlier."

"No, of course not, but is everything all right?"

"Oh. Uh, well, Matt and I went to the Carrollton police station this morning to meet with that detective. I got more information on the case, only on the way back there was an incident on the road. Someone hit us. It was, um, probably deliberate. But that means

I'm making progress," Layne said hastily. "Someone is getting nervous."

Dorothy grabbed the back of a chair, clutching it so hard her knuckles turned white. "Nervous? You mean *dangerous*."

"Hey, I'm okay. Just a sore shoulder. Matt was driving and he's an expert because he used to race cars. I don't think we were in any real danger. The thing is, we were in the Mustang and one of the fenders is pretty crunched." The anguish in her niece's voice made Dorothy sigh.

"It's just a car, Lani. I'm sorry because you love it, but I'm far more concerned about your life."

"I'm being careful. And besides, Matt has his security people watching my house now. Your place, too, so if you see a big recreational vehicle outside, it's them."

"Mine?"

"Just as a precaution," Layne said hastily. "He wouldn't back down about it, so there wasn't any point in arguing."

Dorothy peered out the window, but she didn't see anything that looked odd. "Why argue after getting hit by a car?"

"I don't know. Maybe because he was being so high-handed. I realize Matt feels responsible because he was working at Hudson & Davidson when everything happened with Uncle Will, but that doesn't mean I should accept expensive favors."

Obviously stiff-necked pride ran in the family,

Dorothy thought wryly. The hard part was knowing the difference between being hardheaded and being independent. She would have to give it serious consideration.

"Well, accept all the protection he offers. I couldn't bear it if anything happened to you. And that isn't just because I asked you to start this, Lani."

"I know, and nothing is going to happen. By the way, do you have the documents that Peter Davidson wants you to sign?" Layne asked. "If you don't mind, Matt would like to see them. And I'm also wondering about what's in the partnership agreement. Looking at everything together would be helpful."

"Peter sent the documents a couple of weeks ago, and Will always kept the partnership papers in our safe deposit box. I don't mind Matt seeing any of it, but what good will it do?"

"Maybe none, but he didn't like hearing about that letter from Peter. You should take the originals of everything to your safe deposit box, including the letters Mr. Davidson has sent. I can go with you to the bank and use a hand-scanner to get copies of what's there."

Dorothy blinked. "A hand-scanner? Isn't that James Bond-ish?"

"Yup." Layne laughed. "Now available at your average office supply store—I use one when I'm researching material from books in the public domain at the library. How about going to your bank on Monday morning? I can take the day off."

"All right."

"Great. I'll come over and make copies of everything at the house, and then we'll go together."

"Fine."

They chatted another few minutes before saying good-night. When they got off, Dorothy peered out the window again. She didn't doubt the presence she kept sensing in the house was William's spirit, but that didn't mean someone hadn't gotten nervous about Layne's investigation and wouldn't try to get in now.

CHAPTER FIFTEEN

THE NEXT DAY Layne compared the date on the phone message from Uncle Rob with the dates of the embezzlement. She was briefly excited when they matched, but she was a long way from proving anything. Since Rob couldn't be certain of exactly when his brother-in-law had visited him, she still needed something else to corroborate an alibi.

She continued entering dates of the thefts into the calendar grid, looking for a pattern. The autopsy report remained in the envelope; she hadn't been able to bring herself to read it again. All those words, horrid medical terms and graphic descriptions, as if Uncle Will hadn't been a real person. The medical examiner was just doing his or her job, but that didn't make it any more pleasant. Anyhow, there hadn't been anything she'd seen that raised any flags.

Layne swallowed the last of her iced coffee. The weather had turned beastly hot again and caffeine was a bad idea, but she was drinking it anyhow.

Toto lay on the hardwood floor in front of the oscillating fan. He became alert at every sound, tilting his head at a particular angle as he decided whether or not he needed to investigate. Obviously he was more than Riley Flannigan's pet; he was a trained guard dog. Still, she found it hard to be annoyed with Riley for charming her into keeping Toto in the house—Toto was excellent company and a perfect gentleman.

"Hey, boy," she said, stretching out a leg to stroke his back with her toe. He gave her a pleased canine smile, his tail swaying back and forth.

After Uncle Will's death she'd gotten into the habit of taking Aunt Dee to church every week, but she'd begged off the night before, hating to have Dee see the damage to the Mustang. Not that she couldn't have used the Volvo—Matt had left the keys on the coffee table, completely ignoring her objections.

Layne frowned.

Matt honestly didn't seem to understand that some people cared about dignity and self-reliance. Besides, while it might be nice to let him take care of everything, he wouldn't be there the next time something went wrong. Hell, Layne was astonished he'd stayed with the investigation as long as he had. Matt Hollister was infamous for having a short attention span about everything—sports, places...women.

Especially women.

They'd spoken earlier. His stepfather had said that releasing a list of employees was a legal issue, but had found a way around it...by providing an employee cookbook. Matt had offered to bring it over, but she'd claimed to have more than enough to keep her busy. The truth was, she needed some space. After a series of phone calls to Hudson & Davidson employees, she was burned out for the day. Lord, they disliked talking about the thefts.

Layne touched her bruised collarbone.

And maybe she'd alarmed someone enough they wanted to kill her. She was scared, but also elated because it was a sign that she was on the right track.

LAYNE PULLED INTO the Eisley Foundation visitor parking lot on Monday morning and waved at Riley, who was trailing her in his truck. Apparently "watching" the house included keeping an eye on her, as well. Though she didn't like admitting it, his presence was reassuring.

"Don't you ever sleep?" she asked, walking over to the truck.

"I can sleep anywhere."

Hmm. Layne wasn't sure what to make of Riley. He was attentive, charming, seemed to like her...and was on Matt Hollister's payroll.

She reached in to pat Toto. Rather than leaving him alone in the house for the day, she'd knocked on the door of the van early that morning—much to the displeasure of the team inside—and left him with Riley.

"Well, see you both later."

He smiled. "Count on it."

Inside the lobby, Layne stopped at the reception area. "Hello, I'd like to see Matthew Hollister."

"Do you have an appointment?"

"No, but I'm acquainted with Mr. Hollister."

"Really?" It was a different receptionist from

Layne's other two visits to the building and her expression was skeptical. She probably saw Layne as someone well out of Matt's league and unlikely to know him. It was true…which made it doubly annoying.

"Just let Matt know that Layne McGraw is here," she said tartly.

"Mr. Hollister's assistant has left for lunch and I have no intention of disturbing him."

"That's ridiculous."

"I'm following our standard protocols. Mr. Hollister does not have time to see every starry-eyed young woman who wants to meet him."

"I've met him." Layne gritted her teeth. "And believe me, I'm not starry-eyed when it comes to Matt Hollister. But if you don't want to call, I'll do it myself."

The receptionist gave her a superior smile. "If you actually *had* his number, you'd know it rings on his assistant's desk. Now, I must ask you to leave."

"I'm talking about his private line."

Layne turned around and began digging through her purse for her cell phone. She should have called ahead, but instead she'd stopped at the *Babbitt* to print out what she'd scanned, then rushed into North Seattle, upset about the bombshell Aunt Dee had dropped at the bank. Dee was going to start calling real estate agents about selling the house, which meant her financial situation must be growing worse. So if Matt *could* find something in the sales agreement to show Peter was cheating Aunt Dee, it would be a huge help.

There.

Her purse was so big, the phone had a habit of hiding in the oddest places. Layne turned it on and waited for it to cycle.

The elevator opened and she was vaguely aware of someone stepping out. "Thank you for coming, Mr. O'Brian," the receptionist said. "This young woman refuses to leave."

Layne looked up and saw a large rottweiler bounding over with a happy bark. He gazed up, tongue lolling from the side of his mouth.

"Finnster, *back*," a man said sharply.

"Finnster" ignored the command, sinking down and rolling over on his back. Layne obliged by rubbing his tummy, but her mind was racing. It was the friendly dog she'd played with outside her aunt's house a few weeks before—encountering two clownish rottweilers would be unusual, but two with that same notch in the right ear?

She straightened and looked at the man who'd called to the rottweiler. He was medium height, with a solid, muscular build, and a hard, unsmiling face. She also recognized him; he was the security guard who had followed her to the parking lot the first day she'd come to see Matt, here at the Eisley Foundation.

"You were outside my aunt's house, weren't you?" she accused. "A few weeks ago. You and your dog. Matt sent you to spy on us."

"It was my idea, Ms. McGraw," the guard assured hastily. "Matthew didn't have anything to do with it. I was simply doing a security check and brought Finn with me."

Layne's eyes widened. The guard had a distinctive Irish brogue, and Aunt Dee had mentioned her new friend was from Ireland. It was too big of a coincidence to ignore.

"*Oh my God,* you're the guy making up to Aunt Dee at the art gallery," she said, appalled. "Do you know what she's been through? How could you *do* that to her?"

"Let me explain. My name is Connor O'Brian—"

"Don't bother." Layne didn't want explanations, she wanted to get as far from Matt and his security people as she could possibly get.

She slapped the door opened and marched to the parking lot.

"Are you okay?" called Riley from his truck.

She ignored him and got into the Volvo, hating that she'd talked herself into using it that morning. The only reason she had was its air-conditioning—temperatures had been predicted to climb to a hundred.

The noontime traffic was heavy and it took longer than usual before she got back to her house. Every now and then she caught sight of Riley's truck in her rearview mirror, but it was no longer reassuring. A bright red sports car zipped ahead of her at one point and she scowled, only to decide it was wildly improbable that Matt would chase her anywhere.

She was wrong.

He was waiting at the house, along with Connor

Ratfink O'Brian. Layne parked and threw the Volvo keys at them. She marched up her walkway, but when they followed her onto the porch, she wheeled around.

"Leave, both of you, and take all of…of *that* with you." She made a gesture that took in the Volvo, the security van and the rottweiler, who was looking at her with distress in his eyes. Honestly, how could these security experts have such nice dogs? She hadn't made up her mind about Riley and Toto, but Finnster was obviously an innocent dupe.

Matt crossed his arms over his chest. "Layne, be reasonable. I asked Connor to do a security check the night of the gala. That was before I got to know you."

"And I didn't intend to hurt Dot," the other man added, lines sharply drawn on his features. "Going to the gallery was my idea alone. Your aunt intrigued me and I wanted to meet her."

"Like I'd believe either one of you. *Go away*," she said and slammed the door in their faces.

How could she have let Matt get to her? For Aunt Dee there hadn't been a reason to suspect Patrick of being anything other than he appeared, yet even her aunt had been mildly suspicious of him at first.

Aunt Dee.

Electrified, Layne grabbed the handset sitting on the couch and called her aunt. She needed to know about Connor or Patrick or whatever his real name might be.

CONNOR PROMPTLY COMMANDEERED Riley's truck and drove to Dot's home. He strode up the walkway and rang the bell. The door swung open and Dorothy's eyes darkened with fury.

"You."

Obviously, Layne had wasted no time alerting her to the deception played on them both.

"Dot, let me—"

The door slammed in his face...eerily reminiscent of how her niece had ended the conversation not a half hour earlier. The temper in her eyes had mirrored Layne's ire as well. Plainly, Dorothy wasn't going to be as understanding as he would have wished.

Connor rang the bell again and called through the closed door, "Dot, I didn't do it to hurt you. You're a beautiful woman and I wanted to get to know you. It's as simple as that."

That, and being reminded of the sister he'd been too busy to comfort when she needed it most. It was a sad thing to meet a woman you desired, and know the timing was wrong for anything except friendship.

"Go to hell."

"I've already been there." He leaned on the doorjamb, instinctively turning his head to do a visual perimeter sweep of the property.

"Then go back and leave me alone, Patrick. Or whoever you really are."

"My full name is Connor Patrick Donovan O'Brian. Patrick is fine—it's what my family calls me. Let me in so we can talk."

Silence greeted him. Though aware that the security team on the street had to be listening, he rang a third time, followed by several raps on the door.

Still nothing.

"Damned stubborn women. Both of them," Connor muttered, walking toward the security van. He didn't intend to give up, but he'd give her time to cool down. Meanwhile, at least he didn't have to be concerned any longer that she'd spot him when he checked on the security team.

DOROTHY RETURNED TO her kitchen and slammed a lump of bread dough onto her kitchen counter, giving it a hard thump.

She didn't know what Patrick wanted out of the whole thing, just that he'd lied. William had never lied to her. She should have remembered that instead of worrying that he'd had an affair.

But Patrick or Connor or whatever he called himself had deliberately lied throughout their acquaintance.

She dusted flour over the dough and began kneading it, trying to lose herself in the familiar pattern. Making bread was therapeutic. She hadn't needed it the past few days, though. Learning that her vague fears about William were groundless had taken a huge weight from her shoulders. But now she didn't know what to feel. Layne had offered to come over and keep her company, but this was something she needed to work out on her own.

Forward, roll back, forward again. Another dusting of flour. The dough slowly gained the necessary consistency and Dorothy put it in a bowl to rise.

Unable to resist, she went to the front window and looked out. She didn't see Patrick, but a blue truck was in her driveway and she assumed it belonged to him.

Several unladylike words came to mind as she dropped the curtain. She rarely cursed, but it didn't mean she couldn't when the occasion demanded. The words even slipped out at times, though she *had* been raised by an old-fashioned father with strong views about how his daughters should talk and behave.

To think she'd believed Patrick and her father would have gotten along because they were cut from the same honorable cloth.

LAYNE WANTED TO stay angry with Matt, but as the afternoon wore on, she kept remembering the expression on his face, sort of worried and frustrated and regretful, all at the same time. It hadn't kept her from blowing up, but it was enough to make her wish now that she hadn't.

After all, he'd been in the Mustang with her when they were hit. If Peter Davidson *was* involved, then he'd nearly killed his own stepson.

The doorbell rang shortly after four. "Layne, it's me," called Matt.

A lingering flicker of annoyance went through her. "I told you to go away."

"Please let me in."

She gave a tug to the thin, sleeveless T-shirt she wore, trying to pull it over her belly button. It was miserably hot, so she wasn't wearing a bra, and her short shorts were barely more than bikini bottoms. And he probably wouldn't even notice.

With that sour thought, Layne sighed and opened the door. Matt held an enormous bunch of flowers and three bags.

"Aren't flowers a little trite, *Mr.* Hollister?"

"Flowers are never trite." He thrust them into her arms and stepped inside without waiting for an invitation.

Layne looked at the bouquet. The few guys who'd brought her flowers had gotten things like daisies, saying they suited her personality, while Matt was offering her lovely blue Dutch irises with baby's breath, peach tulips and white roses. It was the most beautiful thing she'd ever seen. And he probably brought the same bouquet to every woman.

"I told you to get lost."

"More or less, then you slammed the door in my face so hard I expected the glass to shatter the way it does in the movies."

"Oh." She hadn't thought about *that*.

Layne cast a quick glance at the leaded, beveled glass; surely she would have noticed any damage before now. Not seeing any, she went to the kitchen and took out vases for the flowers.

"Mr. Two-Faced O'Brian showed up at my aunt's

house and tried to talk to her," she said over her shoulder. "He's the security chief you've talked about, isn't he? The one with connections?"

"Yes. If you hadn't been so ticked earlier, we could have discussed it rationally." Matt stopped. "Uh, that is—"

"Don't try backtracking—you already said it." Layne turned and crossed her arms over her bare stomach. "I wasn't being irrational. I had every reason to be furious. Don't try denying that you and that duplicitous rat were way out of line. It's one thing to check someone out on the internet, another to spy on them."

Matt put the bags he carried on the counter. "Whatever. I brought a peace offering. Cherry Garcia ice cream and the makings for deli sandwiches."

"Isn't that what the flowers are for?"

"Anybody can bring flowers as an apology. Cherry Garcia, on the other hand, is good for any occasion." Matt put several pints in the freezer.

"Some people might say you have a fetish about that stuff."

"Only the ones who've never tasted it."

He set out sandwich ingredients on the counter—crusty bread and deli meats and cheeses and garnishes like pickled peppers. Layne hadn't eaten lunch, her appetite killed by the heat, yet her stomach rumbled at the rich scents. Trust Matt to show up with regular food, instead of a fussy gourmet meal. Not that he'd gone to the deli counter at the supermarket.

He'd probably purchased everything from a high-end delicatessen where it cost four times what any other place would charge.

Unable to resist, Layne sampled something from a container marked *cornichons*—which turned out to be teensy little pickles. She ate another. They were very good, and probably *very* expensive. Spending much time with Matt was hazardous if you didn't want to develop lavish tastes. It was also dangerous when you were a woman with the unfortunate habit of being taken for granted by her boyfriends.

Layne had always wondered what it would be like to be pursued and adored the way her sisters were—in other words, how would it feel to be the kind of woman who was given extravagantly feminine flowers instead of bouncy girl-next-door daisies. Not that daisies weren't pretty, but they said something about a man's impression.

Sighing, she put one vase of flowers on the kitchen table and another in the living room. She couldn't make herself into something she wasn't, but being around Matt was the ultimate downer because he'd been with the most beautiful women in the world and he had to be making comparisons.

Back in the kitchen Matt handed her one of the bags he'd brought. "That's the cookbook from Peter, plus the contact and background info my security people have found for the employees on the recipe contributor list."

A stack of paper was inside with the book and she scanned the first couple of pages.

"Hey, do you want to make your own sandwich or want me to make it?" Matt asked, popping a Greek olive in his mouth.

"I'll do it."

Refusing to eat would be silly, and Layne's mouth watered as she sat at the table and bit into her thickly piled sandwich.

Matt's was even thicker than hers, and he gazed at it with satisfaction. "This is a masterpiece. By the way, why did you come by my office today?"

"I got copies of the sales agreement and stuff."

He frowned. "All the documents we've gone through lately have been photocopies. You don't trust me with the originals?"

"It isn't that—any important originals are in a safe deposit box. Either mine or Aunt Dee's."

Matt carefully set his sandwich on his plate and wiped his hands with a napkin. "Any special reason?"

"Just being careful. Someone may have tried to break into the house, so I got a box to protect important documents and told her to take anything critical to hers."

"Damn it," he exploded. "Why didn't you tell me?"

"I thought I was being ridiculous at the time, though now it doesn't seem so far-fetched."

"You think? And what about your aunt? She could be at risk, as well. Did you consider that?"

"Of course I did," Layne said, exasperated. "She has a top-of-the-line security system and I make sure she uses it."

THE KNOT IN Matt's stomach tightened. The best security system could be circumvented. Layne had to know that, even if she didn't have one herself.

"Besides," she continued, "like I said, I thought I was being ridiculous. And now your security people are out there, so it's okay, even if they *are* being supervised by that two-faced Connor O'Brian."

Matt poured lemonade into glasses and handed one to Layne. Let's see, so far she'd called his security chief two-faced and a duplicitous rat...and God knew what else in private. But she was eating the food he'd brought and hadn't run his flowers down the garbage disposal. Obviously Layne was more concerned about her aunt's feelings than her own.

It was fascinating to see someone so passionate on behalf of a loved one. Not that his mother didn't care about him, but Katrina lived in an ivory tower and was barely aware of what was going on in his life. And he no longer knew what to think when it came to Peter.

As for Matt's father, he was a charming hedonist with only rare flickers of parental concern. Spence had eight children...no, *nine,* Matt corrected himself. One of Spence's girlfriends from two years ago had gotten pregnant; their son was fourteen months old now and lived with his mother in Australia. That made nine children with eight different women. How many people had so many ex-stepmothers they couldn't keep track of them all?

Hell, the more Matt learned about Layne's family, the more screwed-up his own looked. And that was taking her frustrations with the McGraws into account—they might drive her crazy, but it was only because they cared about her.

"What was that?" Matt said, realizing Layne had said something.

"I haven't had a chance to tell you—Uncle Rob finally called and he says that Uncle Will visited him several times in Aberdeen when my aunt was away."

Matt was confused. "*Finally* called?"

"Uh…I guess I didn't tell you about that, either." Layne explained about the phone message she'd found and where that had led her. "Except Uncle Rob can't verify specific dates," she concluded. "Only that it was always on a Thursday and Uncle Will always came as promised."

"Who took the phone message? Maybe between the two, it's good enough to be an alibi."

Layne looked discouraged. "There was no signature or even initials. The thing is, it's very unusual—informal, shorthand texting language, which probably isn't customary for a financial management company. So far nobody at Hudson & Davidson remembers an employee writing messages that way. It's an outside chance the author would remember taking the call, but at least they could say it was their handwriting and whether they thought the date was right."

"We'll just have to keep calling and asking questions. And now we have a better list of employees to work with."

If anything, Layne's face turned even more downcast. "It's awful talking to those people. They're nervous and defensive. I understand how they feel, but it's tough getting information when people are afraid they'll be accused of embezzling."

"I'll help with the calls. They might not be so concerned about speaking with me."

"Maybe, maybe not. I'm careful about what I say, but somebody is telling them I want to clear Uncle Will's name by any means possible."

Matt really hoped the "somebody" wasn't his stepfather.

"By the way," Layne said, "I don't have room for the Volvo in my garage, so you need to have it picked up."

"It's fine in the driveway. I told you, it's just one in a fleet of vehicles. We'll never miss it."

"No."

"What's the big deal?" Matt demanded, exasperated. "It's fully insured and free of charge."

She made a disgusted sound. "I work for a living and expect to pay my way. Just because you won't miss it *isn't* a good enough reason for me to accept the loan of an expensive car. You may have gotten used to giving money away at the Eisley Foundation, but people have dignity, you know. And pride. You can't just wave a checkbook and think it's the answer to everything."

Matt's frustration doubled. "I'm *not* waving a checkbook. How about this…I don't want to see one of my few friends get hurt and the Volvo is insurance. Surely *that* doesn't wound your dignity."

Layne blinked and Matt was a little startled himself.

He *did* have friends, though not that many. There was Terrence from childhood. Connor, though the Irishman would probably snort at the suggestion. And a couple of people from college. He didn't count anybody from his former party days—once they had realized he was serious about doing something real with his life, they'd dropped him cold.

Matt was also fond of his siblings—most of them, at least—though they'd never been close. He'd enjoyed Tamlyn's recent visit and had seen April and Oona not long before taking over the Eisley Foundation. Melanie had just graduated high school and was a sweet kid, unlike Pierre, who was a pain in the posterior. Hopefully he'd straighten out before some nanny had him shot. Aaron and Jake were nearest to him in age and they talked relatively often. Of course, usually Jake could only be reached by satellite phone since he spent most of his time in the Himalayas or somewhere equally remote.

In a way, Matt had more in common with Jake than with Aaron or the others. He knew the adrenaline rush of pushing yourself to extremes, and that was what Jake did, getting his photographs.

"How about it, Layne?" Matt murmured. "You're the type of person who values friendship."

A peculiar look went across her face and for some reason she was staring at the flowers in the middle of the table. "We're not friends, Matt. And we never would have met if it wasn't for the case against Uncle Will."

"That doesn't mean we can't be friends."

"Fine, I'll use the Volvo. But only until I get the Mustang fixed."

"Until they catch whoever tried to run us off the road," he qualified. "The Mustang stands out like a beacon."

She didn't look happy, but she finally nodded. "Okay, until then."

CHAPTER SIXTEEN

"LET'S GO OUT to the patio to go over the new paperwork," Layne suggested when they were finished eating. "It's stifling here in the house."

Matt glanced into the backyard, seeing the appeal. It was shaded by trees and there were sturdy chaises available in a very private setting.

Stop, he ordered.

Layne wasn't offering anything intimate; she was looking for a place to work in the fresh air. Nonetheless, she was getting to him. The first time he'd seen her he hadn't noticed the red and gold glints in her silky brown hair, or the way every emotion could be read on her expressive face. As for her smile…when she really let loose, it was breathtaking. And while she wasn't tall, she had great legs. Her skin was like silk and she had the prettiest breasts—not large, but nicely proportioned.

Today she was barefoot and wearing some sort of skimpy, sleeveless knit shirt that laced up between her breasts and ended well above the waistband of her shorts. And all of it sort of stuck to her damp skin, begging to be peeled off.…

"Uh, sounds good," Matt said hoarsely.

Fortunately Layne pulled out a cushioned chair at the outdoor table, rather than one of the comfy chaises, saving him from making a mistake he wasn't sure he'd regret.

She had two copies of the partnership agreement, and they read in silence, only occasionally stopping to compare notes. The language was standard. William Hudson had sold half of his company to Peter for a very reasonable price, with everything, including business decisions, to be shared equally.

"No strange 'in event of death' language or other questionable clauses," Matt murmured at length.

"I don't think Mr. Davidson is disputing that Aunt Dee owns half of the company, just that she shouldn't get anything because of what happened. And now she's so discouraged, she's talking about selling the house."

Layne was rubbing the back of her neck and Matt almost got up to massage it when he remembered the security team had installed cameras to help keep an eye on things. Did they pick up sound, as well as video? If so, the team could hear every word being said, on top of seeing them.

The sense of privacy vanished and he suddenly understood why Layne and her aunt were so upset. He'd lived with so little privacy all his life, he should have seen it earlier. Yet even Terry had complained about the loss of privacy that came with a major illness, and that was practically the *only* thing he complained about.

"Er…how about going back inside?" Matt asked.

Layne seemed surprised, but she agreed and they settled on the couch in the living room in front of a table fan. *Much better,* Matt thought, though he'd enjoyed being outdoors before remembering the hidden video cameras.

Matt fingered his copy of the partnership agreement. Layne was pale and she'd lost weight since the first day they'd met. He'd have to think if there was anything else he could do to help in a way that wouldn't offend her. Thanks to Spence and Gordon Eisley, he had more money than he could ever spend, no matter how hard he tried. Perhaps he could help Dorothy with her mortgage—it would certainly make Layne feel better if her aunt's financial situation improved.

You can't just wave a checkbook and think it's the answer to everything.

Matt gritted his teeth. Okay, maybe Layne was right about him and his checkbook, but waving it seemed to be the only effective thing he *could* do at the moment.

"Here's the sales agreement, and the papers Mr. Davidson wants Aunt Dee to sign," Layne said a few minutes later, handing him a thick bunch of papers.

The sales agreement seemed equally straightforward aside from a paragraph stating the payment would be placed in a special account and distributed per a separate contract between Peter and Dorothy. Well, that and another clause that showed Peter would continue to receive a tidy percentage of the company's income for ten years in exchange for eight hours of investment consultation each quarter and serving on their board of directors.

Was Peter's expertise *really* worth so much? He was brilliant in the stock market, but it could also be intended to keep Dorothy from receiving more. It would be easy to do—accept a lower sales price and negotiate a handsome consultation fee in exchange.

As for the contract Peter was asking Dorothy to sign—it was short, dry and to the point...possibly because Peter didn't want an official paper trail, referencing the embezzlement. It was the letter written to Dorothy, providing various sums and calculations, that helped the most. Matt reviewed the numbers he'd been scribbling on a sheet of paper about the sale of Hudson & Davidson. No matter how he worked the amounts, it didn't look good.

Layne prodded his leg with her toe. "Did you spot something that might help?"

"I'm still looking. How about some ice cream?"

"I'll get it." Frowning, she got up and a few minutes later returned with a heaping bowl of Cherry Garcia for him, and a more modest one for herself.

"You need to eat more," Matt said, trying to switch bowls with her. "You've lost weight and you don't have any to spare."

"Gee, thanks. Women just love being told they're too skinny."

"I'm not criticizing. I just mean you've generally

lost weight. Your cheeks are thinner and your waist narrower. It isn't healthy." He stuffed a huge spoonful of Cherry Garcia into his mouth to keep from saying anything else.

MATT'S IRRITABLE REPLY told Layne he was genuinely upset.

"Is that why you keep feeding me?" she asked lightly.

"I feed you because we both have to eat, but now that you mention it, *somebody* needs to make sure you're properly fed."

She tried to filter his comment through her that's-just-chauvinistic-bullshit meter, but it was hard to measure when he was plainly unhappy about something. She liked Matt; she just didn't want to like him too much. And she *had* lost weight. Trust a man with an eagle eye when it came to women's figures to notice a few pounds' difference.

"Matt, quit saying dumb things and tell me what's wrong."

He swallowed another bite of ice cream. "All right. No matter how I look at it, the figures are a stretch, even *without* taking the consultation fee clause into consideration."

Layne scrunched her nose. "You noticed the consultation fee, too. Pretty clever. The buyer gets a lower sales price, and Peter receives the same amount of money in the end."

"There are valid business reasons to structure a

sale that way, including managing tax liability. But it could also be to keep Dorothy from receiving any- thing more—he might figure your aunt won't fight him unless it appears outrageous."

"Or not at all, with his threat to bring everything out again about Uncle Will. He knows it would hurt Aunt Dee to have the case dragged into court."

"That, too," Matt affirmed sourly. "It's lousy and unethical as hell. Offering your aunt twenty-five thousand dollars is practically an insult."

Whoa.

Apparently all of the censors had come off Matt's vocal cords, but Layne couldn't deny how question- able it looked.

"And what if Peter *did* have something to do with the thefts?" Matt continued furiously. "What if he killed your uncle? My God, *he's married to my mother.*"

Layne put her hand on his arm. "I know it proba- bly won't be any comfort, but I want to believe Uncle Will didn't entirely misjudge his friend. And they *were* good friends, Matt. Once, a long time ago."

He let out a long breath and lifted her hand, look- ing at her fingers as if he'd never seen them before. Very carefully he pressed his lips to her palm, his breath warm against her skin. Heat burned instantly in her abdomen.

"Matt…"

"Don't say anything." Matt put his bowl on the table and tugged her closer. He touched the tip of his tongue to the hollow of her throat, tantalizing her, then caught her mouth in a deep kiss.

Every inch of Layne's skin burned, only it wasn't the sultry air of a too-warm summer day—it was heat spreading from his hungry hands, exploring and moving clothes out of the way.

She gulped as Matt's fingers slipped beneath her shorts, pressing against her center, dipping into the slick, dark space.

Part of her wanted to be annoyed about his obvious level of experience, but she already knew he must have been with more women than she would care to count.

"You're not concentrating," Matt breathed against her lips.

He touched her again, fingers sliding deeper, and all thoughts of other women vanished.

All at once the muscles in Matt's shoulders bunched as he lifted her.

"The bedroom is upstairs, isn't it?"

She nodded and held on to his neck as he trotted up the staircase, the newel post and polished wood railings flashing past. He stopped on the upper landing and looked around.

"Which door?"

"On the left."

It was half-closed and he nudged it open. "Nice," he whispered.

Her pulse slowed. "Except you don't think it suits me, right?" Layne loved her bedroom, though she rarely let anyone in the family see how it was decorated. As a kid, she had filled her room with books and sports gear and pictures of famous newspeople. *Now* she had antique oak furniture to match the oak floor, including a high, four-poster bed, covered by a quilt in peach and sage-green. Full, soft white curtains hung at the windows and her photographs were enclosed in delicate porcelain frames.

It was beautifully, riotously feminine.

And she didn't want to see her sisters or mother roll their eyes and make jokes about tomboy Layne McGraw choosing such incongruous decor.

"I think it looks just like you." Matt kissed her throat before laying her on the bed.

Even if he wasn't being sincere, Layne enjoyed hearing him say it. People often acted as if she was a sturdy, pint-sized version of the Little Engine That Could, instead of a woman.

Matt cupped her bottom, and Layne instantly lost interest in how anyone else saw her. Then all at once she remembered that the condoms in her bottom dresser drawer were probably expired, not having been needed in a while.

"Uh...." Layne wriggled upright, ignoring the hungry, grabbing demand between her legs. "Not to throw cold water on this, but do you have condoms that were made since the last ice age?"

Matt's eyes gleamed. "A woman after my heart." He reached into his back pocket and pulled out his wallet, extracting two plastic-wrapped condoms. "They're only a few months old."

She let out a relieved sigh. Making love with Matt was insane, but she might *go* insane if they couldn't finish what they'd started. "Good."

He kissed her again and unfastened the thin laces between her breasts. It was only when he spread the edges open and stared at her shoulder that Layne remembered the dark bruise over her right collarbone.

"What happened?" he demanded.

"It's nothing."

"It isn't nothing." Matt traced the purple edges of the bruise, an intense frown on his face. "Is this from going off the road?"

"It was just a freak thing. I'd twisted around to look out the back window when we were hit. I was thrown against the door at an awkward angle, that's all."

He said something Layne couldn't catch, then began kissing the discolored area, so gently she was barely aware of the touch.

Matt's hands got busy, exploring the peaks of her breasts, and not to be outdone, she pulled the tails of his shirt free. He obliged by drawing the garment over his head, tossing it carelessly aside.

Ooh...my. Layne sucked air into her lungs.

His body was hard, lean and muscled in all the right places. He certainly didn't have anything in common with her last boyfriend, a guy who'd begun to spend too many extra hours at his desk drinking cappuccinos and taking the elevator instead of the stairs.

An instinctive urge to cover herself went through Layne. If only it were dark, then she wouldn't wonder as much if he was looking at her and making comparisons. Yet her thoughts scattered as he sucked gently on one of her nipples, teasing the tip with his tongue, seeming to know how long and how much would send waves of need through her body.

Her shorts and his jeans went the way of their shirts and she laughed as her panties flew upward, only to be caught on one of the tall posts at the end of the bed.

Matt seemed particularly pleased about something, probably his aim, or lack of it.

"Mmm, boxers," she said, pulling at the waist of his dark navy underwear.

"Disappointed?"

"Uh-uh."

He settled into even more dedicated foreplay and Layne's pulse raced impossibly faster. Finally he stripped the cover from the condom and invited her to roll the sheath down his swollen length. A moment later he eased into her, moving slowly.

Layne gasped as her body stretched to accommodate him; she couldn't remember ever feeling so filled. But that was the last clear thought in her head. All else fled as Matt began thrusting, fast and hard, then slow and lazy, nearly withdrawing completely before returning until she finally exploded into a million pieces.

IT WAS AFTER dark when Matt's eyes drifted open. Layne was curled against his side, her breathing slow and even. Her lacy panties still dangled on a high bed post, and he smiled, remembering how she'd laughed when they sailed there, instead of getting upset because things weren't all rose petals and champagne.

His gaze drifted around the feminine room. She'd expected him to be amused by it, but it was like the rest of her home: simple, tasteful and uniquely Layne. No wonder she'd viewed his penthouse at the the Eisley Foundation building with confusion. It was no more personal than a hotel suite.

Layne stirred against him and he brushed his fingers over her silky brown hair; he was relaxed and sated and still wanted to make love to her again.

"You awake?" she whispered.

"Barely."

"Me, too."

Matt kissed the top of her head. Having sex with Layne was undoubtedly a mistake, but he'd have to deal with it later. He was too damned relaxed. It was the first time in weeks he'd felt this good, and the bizarre part was that Layne was both the cause of his tension and the cure.

For the most part, Matt didn't care if people understood why he'd returned to Seattle, but it suddenly seemed important for her to know that he wasn't just dabbling.

"Layne, do you remember me telling you about getting Remy Saunders to head up a research project?"

"Yeah, for ALS. It seemed like a big deal."

"It is, and I should have told you why that project is so personal. You see, my best friend from childhood was diagnosed with ALS in January last year."

Layne lifted her head and looked at him in horror. "That's terrible. For anyone, but especially for someone so young."

"He's just a few months older than me. When things used to get crazy on the party circuit, I'd go visit him for a couple of days. He never judged me, and he didn't envy me, either—he was simply a friend who accepted who and what I was."

"We all need someone like that."

"I'm not sure how well I understood it before, but I do now. And when he called about the diagnosis…." Matt's throat closed for an instant. "Hell, it was as if someone had punched me in the stomach. All I could think was *not Terry*. Not my friend."

"It must have been awful."

"It was the worst day of my life. When I got off the phone, I punched the wall so hard I broke two bones in my hand. Bad things aren't supposed to happen to people like Terry. He's doing something real in the world, while all I'd ever done was play and live hard. And even with all my money, I couldn't fix it."

Layne silently held his hand, the way she'd done earlier.

"After a while I realized that the Eisley Foundation might be able to do something. But first I had to convince my grandfather. He wanted proof that I was serious and wouldn't just abandon the foundation if I got bored."

"So that's why you started working at my uncle's company."

"Yeah. Peter knew what I wanted to do and created a position for me in the investment division. I worked hard, Layne, maybe to prove to myself that I could do it, as well as my grandfather."

She didn't say anything for a long minute. "So, when all of this started happening, you must have wanted to show loyalty to Peter, not just because he's your stepfather, but because he had faith in you when no one else did."

"Exactly." Matt was grateful that Layne understood. "It's still hard to believe that he might be trying to cheat your aunt. A month ago I would have sworn he was a stand-up guy. God, maybe I *shouldn't* be director of the Eisley Foundation if I have such poor judgment."

Layne's eyes widened. "Are you looking for an excuse to quit?"

"*No*. I've made promises and I'm going to keep them, I just wonder if my critics might have a point about me."

She didn't say anything for a long minute, then sank back against her pillow. "Everybody makes mistakes. It doesn't mean they have bad judgment."

"I suppose."

"And I have to say that discovering you have a few cracks in your supreme self-confidence is reassuring. Nobody likes people with a god complex, you know."

Matt choked, both with surprise and laughter. Layne said the damnedest things, neatly poking holes in his ego. Yet the merry look in her eyes sobered quickly.

"Matt, you realize that finding a cure or effective treatment could take years, or even decades."

"Or forever. But I have to try. Terry isn't giving up. He's a teacher and intends to *keep* teaching, even when he...*if* he becomes confined to a wheelchair."

"Does he live in the Seattle area?"

"He has a place in Bellevue. His dad was my grandfather's head groundskeeper at the mansion. That's how we got to know each other. I'd come home from boarding school during the summer, and his dad would bring Terry with him to work. We did everything together...got in trouble, snuck into R-rated movies, had our first crush on the same girl, went hiking and swimming in the Puget Sound."

"Yikes." Layne shivered, despite the heavy, sultry air in the bedroom. "Even in summer the Sound is freezing."

"You don't notice it as much when you're eleven."

"I suppose not. So with all that, Terry became family."

Family.

Matt nodded. That's exactly what Terry was—a brother, the same as Aaron and Jake and Pierre.

LAYNE FELT MATT'S arm tighten around her.

Damn.

All this time she'd wanted to believe he was playing at philanthropy the way he'd played at everything else, but his raw honesty was impossible to discount. What a shock it must have been, learning his closest friend might die within a few years.

Damn. Damn. *Damn*.

She'd never had casual sex before, and it was obvious there was nothing casual or uncomplicated about Matthew Hollister either. When she'd gone to the foundation that first day, she'd seen him as little more than a plastic Ken doll, only to discover he was a whole lot more.

"I've been thinking," she said. "You might have better luck getting things done if people knew what you're trying to accomplish and why. People can do amazing things when they're inspired."

"Terry deserves his privacy."

"Talk to him. Ask whether he minds if you say 'a close friend' is dealing with the disease, and that's why you came back to Seattle to start an ALS research project."

"The press might discover he's the friend."

"He still might say it's all right. Surely he knows why you took over the foundation from your grandfather."

"Of course. I don't want to give Terry false hope, but I thought it might help to hear what we're doing. He won't accept anything else."

Layne thought about the Volvo in her driveway. It

was a good bet that Matt had also wanted to help his friend financially.

"It's odd," Matt said thoughtfully. "I was originally going to take every penny of our annual budget and put it into searching for a cure, but I realized that would be irresponsible. And Terry agreed. Instead I'm evaluating the merits of each project or contribution and making sure the funds are being spent productively."

"It sounds like a good plan."

"Thank you." Matt gave her a long, lingering kiss that was more sweet than sexy.

Sleep began overtaking her again and she yawned. There were never enough hours in the day to get everything done, so she tended to sacrifice her rest. Even now she felt as if she should be doing something instead of snogging Matt Hollister. *Snogging*...Layne suppressed a laugh. She'd never even *heard* that word before the Harry Potter books hysteria, now it was part of her lexicon.

Things changed.

Even Matt changed.

"You know what?" she murmured. "You may not be big on commitment, but you've taken over the Eisley Foundation for your grandfather, and are determined to find a cure for ALS. That sounds like a commitment to me."

CHAPTER SEVENTEEN

"I'LL DO THE next call," Matt offered.

Layne promptly handed him the phone and a copy of the Hudson & Davidson employee list pieced together from the cookbook.

They were working at Matt's penthouse and she took a moment to look out at Lake Union. It was early evening and there was still plenty of light in the summer sky. A seaplane took off as she watched, probably carrying tourists for some aerial sightseeing over Seattle.

"Do you still think it was a man in the SUV that sideswiped us?" Matt asked.

"It was just an impression. But more than one person could be involved—male or female."

"Fair enough. Though I suspect there are fewer women in prison." He quirked a smile at her. "That damned testosterone, right?"

"You said it, not me."

Over the past few days, they'd spent practically every free minute working...and nothing else. Layne knew she was becoming too fond of Matt, but didn't know what to do about it. His reputation still bothered her, but he was decent and smart and struggling to figure out his new life. He couldn't help his feelings about marriage and children. Perhaps if she'd grown up in his unusual family, she'd feel the same way.

And she might as well face it—his past was mostly a problem because men like Matt Hollister did *not* end up with women like Layne McGraw. One of her sisters, sure. Matt was one of the beautiful people and so were they. Not that she wouldn't want to punch Jeannie's lights out if she looked at Matt again…

Urghhhh.

Layne wanted to scream. Jealousy was ridiculous. Instead she gave Matt a tight smile and pointed to the list. "Who's next?"

"Let's see, Phyllis Kemp, now in the travel industry. Fifty-seven, never married, worked as an assistant in the accounting area."

There were annotations next to each name, including information they'd learned through their calls and data that the Eisley security staff had gotten about them. The group still working for Hudson & Davidson was particularly touchy about inquiries, possibly afraid that saying anything could get them fired. And maybe they weren't far wrong with a man like Peter in charge.

A number were already employed elsewhere since there had been layoffs following the scandal. Others had retired, some apparently because they didn't like the personnel decisions Peter had been making. The ones working other jobs weren't quite as uptight, but the retirees were easiest to contact—they had pensions and weren't worried about their livelihoods.

Matt dialed the number and waited. "Hello, is this Phyllis Kemp?" He nodded as he listened. "This is Matt Hollister. I think we met when we were both working at Hudson & Davidson last year. I saw your name on several recipes in the employee cookbook. They look delicious."

He went on charming Phyllis the way he'd managed to charm most of the women he had called. Layne didn't think it was simply name recognition; his voice was mesmerizing, low and sexy, with the right touches of humor. Still, the conversation inevitably got tenser when he arrived at the reason for phoning and a request to put Phyllis on speaker phone. But he obviously got a yes, because he pressed the button.

"We're on speaker now," he said.

"I don't know anything about the thefts," Phyllis announced. "Mostly I remember being shocked when Mr. Hudson was accused."

"I'm not trying to make trouble," Layne interjected, mentally making a note that the other woman hadn't said *guilty*. "I just want the truth about Uncle Will."

"Mr. Hudson used to have photos of you in his office," Phyllis said unexpectedly. "I'd see them when I took meeting notes in there."

"He was a second father to me."

"Hmm, yes. You know, I've heard from some

people at the firm. They aren't comfortable with your questions."

Layne let out a breath. "I know, and I'm really sorry to bring this up again, but my aunt and I need to make sense of what happened. Surely you can understand that."

"I can't give Mr. Hudson an alibi. I didn't work that closely with him."

"But maybe you can help in another way. For one thing, how are phone calls handled at the firm? I have a phone message that was apparently taken when Uncle Will's voice mailbox was full."

Phyllis chuckled. "Oh, that. He liked to take his own calls, rather than having his assistant screen them. Of course, if he wasn't available he was *supposed* to transfer his number to Emma, but he'd forget and the box would fill. When that happened, the call was automatically routed to any available assistant. We'd put the message on his desk. Is it important?"

Layne eased herself down to the floor near the phone. "Apparently he had plans to visit his brother-in-law on one of the nights in question. We're trying to confirm it since my other uncle doesn't remember the date of the visit. We don't think the message was taken by Emma Farnon."

"It's been months—that's a long time for anyone to remember taking a phone call."

"I know it's a long shot. The police should have looked into it at the time, only they—" Layne stopped when Matt nudged her, shaking his head. He was right—complaining about the police wouldn't help. "Anyway, I'm following up on everything."

"Any one of us could have taken it."

"Except the message is very distinctive, written in texting shorthand."

"Oh, Lord, that was Brandi Porter," Phyllis said, sounding disgusted. "We could never make her understand that it didn't look professional."

"Brandi Porter?" Layne repeated as Matt flipped through the list. It was alphabetical and he turned the page around so she could see it—the surnames skipped from Polke to Proctor. "Uh...how long has she worked for the company?"

"Not long, and she isn't there now. Hudson & Davidson had a contract with a temp agency, but they weren't used that much. Brandi got sent over when we had a cold going through the staff. She worked for a few weeks, and then just didn't show up one day."

"What was she like?"

"Young, pretty, *always* distracted. She was late a lot."

Layne wrote Brandi's name and the information on a separate sheet of paper. "Are there any other temporary employees you remember working there last fall?"

"No...the company is so big, we could usually shift people around in case of illness."

Matt leaned closer to the phone. "Phyllis, can you think of anyone who might have been acting suspiciously? Somebody spending money too freely?

Maybe a new car they shouldn't have been able to afford, or something else that stood out?"

"Not really," she replied slowly. "But I don't pay attention to that sort of thing. One of the accountants *did* go to Hawaii over the Christmas holidays. It was Roger Lewis. He took his girlfriend and bragged about impressing her with the best hotels and restaurants."

Matt found Roger's name on the list and made a note next to it. Most of the interviews had been like that, little bits of information thrown out, sometimes a name, often innocuous.

Layne was still sitting on the floor when they'd finished.

She looked up at Matt. "Brandi Porter sounds interesting. She might remember more, simply because she only worked at the company a short time."

"I'll have Connor look for her contact information." Matt was focused on the employee list, his face grim. "I'd forgotten we had a few temporary employees. I wonder how many other names aren't here?"

Edgy, Matt got up and brought Layne a bottle of sparkling mineral water. He had to admit, his tension didn't just stem from his growing doubts about Peter. Layne was twisting him up worse than a spinning top.

Not that they'd argued.

Ever since Monday she'd kept things friendly. He ought to be grateful for it; a woman like Layne

McGraw could easily read more into their night together than was warranted. Nevertheless, it was annoying the way she'd brushed it off.

They'd gotten up after midnight, eaten another sandwich, made love a second time, and then...

Matt scowled as he recalled waking up the next morning to see Layne searching through a dresser drawer, clad only in a damp bath sheet. She'd been brisk, friendly and in a hurry to rush off to work.

With the other women he'd known, he would have expected an unspoken agreement that the sex had been pleasant but didn't require analysis. But not with Layne. She fell into a category of "Danger: could be looking for commitment" women that he'd always avoided in the past. Because of that, he'd expected her to analyze everything to death.

Instead she'd stayed silent, and it was bugging the hell out of him.

"Do you think it's too late to call someone else, or should we leave for your house?" he asked.

"We'd better wait until tomorrow. But you don't need to go with me or stay there."

"I won't sleep unless I know you're okay." He'd insisted on staying over as extra protection, much to Layne's disgust.

She snorted. "With the cavalry stationed outside? *Please.* Of course I'll be okay. I can't sneeze without someone saying bless you."

Matt winced. Layne did not enjoy knowing there

were video cameras around the house. "I swear, there are no video or listening devices in the house."

Thank goodness.

Their horizontal activities would have been broadcast to the security van, and Layne would be more justified than ever wanting to strangle both Connor and him.

"If you're worried about it, we could also sleep here," Matt said. "I've got a king-size bed. Plenty of room for two."

"And join the legions of women who've gone on safari there? I don't think so."

"Hey, I haven't had a single overnight female visitor here except for my sister Tamlyn."

He wanted Layne to believe him, but he didn't know why he cared. Besides, she'd probably just say women preferred their own beds.

"Oh, I forgot. I brought my advance copy of the *Babbitt* for you to see," Layne said, suddenly looking apprehensive. She got up and pulled the news magazine from her bag.

The pages were folded back to an article about Peter. Like the one published a few weeks before, it wasn't outright critical, but there was a subtle tone that made Peter sound like a prick.

A grim humor went through Matt.

Peter actually might *be* a prick.

Or worse.

"If Mr. Davidson sees the article, he'll probably assume I'm responsible," Layne said. "But I swear no one has talked to me at work, and I haven't been asked to research anything on him or the Eisley Foundation."

"Don't worry about it." Matt tossed the magazine onto the floor. "A few criticisms aren't going bother Peter once I confront him about the sale of Hudson & Davidson."

Layne still looked concerned. "Those criticisms are in print for everyone to read. Won't it upset your mom?"

Matt tried to keep his expression neutral. It would hurt Katrina a whole lot more if she discovered her husband was a vengeful, unethical businessman who was trying to cheat the widow of his best friend. He leaned over and tugged Layne down on the couch; he liked having her warmth next to him...liked it too much. She stiffened, then relaxed.

"Like I said, don't worry about it," he murmured. "If Peter has nothing to hide and hasn't done anything wrong, he shouldn't care what the *Babbitt* has to say."

"False words can still do damage," Layne said seriously. "We were lucky there was only limited press coverage about Uncle Will and the thefts. They didn't accuse him, but the implication was unmistakable."

"We'll have to wait and see what happens. Peter may not think anything of the article."

"I suppose. So you're going to confront him?" she asked.

"Have to. You don't want to believe your uncle was that wrong about him, and neither do I. But people change. My stepfather mentioned losing his first wife in an accident. Maybe he wouldn't let himself care as much about anyone after that."

"I hope that doesn't happen to Aunt Dee."

"I'm sure it won't."

Matt kissed the top of Layne's head and held her closer. It was a struggle, not wanting her to think he'd changed his mind about long-term relationships...and wanting more time with her. She was an amazingly generous, responsive lover.

"By the way, how is your shoulder?" he asked.

"Getting better. Instead of a lovely purple, it's now an impossible to color-coordinate green, yellow and reddish-brown. I had to settle for basic black."

Since she was wearing jeans and a green T-shirt, Matt's mind instantly flashed to a black bra and panties. Now he *really* wasn't going to sleep tonight. He'd gotten a brief look at Layne's underwear drawer the other morning, a rainbow of silk and lace. Layne obviously indulged her feminine side in private. Was it because she'd gotten teased as a kid about being a tomboy, or because she didn't think she could compete with her older sisters?

"Layne, you mentioned spending most of your free time with your aunt and uncle while growing up."

"Yeah. I was the surprise kid the folks didn't know what to do with. When Aunt Dee and Uncle Will moved back here, Jeremy was already a competitive athlete and the twins had their music and ballet classes and school activities. Everybody was crazy busy. I was too young to leave alone, so Mom asked Aunt Dee if she could start watching me after kindergarten. Before long I was in Carrollton most of the time."

"Do you think your parents feel guilty about that now?"

Layne tilted her head to look at him. "Why would they? Aunt Dee and Uncle Will were wonderful and I could be myself with them. Besides, Mom and Dad were so busy with their medical practices and the other kids, they really didn't have time for me."

"Maybe they feel guilty because they weren't there for you and that's why they nag you so much. Your sisters and brother could even be envious of the relationship you had with William and Dorothy."

"Maybe." Her eyes were thoughtful, then all at once she sat up. "Oh, I need to call Aunt Dee before it gets too late. She'll worry if she tries the house and doesn't get me." She scrambled away and hunted through her purse for her cell phone.

Matt tried to be philosophical about it. At least Layne had let him hold her for a few minutes. And it wasn't as if he wanted to seduce her.

Liar.

He wanted back into her bed.

But for once in his life he should be thinking about what someone *else* needed and wanted.

DOROTHY MIXED THE paint on her palette into the desired shade of sunrise-pink and tried to clear her mind of everything but the tranquil mystery of a mountain lake at daybreak. She didn't have a photographic memory for information, but she could think of something she'd seen and it appeared instantly in her mind. Colors, the arc of a branch or the stately height of a tree. The sway of wildflowers in a breeze or the wildness of an animal, ready to flee at the hint of a threat. They were all stored in her memory.

The phone rang as she reached for a brush and she grabbed the handset instead.

"It's me," said Layne when she answered. "How is it going over there?"

"Let's see, I still have a van parked near my house, presumably filled with those security experts you told me about. And Connor Patrick O'Brian rings my doorbell several times a day, but when I don't open it, he leaves gifts, like tins of apricot tea."

"He's still trying to be forgiven, then."

"Apparently. So, how is it going with you and Matt?" she asked casually. She'd quickly spotted the signs of two people who'd taken their relationship to a physical level and were in the backing-off stage.

"Oh, the same," her niece replied in a careful voice. "You know how it is."

"He's there, listening?"

"Yup. We're still at Matt's penthouse."

Dorothy got up and moved restlessly around the studio. "Has Detective Rivera found anything out about that SUV?"

The little sleep she'd gotten the past few nights had

been broken by nightmares of Layne in the Mustang, careening into a ravine or tree or another car. At least that was one positive about Matt Hollister's involvement—he'd kept her niece safe.

"There isn't much to go on since the license plate was covered," Layne replied. "Rivera is looking into whether anybody on our list has a gray SUV, but he doesn't know if he can get a search warrant, even if they do."

"What about how detectives do it in the movies or on TV? Just follow the suspect to see if there's damage to the vehicle, then sneak a sample of paint and send it to the lab."

"I don't think he's that kind of detective. Hollywood doesn't worry about evidence being thrown out of court. Well, not unless it's a convenient plot device. Since when do you watch cop shows?"

Dorothy smiled reluctantly. "I don't now, but Will enjoyed them sometimes, and I watched with him."

"Okay, you're excused. Sleep well."

"You, too."

Just not with Matt, Dorothy wanted to add as Layne said goodbye. Nothing had changed her mind about the man. She still didn't think he was right for her niece; he was too charming, too rich and *too* experienced. All you had to do was look at a magazine article about him to know his female preferences—pictures told a thousand words, and the ones of Matt Hollister always had a blonde beauty standing nearby.

Sighing, Dorothy picked up her palette and began

blending the reflected color of sunrise into the lake water. The canvas was large, but though she'd spent some of her sleepless hours in the kitchen, many others had been spent in her studio. The painting was nearly finished.

But it wasn't just worries about Layne and her finances keeping her awake; Patrick's trickery was also on her mind. She felt violated and cheated and still so furious with him she could hardly see straight. She was even angry with William for creating a perfect world for them to live in, then leaving her alone as it crashed down. It had left her vulnerable to lying snakes with ulterior motives. Wasn't losing her husband under such circumstances enough to teach her not to trust anyone so easily?

All at once a new picture came into her head and Dorothy put a fresh canvas on her easel. She squeezed paint onto a second palette and began applying it in broad, bold strokes, letting emotion guide her. A sunset this time, one that was wild and furious over a churning ocean with towering waves.

It was 2:00 a.m. before she stopped, and when she did, she was calmer. Strangely, the painting was one of the best she'd ever done. Turning off the lights, she curled up on the daybed along the wall, the canvas illuminated only by moonlight.

Perhaps now she could sleep.

CONNOR SAT IN his Jeep, watching Dot's house and street. The protection detail knew he was there every night, but they were too wary to question it. All except Riley, whose sense of humor was becoming dangerous to his health.

Each evening Connor had watched the blue of the summer sky gradually deepen until stars winked into view. While they'd passed the summer solstice, this far north of the equator they still had daylight until nearly ten o'clock. And each night the lights in Dorothy's windows rarely turned off until the early morning hours.

He tapped his fingers on the steering wheel, his gaze continually sweeping the neighborhood. It was possible the attack on Layne and Matt had just been a warning, an attempt to scare them off the investigation.

Or maybe not.

Connor admired Layne's determination to prove her uncle's innocence. But poking a snake wasn't a good idea, especially when you didn't know where the snake was hiding its head.

CHAPTER EIGHTEEN

LAYNE WALKED OUT of the *Babbitt* offices on Friday with Annette and Regina, trying to look inconspicuous. Matt had asked her to stay inside for lunch until everything was resolved, and while she hadn't promised, she'd said it wasn't a big deal because she usually ate a sandwich at her desk.

Unfortunately, she'd forgotten her promise to help with the wedding shower for Phil Stanton and his fiancée. And honestly, who would try to hurt her in broad daylight, with half of Seattle's office workers taking lunch, as well?

"Layne, what do you think about getting cupcakes for the wedding shower?" Regina asked. "They can make them look like a cake, but it's easier to serve and very fashionable."

"It is?"

"Oh, you." Regina affectionately hooked her arm through Layne's elbow and pulled her forward. "How will you ever plan your *own* wedding if you don't know these things?"

Layne's heart gave a painful bump as she thought about Matt. No. Absolutely *not*. She wasn't going there. Matt had made it clear he didn't plan to ever get married.

She waved her free hand. "I'll just go away to get married and not worry about the fussy details."

"Mmm," Annette said dreamily. "Destination weddings can be fabulous. But I still want a formal occasion, with white roses and tulle everywhere."

"How about some color to perk it up?" Regina asked practically.

"Yeah, peach tulips would be nice," Layne added.

Annette turned to her with an astonished expression. "*Perfect.* What made you think of it?"

"Just did."

Actually, Layne had been remembering the flowers from Matt. They were starting to fade, but were still lovely. Not that she could say anything about them. Her friends would ask questions and she didn't want them to suspect there was a man in her life, however temporarily. They'd never leave her alone about it.

"We'd better hurry if we want to get everything done," she said.

"Gifts first," Regina pronounced. "The right gifts can take forever to find and we only have two weeks. We can always order the food from McGinte's if we run short on time."

"Everybody uses McGinte's," Annette objected. "It'll look as if we didn't try to do anything special."

"Everyone does it because they're good and reliable," Regina retorted. "Don't forget what happened with The Other Place."

Annette shut her mouth. The Other Place, previously known as Jeri's Catering, was infamous because two Christmases ago they'd delivered the wrong food order, thirty minutes before the end of the party. It wasn't the caterer's first mistake with a *Babbitt* order, but it was their last.

They went down to their favorite galleria. By unspoken agreement they fanned out in each shop, looking for anything suitable. It was hard. The forty-something couple still hadn't registered anywhere and Phil was unfailingly cheerful without ever saying anything important.

Layne was evaluating a crystal vase in the third store when a low "psst" caught her attention. It was Matt on the other side of the glass shelves, looking furious.

"What are you doing here?" she whispered around bookends depicting the Seattle Space Needle.

"*Guess.* I thought you ate lunch at your desk."

"I usually do." Layne cast a quick glance around, checking both for her friends *and* whoever had called Matt to tell him she'd left the *Babbitt.* Honestly, this wasn't kindergarten; she was capable of making her own decisions. "I thought nobody from Eisley security was covering me at work."

"Yeah, *because* you eat lunch at your desk. Fortunately I asked Connor to keep a guy on, in case you pulled a stunt like this."

She put the vase back on the shelf. "It isn't a stunt. Annette and Regina asked if I'd help with a wedding shower, but I'd forgotten until they suggested going out to shop at lunch."

"You could have called me *before* leaving."

"Nobody is going to try something in the middle of the day."

"You don't know that." Matt sounded harassed and she almost felt sorry for him. "Just don't do it again."

Layne frowned. "Do you know something I don't?"

Matt got a "busted" expression. "I was going to break it gently, but somebody tried to get access to your safe deposit box a few days ago using a fake ID."

"How come you know and I don't?"

"The bank supposedly left a message on your home phone for you to come in and have everything transferred to a new box, with new keys. Luckily Connor has those connections I've told you about. When I told him about your safe deposit box and that you suspected an attempted break-in at the house, he looked into it. They know you at the bank and called the police when it happened, but the woman got suspicious and left. She had your key, Layne. Somebody didn't just try to break into your house—they *got* in and stole it."

Layne gulped.

She could have been followed to the bank and overheard asking for a large box, suitable for documents. It hadn't been a private discussion. Or somebody could have gone through her recycle bin and seen the bank's discarded safe-deposit literature.

"The bank gave me two keys. I put one on my ring and the spare in my jewelry box."

"That's probably where most women keep something like that."

"Layne?" called Annette from across the shop. "We're going next door, unless you found something we should consider...?"

"No, but I'm still looking," she called back. "I'll be there in a minute."

Matt waited until the two women had disappeared, then came around and took her arm. "I've called Detective Rivera, so he's on it. Shall I have Connor sweep your house to be sure there aren't any surprises left behind, like a bug?"

"Does it *have* to be Connor?"

"I'll ask Riley. He's as good as Connor with electronics."

"Fine." Then her eyes widened. "Oh my God. If there *is* a bug, that means someone could have heard us in...uh...my bedroom."

"Don't think about it," Matt said hastily. "And try not to give your protection the slip again."

"You can't try to give someone the slip if you don't know they're there."

"Whatever."

He left and Layne hurried next door to find her friends. They were debating whether Carl Abernathy would like to "give" a basket of luxury spa items for the bridal couple. Not being a gift-shopping, wedding-shower-throwing type of guy, he'd tossed them two hundred dollars to help pay for the food and a present.

"Come on, we're talking *Carl*. He'd fire us on the spot," Layne announced. "Spa items? And the label says, 'for the Perfect Sensual Retreat with Your Man.' He'd have a stroke if his name turned up on this."

Regina hastily returned the basket to its display. "Right. What about a toaster or coffee grinder?"

"Not a toaster," Annette protested. "That's passé."

"It's better than making the boss see red and threaten pink slips," Layne said firmly.

She glanced around to spot the Eisley security guy following her, but he must be pretty good at staying out of sight. Things were getting serious, sort of like being in the middle of a movie, except it was a lot more fun watching Julia Roberts evade bad guys than doing it herself.

LAYNE WAITED IN her garden while Riley searched the house. She'd intended to stay inside, but it was creepy watching him search her personal space, using weird electronic devices to make sure someone *else* hadn't been there, too.

"I supposed Riley has 'connections,' too," she muttered to Matt who was waiting with her.

"Probably. Connor personally selects each member of his staff, and they require certain levels of skill and training and experience to make the cut. And commitment."

"Must be fun. Like belonging to a clandestine organization with limitless funds."

"Not quite limitless," Matt said drily. "But security for personal and business concerns is important to my grandfather. He makes sure our security staff have whatever they need. Well, *I* make sure of it now. Grandfather put a large discretionary fund at my disposal to manage the family concerns,"

"So you do more than run the Eisley Foundation."

Matt shrugged. "Yeah, though I have nothing to do with his company. Grandfather has let a board of directors handle that since he became passionate about philanthropy. And it still makes more profit than he could spend in a hundred lifetimes."

Layne couldn't imagine having so much money, but it made her understand Matt better. Maybe being raised with so much wealth made it hard to find meaningful challenges. For that matter, Matt's own grandfather, after becoming obscenely rich, had looked for new frontiers in philanthropy.

"Did you hear about the argument Aunt Dee had with Connor?" she asked Matt lightly.

He groaned. "You mean the cinnamon rolls. She walked up to the security van with a pan of rolls and knocked on the door. But it wasn't an argument. Connor simply explained it isn't a good idea to advertise that men are stationed in a van, hanging out in the neighborhood."

"It gets better." Layne laughed, remembering the conversation with her aunt early that morning. "Since then she's brought them all sorts of things like banana bread, cookies and sandwiches. Oh, and thermoses of coffee. Then she goes back to get the thermos so she can refill it."

Matt stared. "Connor must be pulling his hair out. I know Dorothy is being thoughtful, but doesn't she understand the team doesn't want attention drawn to them?"

"Being thoughtful is the reason she fed them cinnamon rolls," Layne explained with a grin. "Everything else is to annoy Connor."

"That doesn't sound like your aunt. She's so…" Matt stopped as if hunting for the right words. "I don't know, gracious and ladylike."

"She's a pissed-off woman, not a helpless damsel in a fairy tale," Layne retorted.

Still, she understood what he meant. Since Uncle Will's death, Aunt Dee had often seemed almost ethereal, but now she was angry, vital and bursting with life. At least that was something meeting Connor O'Brian had done; it had woken her up.

"By the way, Connor is looking for Brandi Porter," Matt said. "But there's nothing on her so far."

Layne glanced at the house, then back at Matt, grateful they hadn't discussed Brandi after returning the night before. If there *was* a bug, the person who'd planted it could now be looking for Brandi, as well.

Just then Riley appeared at her back door. "Hey,

Layne. I found a device under the coffee table, but no-where else in the house. I've deactivated it so they'll just think it's stopped working."

"Nothing on the phone?" Matt asked.

Riley shook his head. "Use a cell from now on, though. It's unlikely somebody will tap into the line outside the house but still possible. A cell scanner is also possible, but they're harder to get."

"Okay, thanks."

The two men shook hands and Layne tried to think of everything she'd discussed with Matt in the living room or on the phone with someone else. It wasn't good. All sorts of things had gone on there…including hot and heavy foreplay.

"What about notifying the police?" she asked Matt.

"We should let Detective Rivera know, but my guys have resources that he can't access, at least not until it becomes an active investigation again. Here, use this—it's from Connor."

He pulled a gift bag from his jacket pocket and handed it to her. Inside was a smartphone.

"No."

"Yes. Unlimited minutes. Internet surfing. Every-thing at your fingertips. Don't refuse because it was Connor's idea."

"I'm not, I just can't accept. And it wasn't his idea—you've been trying to get me to take a new cell phone for at least two weeks."

"He suggested it, too. Consider it another loan.

Connor wants to make it up to you and Dorothy and this is one way of apologizing."

Yeah, as if Matt wasn't ultimately footing the bill. For all the bad things the press had said of him over the years, he was generous. And the raw emotions he'd shown when talking about his friend with ALS… Layne's throat still tightened whenever she remembered.

"Only a loan," she relented, feeling herself slide further down the slippery slope she'd worried about when he convinced her to use the Volvo.

But now she was pretty sure she knew one of the things waiting for her at the bottom…a shattered heart.

MATT STILL DIDN'T fully understand why Layne was so stiff-necked about taking anything from him, but he was getting the idea that he should figure it out. And not just because she was someone he thought well of. If he didn't understand more about human nature, his work at the foundation wouldn't be effective.

On the party circuit everyone had been happy to let him pay for things. If the thought had occurred to him that they were leeches, it really hadn't bothered him that much. After all, somebody had to pay and he had plenty of money.

Then there were people like Terry and Layne, who were damned stubborn about accepting anything.

People have dignity, you know. And pride.

Layne's declaration had frustrated him, but she

was right. Leeches didn't have pride or dignity, most other people did. And people in need deserved to be respected, the same as anyone else.

Layne was sitting on the edge of a chaise, and Matt sat next to her. "I hate bringing this up, but was there anything in the autopsy that might help?"

"Not that I saw. I'm going to look at it again, but I've been too busy. Or maybe I'm procrastinating."

Perhaps. But considering the shadows beneath Layne's eyes and the faint hollows in her cheeks, she needed to spend less time working and investigating, and more time sleeping. Now, Matt could think of a way to burn up nervous energy that usually ended in relaxed sleep at the end. In fact, lately it was getting hard to think of anything else.

It was a thought. She hadn't taken their first night together too seriously—something that still bugged him a little—so maybe a second time would be all right.

CONNOR CURSED A blue streak at his computer. He'd gone back to his office, still looking for information on Brandi Porter's whereabouts and kept coming up dry.

The sooner everything was resolved and the case cleared against William Hudson, the better. It wasn't Dot or Layne's safety he was especially worried about—unless they did something off-the-charts idiotic, nothing should happen to them with his team in place—but Dot was making him insane.

Yet a reluctant admiration filled Connor as he thought about Dorothy's defiant delivery of coffee and food to the security van. She was doing it purely to aggravate him. If she wasn't so damned beautiful, he'd…

No.

Dorothy's beauty had attracted him initially, but it was more than that now. She was warm, intelligent and had a lively wit. Her husband's death had wounded her spirit, but not killed it. And somehow, despite everything, she still seemed to have a belief in people.

Except in him, of course.

He didn't blame her for being angry, but it would be better if she cooperated with the security team.

He looked back at his computer. The one thing Connor *had* learned about Brandi Porter was that she'd visited the hospital emergency room several times, a victim of suspected domestic violence. If she'd gone into hiding from an abusive husband, she could be impossible to find.

And there was another alternative, as well.

Sighing, he began searching death records for Washington and the surrounding states.

It was a new thing, feeling like a fool, his world turning inside out because of a woman. The only consolation was that Matt didn't seem to be in any better condition, though he *had* quickly talked himself back inside Layne's house. Matt's intentions, on the other hand, were a mystery, probably even to him.

The phone rang a few minutes later. It was Riley, reporting the discovery of a listening device in Layne's living room.

"Sophisticated," Riley explained. "Longer range than the average off-the-rack bug. Somebody put money into it."

"Crap."

"It isn't so bad. There can't be more than a few places locally that do this sort of custom work," said Riley. "Assad may identify the maker when he takes it apart in the lab."

"Get him on it. But send someone else to hand the device off. I'm rotating the team—you're at the Hudson house tonight."

"Great. Layne said her aunt is making calzones for dinner. Apparently Mrs. Hudson makes the dough from scratch and stuffs it with homemade—"

Connor hung up.

If Riley had been in the room, he would have shot him on the spot.

AFTER AN HOUR trying to reach Detective Rivera, Layne stood in her living room, staring at the coffee table where Riley had found the hidden microphone. Would she ever feel the same about her house? At the moment she wanted to leave it forever.

"Hey, it's okay. Nobody else is getting in here again. We'll make sure of it," Matt murmured.

She grabbed her purse, unnerved that he'd guessed how she felt. "Yeah. Um…I need to go grocery shopping. Aunt Dee is testing more recipes for the *Babbitt* this weekend and I have to get the supplies. I'll talk to you later."

He looked ready to protest but nodded. "Sure. Just give me a call when you're leaving Carrollton and I'll meet you here."

"That isn't necessary. I'm going to spend the night with Aunt Dee." The decision had been spontaneous, but it seemed best. She needed the time to herself.

Layne thought she spotted one of the security vehicles as she drove to her favorite supermarket, but she couldn't be sure.

She wandered up and down the aisles, consulting the recipes Regina wanted tested, putting groceries in the cart and feeling bad about Matt. The investigation was proving hard on them both. Until she'd entered his life, he'd been comfortable with his time at Hudson & Davidson and had liked Peter Davidson well enough to make him an officer at the Eisley Foundation. Now he was questioning his judgment and wondering if his stepfather was going to land in jail for theft and murder or blackmail.

Layne didn't know herself.

Was Peter guilty?

She went back and forth, thinking he was just a skunk who'd abandoned his friend, to questioning whether he'd killed her uncle. Even the "at best" scenario wasn't positive. *At best,* Peter was using blackmail to get away with nearly every penny from the company.

At Aunt Dee's house Layne popped the trunk of

the Volvo and saw Connor striding down the driveway. "What do you want?"

"Just to carry your groceries."

She regarded him. Connor O'Brian was a solid,
no-nonsense man with short silver-and-black hair and
a muscular build. And he was attractive—not in the
way Uncle Will had been handsome, but nice-looking
with a direct gaze. She might get to the point where
she forgave him, but she wasn't sure about her aunt.
Dorothy Hudson had a big heart, but being lied to
wasn't something she'd easily overlook.

"It was just a trick that morning with Finnster,
wasn't it?" she asked. "The way he clowned around
here in the driveway."

"Finn has specialized training. I like seeing how
people act with a dog, and how they act with him. It
tells me something. You and Dot have his unquali-
fied approval."

"But that wasn't enough. You still went to the
gallery."

Connor let out a heavy breath. "She's a beautiful
woman and it seemed the only way we could meet. I
knew it was a mistake and did it anyway."

Hmm.

She turned around and regarded the grocery sacks
in the trunk, thinking about her aunt's face the past
few days…full of life and energy, more vibrant than
she'd been since Uncle Will's death.

"Drat," Layne said. "I forgot to get the irises for
Aunt Dee. I'll have to get them another time."

She lifted a bag and Connor took it from her, scooping up a second, as well, while she got the other two.

Dee met them on the step and glared at Connor, but she didn't stop him from carrying the sacks into the kitchen. As soon as he put them on the counter, she pointed to the door. "Out," she ordered.

"Of course, ma'am."

Connor dutifully exited, but Layne spotted the faint smile on his face. It was probably the first time he'd gotten past the threshold of the house, and she'd given him a hint about Aunt Dee's favorite flower. She just hoped he wouldn't get smug and blow everything.

CHAPTER NINETEEN

ON SUNDAY EVENING Matt sat on his living room couch with Layne as she watched a new documentary on the Great Sphinx of Giza, fascinated more by her intense concentration than by the film itself.

When the credits rolled she made a few additional notes on her pad of paper before looking up.

"Thanks for watching that with me," she said. "I forgot to set the timer to record it at my house. Justin Adler is doing the review for the *Babbitt* and he always asks me to research some of the facts. It's easier if I see it, too."

"That's okay. Archaeology intrigues me."

"Is that why you went down to see the *Titanic?*"

Matt shrugged. "Partly, and partly it was the adventure."

"How did it feel?"

"Like I was a tasteless sightseer in a graveyard," he replied honestly. "Yet I was still fascinated. I wanted to touch the ship and feel connected to it."

"To be part of the story."

"Exactly. It's one of the great tragedies. The whole time I kept thinking, if one tiny thing had changed, everything might be different today. Who knows how it would have affected history."

"Yeah, the what-ifs can drive us crazy."

Matt knew Layne was thinking about her uncle. He lifted her hand and kissed the palm. "I'm hungry for dessert."

"I'm pretty sure it's a choice between Cherry Garcia and Cherry Garcia."

"Not to be clichéd, but I wasn't thinking about that kind of dessert." He stood and tugged her off the couch, unsure if his motive was a desire to distract her...or just desire. But at the moment he didn't care. "My bedroom has great views of the city lights. Very different from this side of the building. Want to see it?"

A TINGLING HEAT spread instantly through Layne's abdomen. Though she'd told herself that sex was out, she'd still gone out and bought new condoms to stow in her purse, all the while thinking what a fool she was.

"Um, sure," she murmured. "I love city skylines at night."

Matt's bedroom was just as stark as the rest of the penthouse, and it was huge. Hardwood flooring stretched to an enormous bed, positioned to take advantage of the vistas through two walls of windows. Like the kitchen and living room, everything was immaculate, the bed neatly made with one corner folded down, revealing navy-colored silk sheets.

A reporter at the *Babbitt* had written a story the year before, talking about how infrequently the average single American male changed his sheets. Celina had obviously never been in Matt's penthouse. He had to have a maid. Nobody kept a place this spotless unless they were OCD, and Layne had spent enough time with Matt to know he wasn't obsessive about anything.

She wavered.

It was the sort of bed that gorgeous, coolly sophisticated women expected. And she couldn't help wondering, *why her?* Why someone so opposite to the tall, perfectly proportioned blondes he'd always dated?

It had to be convenience and the forced intimacy that their investigation had created. Yet the unpalatable thought shattered as Matt drew her into a slow dance, humming quietly.

After a moment she giggled. "That's the theme song from *Gilligan's Island.*"

"Just making sure you're paying attention."

He began humming something else and she laughed harder. "*The Addams Family?* Now *that's* romantic."

"You know your classic TV theme songs, but you're forgetting that Gomez was terribly passionate. He adored his Morticia."

"True."

Matt dramatically began kissing her hand and

moved up her arm to her throat and down her shoulder to the other hand. "Mind if I go around again, Tish?"

"Very well, Gomez."

This time he stopped at her throat and headed toward her breasts as he unbuttoned her blouse.

Layne gulped. "Uh…this is prime-time television."

"*The Addams Family* was in reruns by the time we were born."

"Oh. That's right."

She stepped back and her heel struck the bed, throwing her off balance. They both tumbled to the mattress. She lifted her head and checked the two walls of windows, feeling exposed in the well-lit room for more than one reason.

"Are you an exhibitionist by any chance?" she asked politely.

"Nope." Matt reached up to the wall and touched a button; the lights in the room went off, but it wasn't truly dark. There was too much illumination from the city. "I can lower the blinds if you want it darker. Still feeling exposed?"

She thought about it. Matt could see her, but mostly in shadow. As for someone in another building? Maybe with a pair of binoculars, and not easily.

Layne pulled her blouse over her head and threw it across the room. "I'll deal with it. You got protection?"

Matt grinned. "Not that I was planning ahead or anything, but yes, I picked up a box the other day."

Good. That meant she didn't have to confess to

doing the same thing, though he'd probably be glad she didn't have baby plans on her mind.

She pushed Matt flat on his back and straddled his hips, unbuttoning his shirt and splaying her fingers across the smooth, taut skin on his chest. He wasn't a hairy guy, but a neat arrow of dark fur went down the middle of his chest, disappearing beneath the waistband of his jeans. It was incredibly sexy.

"Not bad, Gomez," she whispered. "I miss the moustache, of course."

Reaching behind her, she unhooked her bra and tossed it aside. In the faint light she could see his gaze focus, humor forgotten as he stroked the slopes and gently rounded curves. He hadn't touched her breasts, but Layne felt her nipples tighten with anticipation.

"What pleases you, Layne?" Matt whispered. "This?"

He teased the aching peaks, then pulled her closer to draw one into his mouth, sucking hard one moment, and soothing her with his tongue another.

Her pants and his jeans landed somewhere and he drew her underwear down her legs, taking his time as he followed their progress with kisses.

Layne spared a thought to being grateful that Matt hadn't pushed the issue of what pleased her. The women he'd known were probably too sophisticated to hesitate about saying exactly what they wanted and where. To hear her friends talk, it was the modern thing to be solely concerned about your own pleasure, not your partner's.

I'm responsible for my own orgasm.

How many times had she heard that?

Another friend had put it bluntly. "My husband enjoys it no matter what, so I might as well take care of myself and let him do the same."

Layne didn't know, but she had a hard time believing give and take had gone completely out of fashion. It was the way two people…

Her thoughts shattered as Matt eased her thighs apart and stroked the aching center between. Her muscles clenched and released and she tried desperately to keep from going off altogether. She grabbed the top of the mattress for leverage and shimmied away.

"You don't like that?" Matt asked hoarsely.

Like it?

Of course she liked *it.*

"Sure, but it's my turn to experiment."

Smiling in anticipation, she kissed Matt's chest, exploring the arrow of hair and the smooth skin everywhere else. He tensed so much it was almost like kissing sun-warmed stone.

Satisfaction went through her—at least right now, at this moment, he wanted her. She'd have to be content with that because it was all she was ever going to get.

Down to his belly button, a gentle dip of her tongue, and then she shook her hair over his groin, teasing his hard length before touching him.

Almost instantly Matt dragged her up his body.

"Experimentation is over," he informed her in a low, rough tone. "Or I'm going to do something I haven't done since I got too excited having sex the first time."

He reached over to a drawer in the sleek bedside table and pulled out a condom. A few seconds later he was inside her and they were moving fast together, the heat building, her boundaries dissolving, everything coming apart. It was wonderful, terrifying, mind-ripping...and she finally exploded, vaguely aware that Matt had followed her a few seconds later.

"Oh, God," he gasped after a few minutes, his breath still coming in deep shudders. "My heart...I may need an ambulance."

"Don't exaggerate. You're only thirty-two. Your heart is fine."

Lucky for me, she thought. Her body was still shaking, though Matt's gentle caresses were helping. She curled tighter to him and closed her eyes. It was early and she ought to be doing something, but sleep was too tempting.

MUCH LATER MATT gazed down at Layne as she slept, illuminated only by the moon and city lights shining in the distance. *Damn.* She had the softest skin and hair. Just remembering how she'd left a trail of nibbling kisses down his chest and belly, until the silky ends of her hair drifted over him like a thousand curious fingers...

Matt groaned.

How was he getting out of the mess he'd gotten

into? He could almost see a future with Layne and it scared the hell out of him. His father married and divorced on a regular basis, breaking hearts and making headlines. The people who got hurt were his wives and girlfriends and kids—S. S. Hollister just went merrily on to his next romance, seemingly oblivious to the wreckage he'd left behind.

If there was one thing Matt knew, it was that he didn't want to be like Spence. Besides, too many marriages ended in divorce, and couples that stayed together often didn't seem happy.

Matt had never committed to having a cat or dog or even a goldfish, much less a relationship.

Still, Layne was right; he *had* made a commitment to his grandfather's charitable trust. He hadn't thought of it that way. He'd just seen something important that he wanted to do. It hadn't been a snap decision. He'd thought it through, carefully weighing the changes it would require in his life, and knowing that it couldn't just be for a few weeks or months. It *had* to be something he'd do for years to come.

But running the foundation was a far cry from considering a long-term relationship with a woman. And that was even presuming Layne wanted anything beyond clearing her uncle's name. At this point he didn't know if she'd get up in the morning and start rearranging the furniture, or pretend they'd never touched each other.

And he still didn't know which one he wanted it to be.

"ARE YOU SURE you won't stay for dinner?" Dorothy asked the next evening as Layne and Matt gathered the documents they'd been reviewing. The stack of boxes in Will's study was finally gone, and they were working on the last of the contents.

Layne shot a glance at Matt. "Uh, thanks, but we're driving into Seattle for the night. We want to call more of Uncle Will's old employees and can't do it too late. Besides, it's creepy at my house right now, knowing someone was listening to me."

Dorothy nodded. She'd agreed to have Riley Flannigan check inside her own house for the same reason, though luckily nothing had turned up.

She hugged Layne goodbye and shook Matt's hand. It was apparent he'd charmed his way back into her niece's bed and Dorothy didn't know how she felt about the whole thing.

The doorbell rang a few minutes later and she hurried to answer. The first thing she saw was a large arrangement of flowers, mostly formed of white Dutch irises.

"Uh...are you Dorothy Hudson?" asked the delivery person, a teenage boy who was trying to look around the bouquet.

"Yes."

"I'm from Da Vinci Flowers. These are for you." The bouquet was extended and Dorothy tried not to fumble as she grasped the vase. "Have a nice evening."

"Wait, I'll get my purse."

The young man shook his head. "I've already been given a tip, ma'am."

Dorothy closed the door and took the flowers into her dining room. They were gorgeous. She pulled the small card from the envelope and read it. "Patrick." One word. Not "I'm sorry" or "Forgive me" or anything else.

Honestly. He was pushing things, signing the name he'd used to lie to her. In the beginning she would have been angry enough to pitch the whole thing into the creek below the house, but the flowers *were* lovely. Dutch irises appealed to her artistic senses, though she'd never captured the cool elegance of the flowers on canvas to her satisfaction. The ones in the vase were white with purple tongues, and there were small yellow tulips tucked here and there for accent.

Dorothy looked out the window and saw Patrick in the backyard, repairing a damaged plank on one of the planter boxes. She was still angry with him, but it was interesting the way he was attempting to make up for his deception. He'd gotten a load of firewood, stowing it at the side of the house. He had carried groceries and cleared brush from the edges of the yard. Not only that, various specialty teas and spices had appeared on her doorstep, along with a small stone box carved from Irish marble, with a Celtic design inlaid on the lid.

Now flowers.

She'd thought about objecting, particularly about the chores around the house, but what was the harm, really? There was a difference between being helpless and doing nothing for yourself, and a reasonable give and take.

She debated, then went into the kitchen and made a very strong cup of milky tea. Stepping out onto the patio, she met Patrick's gaze. "Flowers. *Really?*"

"An Irish breeze told me you liked that kind."

"They're all right." Dorothy handed him the tea. "Here. But don't think I've forgiven you," she warned.

"No, ma'am. But would you do me the favor of not bringing more food to my team? The point is to go unnoticed."

"Ha. You blew that when your men descended on the house like a team of commandos after I accidentally set off the security alarm."

As Dorothy went back into the house she thought she heard a muttered, "And you expect me to believe it was an accident?"

She smiled wickedly and hurried up to her studio to work on her latest canvas. Setting off the alarm *had* been accidental, but only because she hadn't thought of it first.

"I STILL DON'T think you should go," Connor said to Layne and Matt on Thursday. "Somebody tried to break through the firewall on our computer system last night. They didn't get in, but they tried damned hard."

"We're going, or at least I am," Layne told him stubbornly. "I took the day off for this."

After more than a week, Connor had finally located Brandi Porter, now using the last name Holden. Layne had called and left a message, then had to wait until the next day before it was returned. Brandi had reluctantly agreed to meet them in Olympia, Washington.

"I'm going, too," Matt said.

"It could be a trap," Connor declared. "Why did she insist on seeing you face-to-face? You don't know anything about her. She might be dangerous."

Layne made a disgusted sound. "She didn't have time to talk when she called. Besides, seeing her in person was my idea. I want to show her a copy of the phone message. And we're meeting at a restaurant in the middle of the afternoon, not a deserted warehouse in the dead of night. What could happen? Especially since I'm *sure* you'll have your undercover buddies following us."

"They're security experts, not my buddies. I dislike them all equally."

"Yeah, right. We have to go—I don't want to get caught in traffic. Brandi said four o'clock, on the dot."

Layne caught the two men exchanging commiserating glances and slapped Matt's arm.

"Do *not* do the superior male routine," she warned. "Did it ever occur to you that if you hadn't gotten involved, the investigation might have stayed lower profile and nobody would be the wiser? Not that you haven't been a help, of course."

"Of course."

"And you did introduce me to Cherry Garcia," Layne added grudgingly.

Matt grinned. "Come on, Tish, it's time to head for Olympia. Unless you'd rather have another bowl of Ben & Jerry's before we go?"

His tone was perfectly proper, but Layne wanted to kill him. He kept calling her Tish in bed, which is where he'd coaxed her into staying most of the morning, staining his silk sheets with Cherry Garcia while waiting for Brandi to return their call. It was reckless and stupid and she was going to regret it once they'd gone their separate ways, but she hadn't been able to resist.

"Olympia," she said, her eyes daring him to say anything else involving ice cream.

Connor blinked. "Tish?"

Layne glared. "Don't ask. It's a short trip back to the doghouse."

The security chief instantly rose to his feet. "I'll just give my guys a heads-up about your meeting location. They can check it out before you arrive."

"Connor—"

"Discreetly," he assured as he shut the office door.

Layne rolled her eyes. "Honestly, does he think someone will put a pipe bomb in the car when we aren't looking?"

"Who knows?"

Matt looked so grim, she shivered.

They took the private elevator down to his personal parking area. She had gotten her Mustang repaired—

somehow Matt had convinced the insurance company to pay for a top restoration specialist—but it was locked up at Aunt Dee's house for safekeeping. In the meantime she was using the Volvo to go back and forth to work and do other errands.

"Not the Volvo, we're taking that one." He pointed to a silvery gray Mercedes-Benz in the corner.

"You have *two* Mercedes-Benzes?"

"Yeah. I rarely use the sedan and Connor thinks a different car might throw off anyone following us."

"Oh." She dropped into the leather seat. The luxury sedan didn't fit with Matt's jeans, casual shirt and baseball cap, but she supposed rich guys didn't always look as if they'd stepped out of an Armani store.

They arrived with an hour to spare, so Matt drove around the city before turning into the restaurant parking lot.

"Do you think she'll come?" Layne asked. "She sounded nervous."

"Everybody is nervous when we ask them about the thefts."

They went into the restaurant. It was mostly a steakhouse, but there weren't any customers. Layne checked her watch, hoping Brandi wouldn't be scared off because they were early.

They went into the dimly lit bar and Layne ordered soda water while Matt got a cup of coffee. The bartender looked disgusted until Matt tossed him a twenty and said to keep it. They took a booth in a corner and, precisely at four, a woman approached the table, wearing a uniform with "Brandi" on her nametag.

"Ms. McGraw?" she said, holding out her hand. "I'm Brandi Holden now. I was divorced two months ago."

"Yes, I'm Layne. This is Matt Hollister."

"Pleased to meet you." She slid in next to Layne. "I know I was particular about the time, but my schedule is tight because I work two jobs and go to school."

"I just appreciate your seeing me." Layne opened her purse and pulled out a photocopy of the phone message. "Is this your handwriting?"

Brandi stared at the message, a mixture of emotions chasing across her face, then nodded. "Yeah. Is it important?"

"It was taken on one of the days a theft occurred at Hudson & Davidson. I've been trying to establish an alibi for my uncle and if you're sure you wrote the correct date, it might help to show he wasn't there that night."

"I can do more than that. I can't tell you most of the times Mr. Hudson did or didn't work late, but I know he didn't work *that* night. See, my ex-husband had just beaten me up real bad and Mr. Hudson was trying to help. He was going to visit his brother-in-law and said he'd get me to a women's shelter in Olympia on the way to Aberdeen."

"You're sure of the date?" Matt asked quickly.

Brandi swallowed. "You don't forget something

like that—not when you've got busted ribs and a split lip and you're terrified to leave, and just as scared to go home. Mr. Hudson was real worried. He called my cell phone when he got to Aberdeen to see if I was okay and urge me not to change my mind and go back to Darrell."

"I'm glad you got away."

"Me, too. I liked working for Mr. Hudson, though it wouldn't have been for much longer since outside agency contracts were going to be terminated. Temp secretaries, IT, janitorial, everything."

Layne searched her memory, recalling what Detective Rivera had said about Uncle Will not necessarily having the skills to make money disappear electronically.

"IT? You're sure about that one?" she asked.

Brandi nodded. "According to office chatter, the company wanted to recruit its own IT people. The guy from Scullini Computers was there all the time, anyhow, so why not have people in-house?"

Matt and Layne exchanged a glance.

"I didn't have much to do with personnel when I was at the company. Scullini Computers was the IT service provider?" Matt asked.

"Yeah."

"Did he work on my uncle's computer a lot?" Layne said, a hard knot of conviction in her stomach. It wasn't just what Brandi had said, it was remembering that someone had tried to break into the Eisley security system.

"He worked on *everybody's* computers a lot. Look, I don't know if my ex-husband is trying to find me, but please don't tell anyone where I live. It really threw me when you called."

"But what if you're needed to verify Uncle Will wasn't at the office that particular night?"

Brandi bit her lip, then squared her thin shoulders. "Mr. Hudson was a decent guy. If I can help, I'll do it."

"We'll protect you," Matt promised as he scribbled on one of his business cards and pushed it across the table. "Here are my numbers if you need anything."

"Thanks. I have to go now to set the tables for the dinner crowd." She solemnly shook their hands before hurrying away.

Matt navigated the sedan out of Olympia, wishing he could read what was going on in Layne's head. Finally he sighed.

"Layne, the D.A. may claim that your uncle could have driven back to his office and still be responsible for the thefts."

"I know. That's why Detective Rivera needs to get records on the call Uncle Will made to Brandi. If Uncle Will made a call from Aberdeen, there should be data showing which towers handled the call, proving he wasn't anywhere near Hudson & Davidson that evening."

"Call Detective Rivera and ask him."

But Layne was already dialing the smartphone he'd

given her. She put it on speaker, and as soon as the detective answered, began explaining what they'd learned.

"You say this woman is willing to verify what happened?" the detective asked finally.

"Yes, and…."

"Ms. McGraw? Is something wrong?" Rivera prompted at her silence.

Matt saw Layne staring at the phone with a strange expression on her face.

"Oh, God," she said. "Detective Rivera, I just realized…Uncle Will always kept his phone turned on. The GPS data might also be available from the cell phone company, too, or wherever it's tracked. It could prove he wasn't at the company when *any* of the thefts occurred."

"Or at least that the phone wasn't at the office," the detective said. "I'm convinced, but it will take a court order to get the records and we're the only ones who want this case reactivated, Ms. McGraw. But I'll work on it and also check out Scullini Computers. Maybe I can find some leads there."

"Good luck."

"The same to you."

Layne didn't say anything for a long time after turning off the phone. Matt finally reached over and squeezed her hand. "I have an idea. Let's find a nice, private country back road and make out for an hour."

"I don't think so. You said you had work to do, and I need to take a check from the *Babbitt* to Aunt Dee."

Matt knew he should respect Layne's wishes, but it was damned hard. Especially when she had that remote look in her eyes he couldn't fathom.

"All right. But are you coming back to my place this evening? I don't think we should let up on the investigation, which means we still have some phone calls to make."

From the corner of his eye he saw Layne's reluctant expression, but she finally nodded. "Sure."

LATE THAT NIGHT Matt watched Layne as she slept, unable to sleep himself. Each piece of new information or evidence put them one step closer to solving what had happened to her uncle. And one step closer to knowing if he'd made a mistake while working at Hudson & Davidson.

The strange thing was, he'd probably blame himself more than Layne or her aunt would. Maybe it was because he was so new to taking responsibility for anything.

Matt *did* know he'd probably made a mistake bringing Peter on at the Eisley Foundation. He'd made inquiries about the value of Hudson & Davidson, and it was more than evident Peter was trying to get out of paying Dorothy her fair share. He would have to confront his stepfather about it, the question was *where*.

Not in either of their offices.

He wanted to keep Eisley Foundation business and this unholy mess separated. And it certainly couldn't be at the Eisley mansion where Peter and his mother lived.

It would have to be in the penthouse. He could ask Peter to meet him there while Layne was at work.

As to whether Peter had been involved in the thefts? It was possible, but didn't seem likely. While a large sum had been embezzled, it was minor compared to Peter's personal wealth; it wouldn't make sense for him to steal.

THE NEXT AFTERNOON Peter arrived promptly, but Matt avoided his handshake. It was amazing how he'd gone from liking Peter, to barely being able to stand the sight of him.

His stepfather looked puzzled. "What's up, son?"

A muscle ticked in Matt's check. He wasn't Peter's son, *thank God*. Spence wasn't much of a father, but at least there were no surprises with him.

"I've been reviewing the documents you want Dorothy Hudson to sign," Matt said bluntly. "And no matter how I add things up, she should get a huge chunk of that sale. The sales price is well below the value of the company. You'll get twice as much from your so-called consultation fees."

"Son, I—"

"Don't call me that," Matt snapped, unable to restrain himself. "Don't *ever* call me that again. Even Spence Hollister wouldn't cheat a woman out of her husband's estate."

Peter recoiled. "Perhaps I've made mistakes. I've felt betrayed and—"

"You don't know that William Hudson betrayed you."

"But remember the D.A. said it was an airtight case. Then Will killed himself."

"Layne has evidence her uncle didn't commit suicide. He was most likely murdered. And we're going to prove it."

Peter seemed to age before Matt's eyes. "But…but he *must* be guilty."

"Why?" Matt demanded. "So you can keep justifying how you turned your back on him? Or excuse doing everything possible to keep his wife from receiving what she's rightfully owed?"

Peter made a helpless gesture. "I swear I'll rectify that. Just give me a chance."

"You think that's it?" Matt asked in disbelief. "Sorry, and I promise to fix it? You've had months to think about what you were doing. This wasn't something you did in a blinding moment of hurt and anger. I think you've been jealous of William and Dorothy for years because they had what you'd lost when your first wife died."

"I'm happy with your mother, Matt. I love her deeply."

"But that hasn't erased those years of envy, has it?"

His stepfather's face was so gray and drawn that Matt briefly wondered if he was having a heart attack.

"I don't know. It's possible," Peter finally admitted. "What do you want me to do?"

"To start, call the Carrollton D.A.'s office. Tell them you want Detective Rivera put in charge of a new investigation into the thefts and the death of William Hudson."

"Yes, of course."

"And talk to Mrs. Hudson. *In person.* My God, I've read the letter you sent her. You're lucky not to be in jail for blackmail."

His stepfather swallowed painfully. "I…I hadn't thought of it as blackmail. That wasn't my intention. I don't know if I can face her."

"Deal with it," Matt said shortly.

"Very well."

He stared at Peter, wishing he could feel pity for him. Layne was right—everybody made mistakes, but the ones that hurt people were harder to forgive. He wanted to tell his stepfather to resign his position with the Eisley Foundation, but it was better to wait. If nothing else, Peter was a reminder that making decisions out of anger could lead to something even worse.

CHAPTER TWENTY

"Thank you, Detective," Layne said, giving Matt a thumbs up. "I'll talk to you again tomorrow."

After disconnecting she jumped onto the couch and hugged him. He laughed, though he was still disturbed about his meeting with Peter a few hours earlier.

"What did Rivera say to put you in such a good mood?"

"The owner of Scullini Computers lives with a secretary from Hudson & Davidson…Vanna Eastbrook. She was one of the first employees I talked to. And Jay Scullini drives an SUV matching the description of the one that rammed us in the Mustang."

"That's terrific. Not for him, but for us."

"Yeah. Rivera also said the D.A.'s office called, offering their full cooperation, so he shouldn't have any trouble getting a search warrant to see if the SUV has a crunched fender, or one that's been recently repaired. The paint from my Mustang won't be difficult to match since it was a custom job."

Matt smiled, relieved to hear Peter had kept his promise.

He pulled Layne closer, hating the flicker of uncertainty he always saw in her eyes when intimacy was involved. Whether they'd meant to or not, her parents and siblings had done a number on her self-esteem. Layne always seemed to be asking why he was with her. And it didn't help that his conscience was asking the same thing for different reasons.

Why *was* he sleeping with Layne when he didn't want marriage and children, and she did? Where were his principles? What happened to his restraint? For God's sake, where was his self-preservation?

Matt inhaled and his senses were filled with her fresh, sweet scent. The questions vanished along with his self-control.

"How about an early night, Tish?"

"I…I could be convinced, Gomez."

He kissed her deeply, and after a moment she responded, her slim body arching upward. Getting up, he led her to the bedroom and they tumbled to the mattress.

"Lights out," she whispered as he began unbuttoning her blouse.

"Nobody can see us on the bed."

"Matt."

Frustrated, he hit the control for the room lights. Layne was most comfortable making love in the dark, and he knew it was lack of confidence about her body. He just didn't know how to reassure her, or how she'd take it if he tried.

Long after Matt had gone to sleep, Layne lay awake. She was sure the case would be resolved soon and expected Matt to start making noises about them going their separate ways—not that she believed he'd be rude or insensitive about it unless she got clingy. At the very least it would be nice to think he saw her as special, but when she looked in a mirror, she was reminded of how impossible that was.

Layne sighed. Insecurities were the pits, and the ones from childhood were worse than all the rest. And in her case, all she had to do was see her family to have those insecurities thrown in her face again.

But it was interesting what Matt had suggested about her parents maybe feeling guilty for sending her to Aunt Dee and Uncle Will so much. In the beginning she *had* felt unwanted. Her parents were smart people; they must have known. As for the other kids being jealous about her time with Aunt Dee and Uncle Will…?

Layne turned on her back, thinking about those long ago years. She might have eventually gotten a little smug at being the darling of her dashing uncle and pretty aunt. Stef and Jeremy had never acted as if they cared, but could *Jeannie* have gotten jealous? It might explain why she was such a pain sometimes.

It seemed incredible, but anything was possible when it came to sisters. She would have to sort it out after everything was resolved about Uncle Will.

The full moon had passed, but she could see Matt was still sleeping. He was the biggest reason she couldn't relax. By stealing a little more time with him, she was just making it harder for herself later.

Without saying it aloud, she'd tried to make it clear she didn't expect anything for the future, and maybe that was why he hadn't pushed her away. Making love that first day had been spontaneous, an emotional moment on a hot, sultry afternoon. The other times? As much as she hated thinking about it, convenience *had* to be playing a part.

With another quick glance at Matt, Layne slid out of bed and went into the living room. Something had been nagging her, as if she'd missed an important piece of information. Aunt Dee had given her copies of Uncle Will's medical records and Layne had studied them, but she'd found little time to go over the autopsy report again in depth.

Steeling herself, Layne began reading the document.

MATT ROLLED OVER as he woke up. It was just before 4:00 a.m. and he frowned groggily as he realized he'd forgotten to lower the blinds. It was doubtful that anybody could see into the bedroom from the other buildings, but Layne didn't like feeling on display, particularly as the sun was coming up.

He reached for her, frowning harder when he realized he was alone. She'd mentioned wanting to get to work early to make up some of the time she was taking off, but surely not *this* early. He checked the bathroom, then hurried into the living room and saw Layne on the couch, papers spread around her.

"I found it," she whispered.

Matt sat on the coffee table. "Found what?"

"I got to thinking about Uncle Will's medical records and realized I should read them, so Aunt Dee got me copies. Only there didn't seem to be anything important there…until I read the autopsy again. I'd really just skimmed it before, but it's been bothering me, like I'd missed something. Look."

She handed him a folded-back copy of the autopsy report and pointed to the bottom of the page. It stated that William Hudson had a massive overdose of oxycodone in his system, leading to respiratory arrest.

"Don't *women* usually take pills?" he asked.

"That's what movie detectives seem to think." Layne turned to the next page and pointed again. "This says that a prescription bottle for sixty five-milligram tablets was found with Uncle Will's body, filled two months prior to his date of death. But Uncle Will was allergic to oxycodone."

Matt tore his gaze from the dry recitation of facts in the autopsy. "What?"

"It's in his medical records, only I didn't catch it at first because it says Percocet, which is the combination drug. It caused severe itching. The prescribing doctor was Victor Sutcliffe, but for the last ten years Uncle Will's doctor was Ellen Tani. I remember Aunt Dee used to be frustrated that he'd wait to see Dr. Tani when he could get an immediate appointment with someone else in the practice. The label must have been faked or something."

"I'm not sure anyone would consider the different

doctor significant," Matt said reluctantly. "The D.A. could argue that if he was considering suicide, he would have consulted a physician who didn't know about the allergy."

"True. Though why ask for oxycodone instead of sleeping pills? And why do it two months before he was accused of anything? At any rate, the report also shows Uncle Will's stomach contents and blood levels indicate he ingested an estimated thirty pills, but the bottle was empty."

Matt's eyes widened, seeing what Layne was getting at. Where had those thirty missing pills gone? William wouldn't have used them because of his allergy, even if he *was* planning to commit suicide. "Your aunt?"

"She won't even take aspirin, and she certainly would have questioned why Uncle Will had the prescription. They must not have told her what he'd taken, just that it was an overdose. And she was in so much shock, she probably didn't ask."

Nodding, Matt read through the report. It was mind-boggling that someone could have gotten away with murder this way. Everything had conspired together, including Peter's desire to get the case closed and out of public view.

"I wonder how someone got your uncle to take the pills."

"The killer could have held a gun on him, maybe threatened to hurt Aunt Dee if he didn't go along. Or they could have been dissolved in liquid. The autopsy shows there was coffee in his stomach. Uncle Will drank really strong dark French roast, so he might not have tasted something added to it. I'm sure Rivera will have a theory."

Layne covered a yawn with her hand and Matt dropped the report. "Rivera always has a theory, but it's too early to call him. Come back to bed."

"To sleep?"

"Do you have energy for anything else?"

"Probably not."

She still didn't move, so he shoved the scattered papers aside and pulled her down against his chest on the broad couch. Within minutes Layne's even breathing told him she was asleep, and Matt let his own eyes close.

A vague thought went through his head as he drifted off himself—was this what it was like to be married? The give and take, the comforting moments when sex was no more important than everything else you shared?

It should have been alarming, but instead he felt satisfaction. For the first time in his life, he was content, as if he was exactly where he was supposed to be.

DOROTHY GAZED AROUND her studio at the paintings she'd finished in the past two weeks. She hadn't done this kind of work since William's death. Yet that wasn't entirely accurate, either. There was more intensity in what she'd done lately, as if she was finally expressing those months of suppressed anger and confusion. Emotion poured off each canvas, vibrant and undeniable.

Smiling faintly, she headed down the studio staircase when the doorbell rang, but her good humor faded when she saw Peter Davidson on her doorstep. Patrick was behind him, a sturdy, reassuring presence, while Peter looked as if he hadn't slept in days.

"May I come in?" he asked.

"Well…all right." Dorothy stepped to one side and she was glad when Patrick marched in, as well.

"I want to apologize," Peter said as he stepped into the living room. "For everything. It was wrong to take my anger out on you. And, uh…just as bad that I turned my back on my oldest friend. Maybe if I'd trusted William the way I should have, he might still be alive."

That wasn't something Dorothy wanted to think about. Things *might* have turned out differently if Peter had behaved better, but there was no way of knowing.

"I guess it's too late to know, isn't it?" she said. No matter what, she refused to do the gracious thing and let him off the hook. They were talking about her husband's death, not something trivial like being snubbed at a party.

"Yes, you're right, of course." He pulled an envelope from his pocket. "I've reviewed the books at Hudson & Davidson. This is your share of the profits since the first of January."

"I thought the company was operating in the red."

"Technically the profits have been going against the money I used to repay the embezzled funds."

Dorothy lifted her chin. "Then I can't accept."

"Please. I felt very self-righteous about everything until I saw myself through my stepson's eyes. Now I realize how badly I handled everything."

"What does that have to do with money from the company?"

"A lot." Peter sighed. "There's more to consider than what I've told you."

"You said—"

"I said a lot of things, mostly in anger. In the meantime, please accept the check."

Dorothy looked at Patrick, whose gaze was fixed with distaste on Peter, and she suddenly knew that even if Patrick had lied about his name, he'd never do something truly dishonest. Perhaps honor came in different packages, and you had to accept tarnish on the armor along with the rest.

"I can't accept if money is still owed to you," she told Peter firmly.

"It can come out of the proceeds of the sale. You'll be due much more than I...uh...previously indicated. And besides, if William was innocent, everything changes, including some insurance issues."

"Then I'll take it when he's exonerated."

And I hope you choke on it.

Peter reluctantly returned the envelope to his pocket. "Of course. We'll make sure William's reputation is cleared."

CONNOR DIDN'T SAY anything when they were alone. Davidson had obviously come to make amends, at the same time trying not to admit that he'd attempted to cheat his partner's widow.

Dorothy must need the money, and Connor wanted to be frustrated, the way he'd been frustrated with Alleyne over the years for not taking the help he'd offered, but he couldn't be. Dot had faced her husband's greedy partner with a cool grit he admired.

Maybe he'd been wrong in thinking Alleyne was too proud. There was no doubt she often did without, but she may have needed a big brother more than a long string of international money orders.

"Come have a cup of tea," Dot invited. In the kitchen she set out a plate of scones with homemade jam. "You'll have to let me know if those are like the ones your mother used to make."

Scones?

Connor realized it must be a silent acceptance of his apology, and a weight lifted from his shoulders.

"Perfect," he assured her after taking a bite.

For the first time since he was seven years old and standing at his father's grave, he had some faith in the future. His stepfather had gotten him off the streets and put his feet on a straighter path, but it was Dorothy who'd truly gotten into his heart. Friendship was all he could hope for now with her, but who knew what could happen down the road?

A WEEK LATER Layne and Matt were working in Aunt Dee's backyard, both of them eager for fresh air after so many phone calls and hours sifting out possible evidence.

What shocked Layne was that her aunt had actually agreed to let them do the overdue cleanup from winter. Matt had put it tactfully, suggesting that since Dee needed to use the barbecue to test a shish kebab recipe for the *Babbitt,* she let them get it ready. But it was still surprising. Dee was prickly about accepting anything, though it wasn't as if Layne hadn't helped with yard work *before* Uncle Will's death.

Detective Rivera had been excited when she'd called about her findings from the autopsy report. He planned to question the doctor who'd supposedly prescribed the oxycodone and the pharmacy that had filled it. He'd also learned that Jay Scullini had been severely beaten in a mysterious attack eleven months ago, but his witness statement was contradictory and vague. Since Scullini was a known gambler, the police suspected he'd been worked over by a loan shark. The incident was particularly intriguing because it had occurred just weeks prior to the first theft at Hudson & Davidson.

Layne sighed. She ought to feel better; the end was in sight and Uncle Will's reputation would be restored. Yet it wouldn't bring him back, and she felt terrible that Matt's relationship with his stepfather had been destroyed.

"Look who's here," Connor called as he walked around the corner of the house.

"Detective Rivera." Layne pulled off her work gloves to shake his hand. "Aunt Dee, you remember the detective."

Dee nodded. "Of course. What can we do for you?"

"I wanted to tell you that a full investigation is now under way. The department has given me two detectives for my team and I have full access to the cyber-crime lab. And that means I need to pick up Mr. Hudson's computer. The lab is going to analyze the hard drive to show the printer software wasn't simply uninstalled."

Layne exchanged an elated look with her aunt. "Is that necessary with everything else we've learned?"

"I'm just being thorough. The records obtained from the cell provider show Mr. Hudson's phone was nowhere near the company at the times the illegal wire transfers were made, and that more than one call was made from Aberdeen on those nights."

"What about Scullini?" Matt asked.

"A search warrant has been issued for his home and business, but he's disappeared along with his girlfriend and SUV. He's the right man, though. He had a large sum of money in his account this last fall—money he clearly didn't earn with his business. Our cyber experts are tracking it to establish where it originated, but the dates and amounts of individual deposits match the thefts at Hudson & Davidson. Scullini wasn't too bright about that part—probably convinced he'd never become a suspect. Officially this is now classified as theft, not embezzlement."

Matt frowned. "They couldn't find the money before."

"Yes, but they expect to have better luck backtracking the deposits."

"That's great."

Yet he didn't sound as enthusiastic as Layne would have expected. She lifted an eyebrow. "What's bugging you, Matt?"

"If Jay Scullini is on the run, he could still be a threat to you and Dorothy."

"And to his girlfriend," Layne said worriedly. "He has a record of trying to eliminate witnesses, so she's at risk, too."

Detective Rivera shook his head. "I appreciate your concern on her behalf, but we have an APB out and should locate them sooner or later. If you want police protection—"

"Not needed," Connor interrupted sharply.

"But come back tomorrow," Dee urged. "I test recipes for the *Puget Sound Babbitt* and Layne got much more food than was needed. We're going to have shish kebobs, two kinds of potato salad and turtle brownies. *For everyone,* though the security team has to eat in shifts."

Layne grinned as Connor snorted. He'd obviously

been forgiven for his deception, but Dee still enjoyed yanking his chain.

"I appreciate the offer, but I'll be on duty. I just need to get the computer and give you a receipt."

Connor followed as Dee went into the house with the detective, and Layne exchanged a smile with Matt. It was hard not having Uncle Will there, but he would have said to stop crying and keep living. And she hoped that wherever he was, he knew what they were doing to clear his name.

MATT RINSED THE stainless-steel grill before returning it to the built-in gas barbecue. The outdoor kitchen was in good shape other than an accumulation of grime from months of disuse.

"You're pretty good at that. Have you ever considered a career in the housekeeping industry?" Layne teased.

The sun was shining on her hair and she looked like a forest sprite in her green T-shirt and shorts and bare feet. Layne rarely missed an opportunity to kick her shoes off.

He shrugged. "Not housekeeping. But gardening now and then wouldn't be so bad."

Like if we were married and taking care of our yard together. The thought floored Matt. He could hire whatever gardeners and housekeepers he needed, but the part that shocked him was the *M* word. *Married. Marriage.* Making a commitment to someone.

It was one thing to feel as if being with Layne was a perfect fit but…

His racing brain jolted to a stop.

Layne *was* the perfect fit.

She was fun and sexy and made everything an adventure, whether it was scrubbing a barbecue grill or making love. And she had a heart that was so generous and loving, he didn't think he could ever get enough of it. He was completely, utterly crazy about her.

Still…marriage?

His family's track record in that area wasn't the greatest. Aaron seemed very happy with his wife, but his mother certainly hadn't picked either of her husbands that well. And his father was a disaster when it came to commitment. Hell, Spence didn't actually *make* a commitment; he just played at being married.

Matt looked at Layne and thought of the sweet, wonderful way she'd wrapped herself around his heart.

Real commitment was a choice, the way he'd chosen to take over the Eisley Foundation. It was a promise to yourself, as well as to other people, and he had no intention of breaking faith with Terry or his grandfather or anyone else at the foundation. But did he have any hope that Layne would want to take a chance on him?

"Gardening is great. I love to watch things grow." Layne tossed a stick for Finnster, who ecstatically fetched it, joy on his furry face. For the first time in his canine life, he was getting to be just a dog.

A smile grew on Matt's face as he watched. Around Layne, he wasn't a partyer or sportsman or even a billionaire philanthropist. He was just a regular guy, crazy in love with an amazing woman.

Who wouldn't do whatever it took to make that permanent?

CHAPTER TWENTY-ONE

Contrary to what Detective Rivera had said about not having lunch with them, he showed up Sunday afternoon, just as they finished eating.

"Change your mind?" Layne asked. "We have plenty of food."

"Nope. But I wanted to deliver my news in person. Vanna Eastbrook was found early this morning on a back road in eastern Oregon with two gunshot wounds in her shoulder. A few hours later the police arrested Jay Scullini in Reno. Apparently he couldn't resist stopping to play blackjack."

The air seemed to freeze in Layne's lungs. "Is she alive?"

"In serious condition, but expected to make a full recovery," Rivera explained hastily. "And she's willing to testify about the thefts at Hudson & Davidson in exchange for reduced charges. The deal's been approved. Apparently Scullini plotted the whole thing after his bookie put him in the hospital. She claims she went along because she was scared but didn't know Scullini planned to frame and kill William Hudson until after it was done."

"How did he get away with the thefts?" asked Matt.

"He used a skimmer to duplicate the keycard, and another device to record keystrokes for the passwords and access codes. He also knew Mr. Hudson wouldn't have an easy alibi on Thursday nights. His girlfriend would sign him out in the security log, so there was no paper trail showing he was there at those hours."

"Uncle Will probably mentioned Aunt Dee would be out of town," Layne murmured. "But how did Scullini get into the house to commit the murder?"

"Apparently he just rang the bell and said he had an idea of how the thefts occurred. I've already spoken to the medical examiner. Essentially, the official finding of suicide will be reversed and the D.A.'s office has acknowledged they were wrong about William Hudson."

As Connor walked the detective out, Layne hugged her aunt. They were both smiling and crying at the same time. It was finally over. The victory was bittersweet as Layne had recognized it would be, but at least her aunt would know she cleared her husband's name and be able to keep the house they'd built together.

"Matthew, thank you for helping," Dee said finally, giving him a hug, as well.

"Don't thank me…I should have done more when it happened."

"You weren't the one who could have made a difference."

"PERHAPS." MATT'S THROAT tightened unbearably. Dorothy could easily be angry with the world, including him, but she was too decent. If only his stepfather had been more like her, things might be different now.

"Aunt Dee, why don't you go make sure the security team got enough to eat?" Layne asked abruptly.

Dorothy looked from her niece to Matt before nodding. "That's a good idea."

When they were alone, Layne squeezed his arm. "What's wrong? You helped us get to the truth."

"But I'll never know if I was so anxious to start working at the foundation that I missed something. Can you forgive that?"

"There's nothing to forgive."

Matt could tell she genuinely believed it, and some of the pain eased in his throat. "I also didn't see Peter for what he was."

"I think your stepfather is a damaged person," Layne said honestly. "But I still don't believe Uncle Will was completely wrong about him. He recognized that Peter changed after his wife's death, but felt he would come around with enough time. Maybe it can still happen."

"It's too late for me. I'll never be able to trust him again, especially after what he tried to do to your aunt."

"Then I almost feel sorry for him."

Matt raised a disbelieving eyebrow.

"It's true," Layne affirmed. "He lost the relationship he could have had with you. No one can put a value on that."

"You're so amazing. After everything that's happened, you can still say something like that." Matt cupped her face between his hands, loving her so much it was almost terrifying. "I'm crazy about you, Layne. Please tell me you feel the same way."

She stiffened. "Don't say that."

"Why not?"

"Because you might regret it. You're upset. Neither of us can think clearly after this. I mean, everything is mixed up. You can't exactly celebrate finding a killer, and yet it *does* right something terribly wrong."

"And your uncle is still gone."

"Yes. And your stepfather is still a troubled man. So you see, when you've had time to sort things out, you'll change your mind. By tomorrow you'll feel very different."

"No, I won't."

"Fine, then talk to me tomorrow."

Before he could say anything else, she'd vanished into the house.

LAYNE DRAGGED HERSELF into work the next morning after another sleepless night. Though she'd done the right thing by stopping Matt, it had hurt desperately. She loved him so much, but she couldn't take advantage of an emotional situation.

The night before, she'd driven to her parents' house to tell them the news. They'd been thrilled, and probably a little mortified, too, for not believing in their brother-in-law from the beginning. Layne hadn't told them much about her part in the investigation. Her parents might have valued her research skills…for a few seconds. But in the end, it wouldn't change how they saw her. And perhaps they *weren't* disappointed in how she'd grown up; maybe they just felt they'd failed her, the way Matt had suggested.

But at the moment, he was the one who mattered.

She stared at her computer screen, trying to concentrate.

The cooler she'd brought, filled with shish kebob and potato salad for the staff to taste test, was on the corner of her desk. Regina collected it with a delighted smile.

"I'll tell accounting to cut a check immediately for Mrs. Hudson," she said, sneaking one of the turtle brownies.

"Okay."

"Hey, is something wrong?"

Layne was saved from answering when the new message alert sounded on her computer.

Come see me. C.

"Um, I need to see Carl." Layne hurried into the editor's office. "Yeah, boss?"

"I want to know what gives with you and Matthew Hollister."

She stared. "What?"

Carl grinned broadly. "I just got off the phone with him. He's granting us an exclusive interview. He says

I can thank him by giving you a two-week vacation, starting now. What's the story?"

"Well, Matt and I have become acquainted. He's doing good work at the Eisley Foundation and I've urged him to consider going more public about what he hopes to accomplish there."

The *Babbitt* editor rubbed his jaw. "You didn't think to tell me about this friendship, given what we've been printing about his stepfather?"

"No," Layne returned flatly. "You don't own my private life. And if you think otherwise, you can shove this job."

He grinned. "Take it easy, kid. I'm ecstatic. The guy hasn't given a personal interview in years. Grab your stuff and get going. You've got two extra weeks of paid vacation."

Layne went back to her desk in shock. Matt must have lost his mind, though she couldn't deny that having some time to sort everything out in her head was a good idea. Maybe he was doing it to be nice— a sideways thank-you for stopping him from saying something he'd regret. She'd known it would happen...yet a tiny part of her had hoped that she'd been wrong.

"Hey," said a voice as she turned the corner of the building into the parking lot. It was Matt, leaning against the Mustang and holding out a bouquet of red roses. "Okay, red roses *may* be a little trite, but I've never proposed before, so I took a chance."

Proposed?

The word hit Layne like a bombshell.

"But just in case, I also brought these." He reached behind him with his free hand, and the second bouquet was a confection of pink miniature roses and ferns and baby's breath. "You're the love of my life, Layne. Please marry me."

She stared at the flowers. "You don't believe in love or marriage," she said finally. "You think it's a fairy tale."

"I did. Then I met you."

"But I'm not...I'm not blonde and tall like Jeannette."

He set the flowers down on the Mustang, walked over and kissed her. "Who cares? I wasn't interested in Jeannette because you and I had already met. To me you're the most beautiful woman in the world, but that isn't what love is about or I would have fallen a long time ago."

Layne thought about all the times he could have left, instead he'd stuck around through some pretty nasty stuff. He really *had* reformed.

"I know I can do anything if we're together," he murmured. "Even be a good husband and father. You're the reason I'm giving the interview to the *Babbitt* about the ALS research. You said I should get people to listen. And that's what I'm going to do. Please have faith in me...and in us."

Faith?

She believed in him, but she also needed to have faith in herself and let go of the old insecurities. After all, Matt should certainly know what he wanted in a woman.

And he wanted her.

The corners of her mouth began to curve.

MATT KNEW HE'D never seen anything more breathtaking than Layne McGraw with tears in her eyes and a smile so dazzling it could warm the coldest night. He gathered her close.

"What about your father and all that stuff with Peter and your mother?" she asked.

Matt sighed. He still had to deal with Peter. While he hadn't wanted to act in anger, he couldn't have someone working at the Eisley Foundation that he didn't trust. He only hoped his mother wouldn't learn how badly her husband had behaved.

"Peter isn't important," he said. "You are. I've never really fit anywhere until now. I love you and I need you…and I damn well can't live without you."

"Oh, my God," shrieked a woman's voice abruptly. "Layne, what are you doing with Matthew Hollister?"

Matt saw a woman standing next to a man. Both looked vaguely familiar.

"That's Noah Wilkie, the social reporter," Layne whispered. "And Annette Wade, one of my friends. She does the nuptials column."

"That's perfect. Let's give them a scoop." Matt grinned. "She's accepting my marriage proposal," he called to the two *Babbitt* employees. "You can be the first to congratulate me."

Layne laughed and flung her arms around his neck as Annette shrieked again. She still had a million silly questions, but the important ones had already been answered. Besides, she was too busy getting kissed and making plans to care.

* * * * *

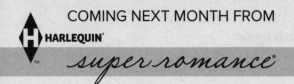
#1938 THE SWEETEST SEPTEMBER
Home in Magnolia Bend • by Liz Talley

Of all the wrong men Shelby Mackey has fallen for, this one's a doozy.
John Beauchamp is still grieving his late wife, and now Shelby's pregnant with
his child. They weren't looking for this, but could that one night be the start of
something much sweeter?

#1939 THE REASONS TO STAY
by Laura Drake

Priscilla Hart's mother leaves her an unexpected inheritance—a half brother! What
does Priscilla know about raising kids? How can she set down roots and give him
a home? Then she meets sexy but buttoned-down Adam Preston. Here's one man
who might convince her to stay in Widow's Grove.

#1940 THIS JUST IN...
by Jennifer McKenzie

Sabrina Ryan never wanted to go home. But, suspended from her big-city
newspaper job, that's exactly where she is. Things improve when sparks fly
between her and Noah Barnes, the superhot mayor. Doing a story on him, she
discovers home isn't such a bad place, after all....

#1941 RODEO DREAMS
by Sarah M. Anderson

Bull riding is a man's world, but June Spotted Elk won't let anyone tell her not to
ride—not even sexy rodeo pro Travis Younkin. He only wants her safe, with him—but
what happens when her success hurts his comeback?

#1942 TO BE A DAD
by Kate Kelly

Dusty Carson has a good life—no responsibilities and no
expectations. But after one night with Teressa Wilder, life
changes in a hurry. Teressa's pregnant and suddenly, she
and her two kids have moved into his house. Now Dusty's
learning what it really means to be a dad.

#1943 THE FIREFIGHTER'S APPEAL
by Elizabeth Otto

To most people, firefighters are heroes—but not to
Lily Ashden. She blames them for a family tragedy and is
in no hurry to forgive. But Garrett Mateo challenges all of
her beliefs. This sexy firefighter wants to win her over and
won't take no for an answer!

superromance

The Sweetest September

By **Liz Talley**

Shelby Mackey would have been happy
to *never* revisit the night she met
John Beauchamp. Well, that's not entirely true.
It was a good night...until the end. But now
avoiding him is no longer an option!

Read on for an exciting excerpt of the upcoming
book **THE SWEETEST SEPTEMBER**
by Liz Talley...

Shelby took a moment to take stock of the man she hadn't
seen since he'd slipped out that fateful night. John's boots
were streaked with mud and his dusty jeans had a hole in the
thigh. A kerchief hung from his back pocket. He looked like
a farmer.

She'd never thought a farmer could look, well, sexy. But
John Beauchamp had that going for him...not that she was
interested.

Been there. Done him. Got pregnant.

He looked down at her with cautious green eyes...like she
was a ticking bomb he had to disarm. "What are you doing
here?"

Shelby tried to calm the bats flapping in her stomach, but there was nothing to quiet them with. "Uh, it's complicated. We should talk privately."

He slid into the cart beside her, his thigh brushing hers. She scooted away. He noticed, but didn't say anything.

She glanced at him and then back at the workers still casting inquisitive looks their way.

John got the message and stepped on the accelerator.

Shelby yelped and grabbed the edge of the seat, nearly sliding across the cracked pleather seat and pitching onto the ground. John reached over and clasped her arm, saving her from that fate.

"You good?" he asked.

"Yeah," she said, finding her balance, her stomach pitching more at the thought of revealing why she sat beside him than at the actual bumpy ride.

So how did one do this?

Probably should just say it. Rip the bandage off. Pull the knife out. He probably already suspected why she'd come.

As they turned onto the adjacent path, Shelby took a deep breath and said, "I'm pregnant."

How will John react to the news?
Find out what's in store for these two—and the
baby—in THE SWEETEST SEPTEMBER
by Liz Talley, available August 2014 from
Harlequin® Superromance®.

LARGER-PRINT BOOKS!
GET 2 FREE LARGER-PRINT NOVELS PLUS
2 FREE GIFTS!

⬧HARLEQUIN®

super romance®

More Story...More Romance